Dark Ages Of The Future

A Collection Of Short Stories

By Justin Mohn

Book cover photos found on Google Images labeled for reuse with modification.

Published on Amazon Kindle on January 29, 2018

Published in print by Amazon Createspace in the United States on January 29, 2018

ISBN-13: 978-1984379177

ISBN-10: 1984379178

Front Cover Image Sources:

Castle - https://pixabay.com/p-2672317/?no_redirect
Upsidedown cross-
https://commons.wikimedia.org/wiki/File:Coa_Illustration_Cross_Peter%27s.svg
Swastika -
https://en.wikipedia.org/wiki/File:Nazi_swastika_clean.svg
Checkered pattern -
http://maxpixel.freegreatpicture.com/Background-Checkered-Design-Abstract-Red-White-313324
Front cover background -
https://commons.wikimedia.org/wiki/File:Lavender_field.jpg

Back Cover Image Sources:

Pentagram -
https://upload.wikimedia.org/wikipedia/commons/thumb/2/2b/Inverted_Pentagram_circumscribed.svg/2000px-Inverted_Pentagram_circumscribed.svg.png
Square and Compass - https://pixabay.com/p-35011/?no_redirect
Cao dai -
https://commons.wikimedia.org/wiki/File:Cao_Dai_white.png
Eye of Horus -
https://commons.wikimedia.org/wiki/File:Eye_of_Horus.svg
Fleur-de-lis - https://pixabay.com/en/fleur-de-lys-symbol-fleur-de-lis-937638/
Checkerboard border -
https://en.wikipedia.org/wiki/Checkerboard

This book is dedicated to those who stand up against evil in the darkest of times.

Table of Contents

Title Page

Copyright Page

Cover Image Sources

Dedication Page

The City……………………………………………………………1

The Law of Jealousy……………………………...…………..57

Heaven and Hell…………………………………………........154

The Music Theory Of Everything.....…………………………178

A Matter of Light vs. Dark ………..…………………..………250

The City (2028 AD)

"Where is all the money going to in the city to cause such economic inequality and crime? It's dividing our community and making us busier and busier down at the station, we constantly need more resources from the taxpayers. The criminals just keep getting smarter, a lot of the criminals nowadays are people who once had bright futures… it's every city's worst nightmare. But where to start looking, and who can we trust to start looking for answers without taking bribes?" the police chief said.

The Mayor murmured something incomprehensible.

"Eeeherrrrrmmllgh," the Mayor murmured.

The Mayor's pale and unfocused grey-blue eyes which were once shiny and determined began to drift backwards so only the whites of his eyes showed. The Mayor was surrounded by four executive assistants, all females wearing black suits, who had eyes with black irises which made their pupils look dilated.

Then the Mayor tilted his head backwards and made a gurgling noise - drool spilling from the sides of his mouth. One of his executive assistants leaned forward and put her ear close to the Mayor's mouth.

"The Mayor says send Officers Black and White to investigate," the assistant said.

"But Mr. Mayor, we've sent Officers Black and White for the past several times, they never come back with any leads, but they happen to have bought new cars and houses uptown in the nicer part of the city… which no other officer their rank seems to be able to afford," the police chief said.

The Mayor gurgled and a bit of spittle sprayed from his lips followed by a trail of discolored slobber down his chain. One of the Mayor's assistants leaned forward and wiped the Mayor's face off with a rag.

“The Mayor says send Officers Black and White, and them only. Remember, the Mayor was once District Attorney of the city, he’s been working on suspected financial crimes like this longer than anyone else,” the assistant said.

Officers Black and White drove their black and white muscle, patrol car with the siren on, speeding through red traffic lights.

“Who do you want to go to first?” Officer White said.

“The Bank,” Officer Black said.

Officer White veered the patrol car right at the next intersection in Center city. After two blocks they turned off the siren and parked in front of The Bank. There was a branch of The Bank near the center of every main city across the nation. Officers Black and White stepped out of the patrol car, both standing over 6 feet tall. They walked into The Bank and straight up to the head teller.

“We’re here to see Mr. Fiat,” Officer Black said.

“Right away,” the teller said.

The teller quickly grabbed the phone on her desk and dialed.

“Mr. Fiat, Officers Black and White are here to see you,” she said.

The teller hung up the phone.

“He’ll be right out,” she said.

A door opened from a room connected to the teller desk station. A morbidly obese, short man in a pinstripe suit and tie stepped out of the door. The man opened the door of the teller station and Officers Black and White walked behind the teller station. Mr. Fiat led the officers to his office.

“What can I help you with gentlemen?” Mr. Fiat said.

“Here to collect dues for the Mayor,” Officer White said.

“This is the second time this month. What happened to our arrangement?” Mr. Fiat said.

“The police chief is asking more questions, so to keep our deal hidden, the arrangement has changed. Remember, one word to the FBI and you get put away for racketeering,” Officer Black said.

“And you would get put away for racketeering as well,” Mr. Fiat said.

“We like prison, we fit in there,” Officer White said.

“Fine… but, you double the price, and I double the price,” Mr. Fiat said.

“There’s no need for that, the Mayor said homeless rates and crime rates are at a perfect level to keep the money flowing,” Officer Black said.

A fly flew by Mr. Fiat’s face and his tongue shot out and caught the fly, which he then ate. Mr. Fiat stood up and cast a shadow of darkness over the officers. Suddenly, his skin turned red and scaly, and his pupils turned into slits.

“There’s also no need to do business with people like me gentlemen, yet you and the Mayor willingly come to us private banks to finance your city, just like every other city in the nation… haven’t you ever heard of a state owned, public bank, or does everyone just prefer to sit and drink at the table with… us? Sure, you could pummel my brains out right here and get away with it, but remember who I serve, remember the power of my master, and my master’s control over the Mayor… along with every other politician, big business, and well, everything. There’s a price for everything in this world, gentlemen, especially when you sit and drink at the table of d..,” Mr. Fiat said.

“Just give us the damn money before we take you up on your other suggestion,” Officer White said, interrupting.

Mr. Fiat sat back down and his skin and eyes returned to normal. Then Mr. Fiat handed an envelope to the officers. Officer Black grabbed the envelope and the officers stood up.

"Do tell the Mayor I said hello… from the other side," Mr. Fiat said.

Mr. Fiat laughed maniacally as the officers walked out of his office and out of The Bank to their patrol car. Mr. Fiat hit a button on his desk and a phone rang.

"Yes, Mr. Fiat?" a female voice said.

"Sheila, who's that new teller who said he had to defer his student loan payments to pay rent the past three months?" Mr. Fiat said.

"Timothy," Sheila said.

"Send him in here," Mr. Fiat said.

Timothy walked into Mr. Fiat's office.

"Jimmy, take a seat," Mr. Fiat said.

"It's… Timmy," Timothy said.

"Well, that's fine, ya know why Jimmy?" Mr. Fiat said.

"Why?" Timothy said.

Mr. Fiat's face turned red and his pupils turned into slits.

"You're fired!" Mr. Fiat yelled.

"Ahhhhh!" Timothy yelled.

Timothy ran out of Mr. Fiat's office and out of The Bank. Mr. Fiat walked to his office door and closed it, sniffing, huffing, and licking at the air left behind by Timothy.

"Ahhhh, thank you Mayor… fear and heartbreak never tasted so good," Mr. Fiat said.

Mr. Fiat laughed maniacally.

Officers Black and White drove their patrol car uptown with the sirens on, speeding through red traffic lights, and parked in the parking lot of The Insurance Company. There was a site of The Insurance Company uptown in every main city across the nation. The officers got out of their patrol car and walked inside the huge, call center site of The Insurance Company. Once inside, they walked up to the security desk.

"We're here to see Mrs. Eris," Officer Black said.

"Just one moment, gentlemen," the security guard said.

The security guard hit a button on his desk. A couple minutes later, a short, skinny elder woman in a woman's suit walked into the massive lobby.

"Greetings gentlemen, come to my office," Mrs. Eris said.

Mrs. Eris held the door open for the officers as they walked through doors of the security checkpoint. The officers waited for Mrs. Eris, then walked in tandem with her on a long corridor overlooking the massive cafeteria. Employees walked slowly to and from lunch tables. It was quiet in the cafeteria and building, other than the sound of the kitchen. All of the employees in the cafeteria stared blankly at their smartphones, moving lifelessly, other than their hands as they played video games and ate lunch.

A group of morbidly obese employees sat together at a lunch table in the cafeteria, their faces showed no emotion, and only two employees at the table talked as they ate. The two employees' eyebrows and mouths were unanimated while they conversed, quietly, so nobody else would hear them and without any body language - without any enthusiasm or energy. All of the employees' eyes were sunken in and dark.

The corridor connected to a hallway which Mrs. Eris and the officers turned and walked down. Ancient Roman era artwork decorated the hallway, many pictures being sexual and or obscene to the modern Western audience. An employee slowly walked by them in the hallway with his head down, unnoticing of the officers and site manager. The young man dragged his feet and hunched his shoulders as he walked. His face was a mixture of pain and confusion but his eyes looked lost and hopeless like he was so letdown and heartbroken that he had given up on life. They stopped at an elevator. The elevator doors opened and a woman ran out crying, pushed by them, and ran down the hallway. They entered the elevator and took it to the top floor.

The elevator stopped. They walked out of the elevator and down a hallway filled with Victorian era artwork with another employee behind them on the phone.

"That car is too old, we're not paying to replace the windshield from a hail storm, just total out the car, cut them a check for the cash value of the car, and resell the car elsewhere, who cares if he can't afford a new one, he shouldn't have filed the claim. What kind of moron puts full coverage on a 1995 anyway?" the employee said.

The employee behind them turned down a hallway just as another employee turned down the hallway in front of them talking on her cell phone, walking towards them.

"Just tell them the only procedure their insurance will cover is amputation, who cares if she has a scholarship, I never had a scholarship for a sport and now I make 6 figures a year. She shouldn't have been in the car driving that late at night. I never had friends to go out to parties with when I was in college, so I was never out that late," the woman said.

Mrs. Eris and the officers walked by the woman talking on the phone.

"And make her at-fault for the accident too, there's more drunk people out at that time of the night, she'll learn her lesson, and we can make more money off her being at-fault because she's young so her rates will go up higher," the woman said.

The woman stopped at the elevator behind them, her voice carrying down the hallway.

"I know she doesn't have collision coverage, tell her she needs to pay out of pocket for a new car since she's at-fault, this isn't a charity," the woman said.

The officers and Mrs. Eris stopped in front of a big, corner office. Mrs. Eris unlocked the door and opened it for the officers. They all stepped inside her office. Mrs. Eris sat down behind her desk, which had a huge window and view overlooking the mountains. The officers sat in chairs in front of her desk, squinting from the sunlight coming in through the window. Mrs. Eris's eyes looked in opposite directions towards the sides of the room such that it was impossible to tell who or what she was looking at.

"The police chief is asking a lot of questions, so to keep everything going smoothly we're gonna need double," Officer White said.

Mrs. Eris's eyes spun around the room when he said "double." Then she smiled. She had brilliant, white dentures. She wore a lot of perfume and makeup, and her hair was obviously fake due to it being a wig of a female's hair in her 20s, when her face revealed she was over 60.

"Double it is boys," Mrs. Eris said.

Mrs. Eris unlocked the main, center drawer of her desk, opened it, reached inside, and grabbed an envelope which she put on top of the desk. Officer White grabbed the envelope.

After the officers left, Mrs. Eris hit a button on her desk.

"Yes Mrs. Eris," a female voice said.

"Tammy, fire the three smartest men in the call center," Mrs. Eris said.

"With pleasure," Tammy said.

Mrs. Eris sat at her desk with her eyes spinning around the room like watermelons on waterwheels. She hit a button on her computer which revealed the footage from an array of CCTV surveillance cameras. She watched as one by one the men were called into their bosses' offices and fired. Then she switched to the cameras in the hallways, lobby, and parking lot to watch them leave the premises while her hand slowly reached between her legs.

"Oh, Mr. Mayor, I didn't know you felt this way," Mrs. Eris said.

She giggled and her head tilted backwards with her mouth open while her eyes rolled backwards so only the whites could be seen. She let out several short, fast breathes.

Back at the Mayor's office, the Mayor's eyes suddenly became even more pale, colorless, glassy, and unfocused while Mrs. Eris caressed herself to thoughts of the Mayor and the city's relationship with The Insurance Company. The Mayor's skin became paler, and his hair became greyer.

Officers Black and White walked into the Mayor's office and put the envelopes of money on the Mayor's desk. The Mayor vomited what looked like potato soup, with little effort, such that it landed on his own chest and lap. One of the Mayor's assistants leaned forward with a rag and cleaned off the Mayor. Another assistant grabbed the envelopes, pulled out some of the cash, and handed it to the officers.

"The Mayor said the city thanks you for your service, here is your commission," the assistant said.

The officers glanced at each other, grabbed the money, then walked out of the Mayor's office.

A couple days later, before the first of the month when rent would be due, Timothy grabbed his gun and went for a drive late at night. He stopped his car in front of a low-income house, in a rundown neighborhood, downtown. He walked up to the door and knocked three times, pausing for a moment before the third knock. A few moments later the door opened.

"What up Timmy," another guy said.

"I'm trying to pick up a few cuts to flip so I can pay rent," Timothy said.

"Fa sho, come in," the guy said.

Timothy walked into the house.

"I thought you said you were done with this shit?" the guy said.

"I was, but I just lost my job, fucking demon of a boss canned my ass the other day," Timothy said.

"Shit man, well let me show you what I got, this shit will really make you see demons," the guy said.

The guy laughed. They walked into the living room which had nothing but an old, ripped up couch and an old, tube TV with a fat back. In between the TV and couch was a table with several bags of white powder on it.

"Damn man, times been rough?" Timothy said.

"Yea well, I got busted a bit ago," the guy said.

"You got busted? What the fuck man, you didn't tell me that! The Feds are probably waiting outside on a sting right now," Timothy said.

"Nah man, I been selling again ever since I got out of jail early for good behavior, haven't got caught yet," the guy said.

"Jesus, just give me the stuff so I can get out of here," Timothy said.

"Don't you want to try it first? It's good stuff," the guy said.

The guy poured a line of white powder on the table from a bag. Timothy put his head down and snorted it through a pen cartridge. Timothy put his head up and sniffed a couple times.

"Damn, that is good stuff, I only got enough for a quarter, wish I had more," Timothy said.

"Hey man, cause I know you're a good guy going through a tough time, I can front you another quarter so you can flip a half, then just repay me later," the guy said.

"Nah man, I'm good, thanks though, I only need to flip a quarter to help pay rent, I don't need that much weight," Timothy said.

"You don't understand, I wasn't asking," the guy said.

The guy pulled out a handgun and put it on his lap.

“Take the half, flip it, pay your rent, then come back and pay me for the quarter I fronted you,” the guy said.

“What the fuck man? I thought we were cool,” Timothy said.

“We are cool… if you take the half. Remember, you’re only cool if you’re in business with me, otherwise you’re nobody to me, just like you were for the past two years while I was in jail,” the guy said.

“Fine, give me the half,” Timothy said.

“Why don’t you take a whole ounce,” the guy said.

Timothy pulled his handgun from his waistband and pointed it at the guy.

“Why don’t you give me my fucking shit so I can get out of here you sketchy mother fucker, now I’m taking just a quarter so I never have to see you again,” Timothy said.

Timothy kept his gun pointed at the guy while he put down the money for a quarter, then grabbed one of the bags of white powder.

“You see what happens when you’re a greedy fuck? Now I’m really never coming back here, because now I know what kind of person you are,” Timothy said.

“Oh, you’re no different Tim, you just landed that job at The Bank so you thought you were better than me for a while, but look where you are again, back in the slums with the yayo!” the guy shouted.

The guy reached for his gun so Timothy shot the guy’s hand. The bullet went through the guy’s hand and into his leg and blood sprayed all over the couch and bags of white powder.

“You fucker!” the guy said.

The guy lunged at Timothy and grabbed Timothy’s gun with one hand and the bag of cocaine with the other hand. Timothy’s gun fell on the floor and the bag of cocaine ripped, causing white powder to puff all over them as the guy tackled

Timothy onto the floor. Timothy headbutted the guy and blood immediately poured from his nose all over Timothy. The guy reared backwards, which allowed Timothy to roll over on top of the guy. Timothy raised his fist to punch the guy but he realized the guy was knocked out from the headbutt, bleeding profusely. Timothy stood up and grabbed his gun and all of the bags of white powder from the table before heading for the door.

Timothy ran out of the house and to his car where he opened the car door and released his armful of white bags into the passenger seat. He quickly calculated he had about one and half ounces of cocaine - several thousands of dollars' worth. Just as Timothy started his car to drive away, a cop car pulled up across the street from him. A police officer stepped out of the vehicle and began walking towards Timothy with a flashlight and one hand on the handgun at his hip.

Timothy reached for his handgun.

"Heard a report of a gunshot, just want to make sure everyone's safe," the officer said.

The officer kept walking closer, pointing his flashlight at Timothy, who was covered in the drug dealer's blood, now inside his car. Timothy quickly calculated he had enough drugs in the car for about 5 to 10 years in prison. Eventually the officer got close enough to see the dozen or so blood-covered bags of white powder in the passenger seat.

"Holy smokes! Get out of the car and put your hands up!" the officer shouted.

Just as the officer began pulling out his handgun, Timothy pointed his handgun out his window and shot several times. The first shot hit the officer in the neck and sent him flying backwards into the middle of the street, grasping at his neck as it squirted blood. The second shot hit the patrol car in the engine area, and the third shot hit the street next to the downed officer and ricocheted into the patrol car's front left tire, causing it to flatten. Then Timothy started his car and drove away into the night.

By the time Timothy made it halfway home, two cop cars were following him with their sirens on. Timothy went into shock – his face became pale, he had cold-sweats, and he was tense and shaking so much that it hurt his lungs and he could barely breathe. Timothy began speeding, faster and faster. The last thing he remembered was a truck coming from the right.

Timothy woke up in the hospital with two police officers, a doctor, and a nurse standing over him.

"Had a crazy night. There was this lunatic here who almost killed an officer in his cocaine frenzy, and we had a group of three guys who used to work together dressed up as farm animals do a string of armed robberies at gas stations and convenience stores," an officer said.

"Well, there was a full moon last night. The moon seems to do this to people, and hey, we had higher than normal birth rates last night too," the doctor said.

"Yea, I think it's called the lunar effect," a nurse said.

"I just call them lunatics," an officer said.

"Well, that's where the word lunatic comes from, Luna – the Moon, and how full Moons makes crazy people tic," the doctor said.

"Did any of those three armed robbers survive?" the officer said.

"Just one, but he's on life-support, he might not make it," the doctor said.

"It was one hell of a shoot-out. We lost an officer from those maniacs and a couple bystanders got injured; and man did they cause a lot of damage, hundreds of thousands of dollars' worth, easy," the officer said.

"The insurance companies must love these maniacs. It's brutal living in some of the zip codes in this city associated with these crimes, it's been making everyone's insurance rates skyrocket for the past couple of years," the doctor said.

"Yea right? The insurance companies always say it's not you, it's the bad drivers and bad area around you that's making your rates go up," a nurse said.

The next day, a young musician named Carl drove into the city for the first time looking to start a new life as many other young people did from around the nation to escape their old lives for the sanctuary of the nature and mountains nearby the city while chasing the American dream. He drove a beat-up 1990 sedan to a hotel, where he put on his only suit and tie. Then he drove his car uptown for his first interview in the city – at The Insurance Company.

Mrs. Eris watched from the security cameras as Carl was led through the lobby by the security guard to the recruiter for the interview. Mrs. Eris hit a button on her desk.

"Yes, Mrs. Eris?" a voice said.

"A young musician… yes… perfect… his soul will taste delicious. Hire him, we will make a plan to feed off his soul for as long as possible before destroying him," Mrs. Eris said.

"Yes, Mrs. Eris," the voice said.

Mrs. Eris took out her dentures and held them in one hand while she caressed them gently with her other hand.

"Misery, doom, chaos… misery, doom, chaos…" Mrs. Eris chanted.

Mrs. Eris's eyes spun around the room as she giggled, which then turned into a hysterical laughter.

There were a dozen people in Carl's training class, and only one other guy besides him. After several months of training, Carl was at the head of his training class and ready to start the job.

"So, today is the last day of training, you'll be sitting in your permanent seats starting tomorrow, and Training Level 2 starts tomorrow," the trainer said.

"Training Level 2?" a new hire said.

"Yeah… during Training Level 2, there will be one *coach* assigned to each of you who will monitor you for the next several months and decide whether or not you can work here," the trainer said.

The trainer emphasized the word *coach* and the room got quiet for a moment after she spoke.

"But what if our coach doesn't like us but we're the best at our jobs?" the other male, new hire said.

"Well, then you're fucked," the trainer said.

The female trainer laughed but her laughter came out in a deep, earthshaking bass tone, and sounded like two people laughing at once, slightly out of sync, like someone else laughed from inside of her, along with her. All the new hires in the room laughed nervously and glanced around at each other.

Just then, a dozen middle-aged men and women walked into the training room. One of the men who walked into the room caught all the new hires' attention because he had deep red skin, and shaved horns coming from his forehead like a bull, and a thin, black goatee. The man was wearing a black suit like the rest of the coaches but had a long red tail hanging from behind him with a triangular point at the end.

"Speaking of the devils, here are the coaches!" the trainer said.

The trainer kept laughing. Then the trainer began reading the list of which coach each new hire had next.

Carl crossed his fingers. He saw the other new hires nervously glancing around at each other and at the man with the red skin.

"Mrs. Anderson will be *coaching* Jill," the trainer said.

One of the coaches walked over to Jill.

"Mr. Peters will be *coaching* Rex," the trainer said.

Another coach walked over to Rex.

"Mr. Baal will be *coaching* Carl," the trainer said.

The man with red skin, Mr. Baal, slinked slowly over to Carl. All of the new hires stared wide-eyed at Carl as Mr. Baal walked over and sat down next to Carl. Then Mr. Baal cupped his hand around his mouth to whisper in Carl's ear.

"How bad do you want this job kid?" Mr. Baal said.

"Well, it's the highest paying one I could find, and I'm trying to set up a music studio to release an album," Carl said.

"Ohhhh, a musician. We'll see how well you fit in around here," Mr. Baal said.

Mr. Baal laughed, then his abnormally long, pitchfork tongue shot out and went inside Carl's ear before retracting back into his mouth.

"Ewwww gross!" Carl said.

"Is something wrong Carl?" the trainer said.

Everyone in the room looked at Carl.

"Nobody saw that?" Carl said.

"Saw what?" the trainer said.

"Ugh, nothing," Carl said.

"Don't interrupt again or we'll have to enforce our disciplinary code," the trainer said.

The only other guy in Carl's training class mysteriously never came back to work one day during Training Level 2, but of those remaining from Carl's original training class, Carl had the best performance metrics and received the most compliments from customers for his customer service.

Carl even had several ideas for products and services which could be profitable to the company, but he didn't share them with anyone because everyone else in his training class eventually graduated from Training Level 2 except him, even the employees who were the slowest learners, performed much worse, and were much less qualified and educated for the job – in fact, it seemed the employees who were struggling the most and were least desirable for the job and company were the ones who graduated Training Level 2 first and were allowed to work at The Insurance Company without being *coached.* The *coaching* sessions between Carl and Mr. Baal were also increasing in frequency over time.

Carl sat in his cubicle on a phone call.

"And, is there anything else I can assist with?" Carl said.

"No kid, you did a great job. Every other time I call in here I just get put on hold, you're the first person to actually help me. Can I talk to one of your supervisors to tell them what a great job you did?" the customer said.

"Sure, I'll transfer you to her voicemail, have a good one," Carl said.

Carl transferred the customer to his supervisor's voicemail. Then he looked to his right and saw the employees next to him had their customers on hold while they whispered a conversation with each other.

Then Carl got an instant message from Mr. Baal.

"Let's have a coaching session," Mr. Baal said.

Carl walked slowly over to Mr. Baal's cubicle and sat down in a spare seat next to Mr. Baal's desk.

"So, I listened to all your phone calls over the week, as usual, and I'm not really seeing the improvement I'm wanting to let you graduate from Training Level 2. Are you sure you can do this job?" Mr. Baal said.

"Yes," Carl said.

"Well, your numbers need to be higher because once you're done Training Level 2 you won't have anyone like me to push you to keep your numbers up so you're numbers are probably going to drop, so we gotta prepare you for if your numbers drop by getting them higher now," Mr. Baal said.

"I'm doing my best," Carl said.

"For this phone call you took yesterday, when you cancel an insurance policy, make sure you read everything on the screen verbatim, and you can still sell a homeowner's policy to someone even though they just cancelled their auto insurance policy, I didn't even hear you make an offer, we need you to make offers on every call," Mr. Baal said.

"Is there anything else I need to do better in order to graduate from Training Level 2?" Carl said.

"Yea, there's just a bunch of little things that you could do better. We expect perfection a certain number of times before we can graduate you, especially you because of your education and qualifications. You're doing really well in offering renter's policies but only average in other metrics like discussing online services – we need consistency and perfection around the board. I'm gonna give you the manual and recordings of flawless phone calls rated 10 out of 10. I want all of your calls to sound like these and go exactly by the manual. Here," Mr. Baal said.

Mr. Baal handed Carl a thick manual and several CDs.

"Go back to your desk and listen to those CDs and read the manual, but don't take too long because the more time you spend on those materials the less time you're on the phone so the more it hurts your metrics, if you don't figure out how to graduate in the next week or two we're gonna have to start disciplinary action and possibly even termination," Mr. Baal said.

When Carl walked back to his desk he noticed there was a red-skinned woman with long horns and a long, pointed tail rummaging through Carl's desk.

"Hey, can I help you?" Carl said.

"Eeek!" the red woman said.

The red woman snuck down the aisle, as if Carl didn't already see her. She scurried away almost theatrically - holding her arms up like a T-Rex and lifting her knees high as she fled down the aisle, turned, then ran across the office before turning down another hallway out of sight.

"Did nobody just see that… person at my desk?" Carl said.

"Who? I didn't see anyone," the girl next to Carl said.

"There was just a… red woman at my desk," Carl said.

Another girl sitting behind Carl laughed.

"Red woman? What are you talking about?" she said.

"With horns… and a tail…" Carl said.

All the girls who sat in the cubicles around Carl stared at him. All the girls had customers on hold. The irises of their eyes which were normally colored were as black as their pupils - either their pupils had dilated or their irises had turned black.

"Have you lost your mind?" one of the girls said.

"Maybe you should see the company doctor," another girl said.

Then the three girls congregated in one of the girl's cubicles, whispering to each other with their customers still on hold while glancing at Carl.

"I used to think he was *so* hot," a third girl whispered.

Carl sat down at his desk and moved his computer mouse. His dual screen monitors came out of sleep mode and revealed all the icons on his screen were missing and there were several insurance policies open with recent changes done to them while he was meeting with Mr. Baal.

"What the Hell?" Carl said.

Carl clocked out of work that night, then walked with his shoulders slumped over and his head down while dragging his feet. Mrs. Eris watched Carl as she sat in her office from the surveillance cameras as Carl slowly walked through the lobby and out into the parking lot to his car. Mrs. Eris hit a button on her desk.

"Yes, Mrs. Eris?" a voice said.

"Gather some of the air from the path Carl took from his desk all the way to the parking lot - his injured soul is oozing out fresh and tasty life force... I can smell his misery from here. And try to gather some dried skin and sweat from off his desk, chair, keyboard, and mouse - also bring me his trash," Mrs. Eris said.

"Yes, Mrs. Eris," the voice said.

Mrs. Eris's eyes began to spin in circles faster and faster as her hand reached between her legs and her other hand squeezed her fake breasts.

The next week, Carl's supervisor called him over to her desk.

"Carl, you're a good guy, but we don't think you're going to succeed at this company. You haven't graduated from Training Level 2 yet, and you don't seem to be fitting in with our culture," the supervisor said.

"But my performance metrics are some of the highest every month!" Carl said.

"You can be the best employee in the company and you won't go anywhere in this company without fitting in with our culture, plus, you made a couple of bad mistakes on some insurance policies last week and you were off the phone for several hours while the IT department fixed whatever you did to your computer that same day," the supervisor said.

"I told you, that wasn't me, someone was at my desk when I came back from my meeting with Mr. Baal," Carl said.

"I asked Mr. Baal and he said you guys didn't even have a meeting that day. Besides, using someone else's computer to open insurance policies is a violation of our ethics and privacy laws, nobody here would ever do that, which brings into question your ethics for saying someone else would do such a thing instead of taking responsibility for your own actions," the supervisor said.

"But..." Carl said.

"But nothing, Carl. We're all very disappointed in your performance and behavior as an employee. We had such high hopes and plans for you. We originally thought you would be promoted fast at this company and find a comfortable career here, but you proved us wrong – you couldn't even make it out of Training Level 2. You're terminated from employment Carl. Please get your belongings and leave the premises," the supervisor said.

As Carl walked out of the office, a security guard escorted him out - to block the view of another employee walking behind Carl with a long bag, collecting air and particulates in Carl's trail.

Mrs. Eris watched the surveillance footage from a secret room down a corridor in the basement of the Insurance Company building. She was with several other higher-up managers, directors, and employees with red skin in a dark room, lit only by candles. A bronze statue of a goat sodomizing the Greek God Pan stood in the middle of the room.

"Let us begin the ritual!" Mrs. Eris cried.

An employee walked a live goat into the middle of the room next to the statue.

"Oh mighty Lord Baphomet! Let the altering of the course of this musician's life cause a chain reaction of negative events to inflict misery, and cause chaos to please you. And let the sacrifice of this animal cause the manifestation of powerful demons amongst all of us who drink its blood while we consume the hopelessness, fear, and pain of this young, powerful musician," Mrs. Eris said.

Mrs. Eris began chanting incantations from an old, tattered grimoire – a book of magic. Two more employees walked into the dark room, one employee with a bag of air from Carl's trail, and the other employee with bags of trash from Carl's desk which was collected over the past several months since he began Training Level 2. The employees huffed and licked the contents of the bags while passing them around the room.

Mr. Baal used a large knife to cut the goat's neck while two other employees held the goat's legs, and a third employee held a bowl under the goat collecting the blood as it drained out. The employees then passed the bowl of goat blood around the room, drinking from it and pouring blood all over their hands and faces. They began painting the floor, walls, and each other with the goat's blood until the bowl was empty and they were rolling around on the floor with the writhing, hollering goat - everyone covered in blood and Carl's trash. Soon, employees began stripping and tearing each other's clothes off, and an orgy began as the goat died.

The police chief, Mayor, and his staff met in the Mayor's office watching the local news. A reporter and cameraman stood in front of a crowd holding signs outside of the Mayor's office.

"Protests have erupted outside of the Mayor's office after the Mayor voted to close 10 more elementary schools, displacing over 1000 students due to lack of public funds. So, the question on everyone's mind is, where are the funds going? Where's all the money at?" a reporter said.

The reporter put the microphone up to a protestor.

"Crimes been on the rise for the past couple of years ever since this Mayor took office, and everyone seems to be broke, except the police and people working for the Mayor," a woman said.

The reporter put the microphone up to another protestor.

"Schools are closing, roads aren't getting rebuilt, no money is going to build new public projects – the money is disappearing and the homeless rates are soaring. Something is going on, something isn't right, it never used to be like this, somethings gotta change!" a man said.

"I don't know what's going on, Mayor, the financial crimes unit can't get any leads through Officers Black and White, and if we don't get some answers soon, there could be riots," the police chief said.

The Mayor sat in his chair behind his desk, staring at the TV. His eyes had become almost entirely pale, colorless, and glazed-over. The Mayor began coughing and splatters of blood appeared on his desk. Then the Mayor gagged several times before he sprayed green vomit like a laser all over his desk, splashing onto the police chief's back and side. Some green vomit squirted from the Mayor's nostrils, leaving tendrils of chunky slime hanging from his nose. One of his assistants used a rag to wipe off the Mayor's face.

"The Mayor said send Officers Black and White, and them only," an assistant said.

"God dammit," the police chief said.

Carl sat in front of Mr. Fiat during an interview at The Bank.

"You know, I run shit around here. I didn't have to make time to interview you myself, but I wanted to, because this is an important role, and I want to make sure I hire the right person," Mr. Fiat said.

"Yes sir," Carl said.

"As internal auditor, you gotta make sure this ship is sailing smooth, without any dirty sails, if you catch my drift. My last internal auditor spent 5 years in the slammer for white collar crimes for not doing his job while a bunch of filth was going on, you know what I mean?" Mr. Fiat said.

Carl gulped.

"Yes sir," Carl said.

Mr. Fiat leaned in over his desk towards Carl. His face came within a foot or so of Carl's face. Mr. Fiat's arms extended across the table, his hands shaking as he held the edge of the table in front of Carl. Then Mr. Fiat's skin turned red and scaly, and his voice sounded unnaturally deep.

"Because when the Feds come knockin, they come knockin hard bitch!" Mr. Fiat said.

Carl leaned far back into his chair and almost fell over backwards.

"Yes sir," Carl said.

Mr. Fiat leaned back to his normal sitting position and his skin and voice turned back to normal as well.

"Perfect, you're hired," Mr. Fiat said.

At the end of Carl's first week, on Friday afternoon, he sat in his office, listening to music while scrolling through the database of home loans. Carl leaned in towards the computer screen and his eyebrows pointed in towards the middle of his forehead. He turned off the music. Then he opened another database of collateralized debt obligations (CDOs). Carl put his hand over his mouth. His hand shook as he opened the database of credit default swaps (CDS). Then his arms fell at his sides and he leaned back in his chair, throwing his head backwards and looking up at the ceiling.

"Oh my God," Carl said.

Carl got out of his chair and walked out of his office to Mr. Fiat's office. Carl knocked on the door.

"Come in," Mr. Fiat said.

Carl opened the door. Mr. Fiat sat at his desk with a large plate of pasta and breadsticks.

"Yes Carl?" Mr. Fiat said.

"Mr. Fiat, I think I found something bad you might want to look at," Carl said.

"Carl, I won't lie, if I stand up right now, I might shit myself, just tell me what the problem is," Mr. Fiat said.

"Upwards of 70% of our home loans are resulting in defaults and foreclosures, the same home loans which are being bundled into CDOs, which are then rated AAA by credit rating agencies, and are being sold to investors. At the same time, we are selling these CDOs to investors, our partner investment firms are buying CDS which will pay off when the CDOs fail, and this has been going on for years… as if someone internally is purposely selling home loans to people without jobs, loans with interest rates that will skyrocket so that they fail, knowing the CDOs from these bundled loans will also then fail even though they are rated AAA, which will cause a payoff on the CDS. Someone's getting rich off of us selling bogus home loans and CDOs by betting on them to fail with CDS!" Carl said.

"You're right, someone *is* getting rich off of fraudulently selling CDOs to investors knowing they will fail and betting against them with CDS, and someone else better keep their fucking mouth shut about it," Mr. Fiat said.

Mr. Fiat stood up and his face turned red and scaly. He seemed to grow in size and casted a dark shadow over Carl.

"But Mr. Fiat, this is securities fraud and possibly racketeering, people could go to jail for this!" Carl said.

"The Feds busted us for something similar about a month ago and the guy in your position went to jail for it, so if you think about it, they probably won't investigate again for a while since they recently did," Mr. Fiat said.

"Mr. Fiat, I'm not going to jail for this!" Carl said.

"Well, do you want a job?" Mr. Fiat said.

"Yea, but…" Carl said.

"Then keep your fucking mouth shut and there will be a bonus in it for you, otherwise get the fuck out of my bank and never come back you goodie two-shoes, fairy loving bastard.

Your parents hate you and wish they never had you!" Mr. Fiat said.

"Jesus!" Carl said.

Mr. Fiat slammed his hands on his desk.

"Don't say that name in my office or I'll scalp you and hang you as a trophy! Right there!" Mr. Fiat screamed.

Mr. Fiat pointed to the wall where what looked like a wig and the skin of someone's head hung.

"That's where I'll hang you! Now get back to work! There's still two hours left in the day, you daisy picking bitch!" Mr. Fiat said.

Mr. Fiat picked up a breadstick and threw it at Carl. Carl ducked and the breadstick exploded against the door behind him.

"Fuck! Theresa, get in here and clean up this mess!" Mr. Fiat yelled.

Carl ran out of Mr. Fiat's office back to his office where he locked the door, panting and sweating.

"Eat it off the floor, you fat whore!" Mr. Fiat yelled.

Mr. Fiat's voiced echoed throughout the bank. Customers in line for the teller glanced back and forth at each other nervously.

The next week at work, Carl sat in his office using the computer to look through the city's accounts such as the municipal water account, sewer account, public school district accounts, etc. Then Carl looked through the city's investment portfolio with The Bank. Carl began shaking his head. He put his face in his palms and began weeping quietly. Just then Mr. Fiat walked into his office.

"What's wrong, did you finally find out your family has been trying to get you killed since you were a teenager?" Mr. Fiat said.

"No… wait, what? It's the city's accounts and investments, Mr. Fiat, something's just not right. The city is paying The Bank millions of dollars for interest rate swaps – for bad bets. The city took out these interest rate swaps years ago to lock in fixed interest rates, and shortly after, the Federal Reserve made interest rates drop to near 0, which locked the city into higher interest rates, and the city has been paying millions of dollars to The Bank for these swaps instead of using those funds for public projects. This is why schools are closing, roads aren't getting worked on, and why the city is falling apart. This is where all the money's going, and why everyone in town is in an uproar on the News!" Carl said.

Mr. Fiat laughed maniacally and his voice deepened to sound nonhuman. His skin turned red and scaly and the light in the room began to dim.

"Yes Carl, that *is* where all the money is going, and if you say anything about it, you'll be fired and never work in this city again. You'll have to go back to whatever rinky-dink town you came from or walk the streets homeless. You must be a really shitty musician for Satan to not want to buy your soul, and you're too good of a person to survive in the corporate world, so you're fucked!" Mr. Fiat said.

"You're a monster!" Carl said.

"You're fired! Get the hell out of my Bank before I call the police you worthless piece of shit!" Mr. Fiat screamed.

Mr. Fiat took a handgun out from his pocket and raised it in the air.

"You have 30 seconds turkey fucker!" Mr. Fiat screamed.

Carl ran out of The Bank, got in his car, and drove to his apartment.

When Carl got inside his apartment building, he noticed there was a man in a black top hat and black trench coat standing in front of the door to his apartment.

"Can I help you?" Carl said.

"It wouldn't be so much helping as much as establishing a mutually beneficial relationship, Carl," the man said.

The man whispered but his voice bellowed a cacophonous voice down the hallway.

"How do you know my name? Who are you?" Carl said.

"My name is not relevant so much as the entity I represent. Because you're a talented musician, you have learned the gears of The Machine by working for The Insurance Company and The Bank," the man said.

"I'm calling the FBI," Carl said.

"What for?" the man said.

"This is a God damned racket. The city puts the taxpayer's money in The Bank and The Bank uses that money for investments which rob the taxpayers of more money, while also secretly rigging home loans and investments to fail to rob investors of money," Carl said.

"Mmhmm. And what else did you find out?" the man said.

"And I'm pretty sure The Insurance Company purposely hires then fires people within a few months to make our resumes look bad which contributes to homelessness because higher homeless rates increase crime rates, and insurance companies profit off higher crime rates by raising insurance rates due to claims and in crime-filled areas. They discriminate against hardworking, young men like me to profit off homelessness and crime. This is probably happening in every city across the nation. I'm calling the FBI," Carl said.

"Whoa whoa, no need to do that, why don't we talk business?" the man said.

"You're freaking me out man, how do you know who I am and where I live?" Carl said.

"Let's just say the entity I represent is all-knowing and all-powerful and has been waiting for you to be chewed up and spit out by The Machine - rejected for who you are so that you may fulfill your destiny," the man said.

"God dammit, ever since I moved to this city, my life has been completely out of my control and full of surprises, I don't know what to believe anymore," Carl said.

"Believe that there is a higher entity with power over you who has been controlling your path all your life whether you know it or not," the man said.

"What the Hell do you want from me?" Carl said.

"We should talk inside, aren't you going to invite me in?" the man said.

"Ugh, fine, let's go," Carl said.

Carl unlocked his door and they walked inside his apartment. Carl closed the door behind them. The man removed his top hat, revealing a shaved horn on the middle of his forehead, and his ears were pointed upwards more like a horse than a human.

"Oh, come on," Carl said.

"What?" the man said.

"You're clearly a demon," Carl said.

"No… not clearly… only when I have my hat removed people can tell," the man said.

The man blushed and his eyebrows arched towards the middle of his forehead as he took a defensive step backwards. He held his hat in his hands up near his chest like an insecure, little boy. His hands were overgrown, pinkish-red, and had shaved, pointed claws instead of fingernails.

Carl sighed.

"Well, get on with it," Carl said.

The man pulled out a several page document from inside his trench coat.

"Read this, sign it, and say goodbye to your old life," the man said.

Carl took the document and sat down at the table.

"Is this a contract from Satan?" Carl said.

"He goes by that name sometimes, other times, he's a she. In short, we will give you 2 million dollars to live off while you make music for us, which we will also market for you, and set up your tours, and take care of you, as long as you take care of our needs. All your sales go back to us until you repay the 2 million dollars, then, once you break past 2 million dollars in sales you will start making a small percentage of royalties from your sales. The contract is for 5 years and requires you to put out at least two albums, then after 5 years we can renegotiate the contract based on sales performance. No tricks, no legal jargon, just making music as a full-time job," the man said.

Carl read terms out loud from one of the pages of the contract.

"Breaching of the contract is punishable by death… I cannot disclose anything about my past careers, I cannot contact anyone from my past… Wait a second here, I just found out the answer to the problem everyone in the city is talking about. I need to tell the police or the FBI that The Bank and The Insurance Company are stealing all the city taxpayers' money and causing homelessness, it's a racket, it's a scam, it's fraud," Carl said.

"It's how every city in the country runs kid. In every city, either the Mayor or police are in on it. The FBI looks the other way to keep the gears of The Machine running. Everyone in power knows insurance companies and banks cause homelessness by firing employees after a couple months of hiring, submerging people in debt, and by structuring bad home loans. There can never be no homelessness - the police know homelessness increases crime and crime stimulates the economy - the police wouldn't have jobs without crime, so they need a constant source of it. And the Mayor knows depositing the taxpayer's money in private banks and investing with private banks is robbing the taxpayers and the city of money to make the rich richer and the poor poorer. Everyone who knows how The Machine really works gets paid to shut up, and this is how we shut people like you up, by turning you into a celebrity," the man said.

"This isn't right... this is so demonic," Carl said.

The man smiled shyly and nodded.

"You're right. And you really don't have any other options. You can try to fight it, but you'll be homeless soon without another job and nobody else in the city will hire you. Everyone who fights it ends up dead or leaving the country," the man said.

Carl sighed.

"I don't have a pen," Carl said.

"Oh, you don't need a pen to sign this kind of contract. Here, give me your hand," the man said.

Carl stuck out his hand. The man held Carl's hand, palm-up with one hand then quickly pulled out a previously concealed knife with his other hand and slashed Carl's palm.

"Ouch! Hey! What the fuck man?" Carl said.

"Sign it," the man said.

Carl signed his name with his blood on the contract as the man licked the knife clean. Then the man slashed his own hand and signed the contract on the witness line. The man's blood was so red it was almost black.

"There, that wasn't hard, was it? The next time you open your bank account you will see a $2 million dollar deposit. Here is the location of the recording studio you will use," the man said.

The man put a business card down on the table.

"Alright, now get the fuck out weirdo before I call the cops," Carl said.

The man sighed.

"Nobody ever lets Amdusias stay for dinner," the man said.

"That's because you're a demon, now please, leave," Carl said.

Amdusias turned slowly and walked out of the door of the apartment.

The next morning, Carl drove to a music studio on the outskirts of the city owned by one of the powerhouse music record labels, Beleth Records. Carl parked in the parking lot which only had a couple other cars. When Carl walked up to the door of the music studio, three imps crawled out of a nearby bush, each imp no more than four feet in height, all with horns, and long pointed tails. One imp had purple skin, one had red skin, and the other had grey skin.

"Come," an imp said.

Carl sighed and shook his head.

"This is already weird," Carl said.

The imps led Carl around the back of the building and stopped in front of a door.

"This door can only be opened by three or more imp drum masters," an imp said.

Then the three imps unleashed a complex, polyrhythmic drum beat against the door with their bare hands for several measures before stopping. The door opened.

A massive, greyish-white man with a disproportionally large, beachball-sized head, huge facial features, and big ears stood at the doorway holding the door open for Carl and the imps. The man also had horns and a tail, and held a large, wooden staff.

"Ronové, take Carl to the music studio – and don't eat him," the purple imp said.

"Bahhh," Ronové said.

Ronové leaned down and grabbed the purple imp by the legs with one hand. He held the imp above his head and put the imp into his mouth, head first.

"Ahhhhhh!" the imp yelled.

"Nooo, don't do it!" another imp yelled.

Ronové chomped down with the imp halfway in his mouth and blood dripped down his cheeks as he crushed and impaled the imp's midsection. Then Ronové pulled upwards on the imp's legs - ripping the imp in half and causing blood, entrails, and tendrils of flesh to hang between Ronové's mouth and the bottom half of the imp. The imp's blood and guts spilled all over the floor.

Carl huddled down in the entranceway, shaking. The two other imps ran down the hallway screaming as Ronové chewed and swallowed the top half of the imp and dropped the other half on the floor. Ronové burped then turned towards Carl.

"Come," Ronové said.

Ronové began walking down the hallway. Carl followed, keeping a small distance from the monster. They stopped in front of an old-style, hand crank elevator which looked new and polished. Ronové opened the golden gates of the elevator and Carl walked in, followed by Ronové who had to duck to fit. Ronové cranked the elevator down to the 13th basement level.

The elevator stopped and they stepped out, then walked down a hallway which had checkered patterns on the walls, floors, and ceiling. The checkered pattern down the hallway created an optical illusion to make it look like there were random bulges, indents, curves, expansions, and contractions, when in reality it was just a straight hallway. It gave Carl a headache to look at and made him stagger as he walked behind the monster.

They stopped at a room numbered 33, and Ronové opened the door for Carl. Carl walked inside a music studio and a regal sounding trumpet played to his entrance. Carl turned and saw Amdusias holding a trumpet in his mouth.

"You again?" Carl said.

"Ladies and gentlemen, the musician Carl is here to record his first album," Amdusias said.

Carl looked around the music studio. There was nobody else there.

“Umm, who are you talking to? We’re alone,” Carl said.

“Oh, no we’re not! There are many spirits here - they’ve come to hear you, and now they tell me Lord Beleth himself is approaching!” Amdusias said.

Amdusias began playing the trumpet, once again, as though for the entrance of royalty. Carl stared at the door. Amdusias began to play louder towards the climax of his trumpet part. Then Amdusias stopped playing. Suddenly, the door to their room swung open and a gust of wind hit Carl, knocking him backwards onto the floor. Then the door closed.

“Lord Beleth said hello. He came and he went, he has much business to attend to, but you should feel lucky that he introduced himself to you, not all new musicians get such an introduction,” Amdusias said.

Carl stood up again.

“What the… Can we just start making music?” Carl said.

“Of course. At that computer you will find your songs,” Amdusias said.

“What do you mean? I have my songs with me,” Carl said.

Carl pulled a notebook and a USB flash drive out of his backpack.

Amdusias laughed.

“You don’t think you’re actually going to record and perform your own music, do you?” Amdusias said.

“Well yea, isn’t that what professional musicians do?” Carl said.

Amdusias laughed again.

“Listen kid, in that computer you’ll find a catalogue of songs that you can choose from to record. Other than that, you can burn all your old lyrics, recordings, dreams, etc.,” Amdusias said.

“Then what do you even need me for if nothing I perform will be my own work?” Carl said.

“For your soul!” Amdusias said.

Amdusias laughed hysterically. Just then thunder shook the building from a storm above. The lights dimmed and flickered for a couple seconds, creating a strobe light effect, and in the strobing light, Amdusias’s head transformed into a horse and the horn in the middle of his head grew to full length - like a unicorn. Amdusias’s laughter thundered like the storm above.

“Ahhhhh!” Carl screamed.

The Mayor and his assistants met with the city budget analysts and finance directors in the Mayor’s office.

“Mayor, we have a problem on our hands. If we don’t do something soon, the city will have to declare bankruptcy,” an analyst said.

“About half of our water bill is for paying interest on bad interest rate swaps, all of our accounts are getting submerged in debt, and we’re losing more money for the schools, libraries, roads, and other public services,” a finance director said.

The Mayor’s eyes had become so pale that from only a short distance away they looked entirely off-white and glossy with no iris or pupils. His hair had become entirely grey and was falling out in strands which drifted slowly onto his desk. The Mayor groaned then fell face forward, bashing his forehead loudly onto his wood desk. One of the Mayor’s assistants pulled him upright as a trickle of blood ran from his forehead down his face.

“The Mayor said there’s nothing to worry about, he’s seen this happen before, it’s just cyclical, by next season everything will go back into the positive and everything will be normal again,” an assistant said.

"But what about the fire that's been burning for over a month now down near the industrial plants?" the director of parks and recreation said.

"Yea, they had to close down one of the plants because of it, and the nearby residents have been complaining of the smell. Pretty soon this town is gonna turn into that town in Pennsylvania that's had a mine fire burning since the early 1960s if we don't do something about it," an analyst said.

"Yea," the other directors and analysts said.

Just then, the lights grew dim and an unholy growl came from the Mayor. The door to the Mayor's office flung open and Ronové stepped into the room holding his long, wooden staff.

"Who is this big, naked ogre? He smells horrid, someone call the police," a director said.

Ronové thrusted his hollow, wooden staff into the sternum of the director of parks and recreation, which made a loud cracking noise. The director only let out a squeak as Ronové hoisted the director into the air, impaled on his staff, then Ronové put his mouth on the other end of his staff and inhaled strongly. Ronové kept sucking… then gulping on his staff – his straw, as blood ran down his chin until the director impaled on the other end of the staff was a bloodless sac of skin and bones. The directors and analysts watched in horror as the Mayor's assistants smiled.

Another director pulled out a handgun and shot Ronové in the head and chest several times until the gun's clip was empty. Thick, purple blood glopped from Ronové's head and chest all over the floor as Ronové screamed in pain.

Ronové's scream shook the room and all the directors and analysts covered their ears and ran out of the door, leaving the director with the empty handgun staring at Ronové. Ronové swung his long staff with inhuman speed, striking the man on the side of the head. The man spun and fell down on the floor, unconscious. Ronové walked up behind the man and speared him through a natural orifice with his wooden staff, then hoisted him up into the air, resting the staff on his shoulder with the man impaled on top as he walked out of the Mayor's office.

One of the Mayor's assistants pulled out a cellphone and made a call.

"Amdusias, it's time. We can't wait any longer, people are going to start talking and realize what's going on. Ronové just made a scene in front of the city's staff in the Mayor's office," the assistant said.

"Oh, Ronové will do that. He really is a friendly demon if he's on your side, and he usually just eats farm animals. I've known him for thousands of years…" Amdusias said.

"Amdusias, the plan," the assistant said.

"Oh right, I have just the person for the job," Amdusias said.

Amdusias laughed and hung up the phone. Amdusias hit a button on the desk of the audio workstation where he sat in the music production room and spoke to Carl from a speaker. Carl was recording music in the room next to Amdusias, on the other side of a see-through, sound-proof glass wall so Amdusias could see him and communicate through the speaker.

"Oh Carl, when you're done that recording, come out here and talk to me," Amdusias said.

Several minutes later, Carl walked out of the recording room into the producing room where Amdusias sat.

"Carl, I need you to record this song, right now, we're going to release it as a single ASAP. It'll be your debut single - you'll be huge! We'll put you all over the radio and internet across the world, then we're gonna dye your hair blonde and pierce your nipples then put you on the media," Amdusias said.

"What happened to me at least getting to pick what I want to record from that catalogue? Now you're telling me what I have to record?" Carl said.

"Well Carl, did you read the contract? You can pick what songs you want for the albums, but Section 7B clearly states that we have the rights to make you release up to 5 singles or bonus tracks per contract lifespan, so that means you're doing this single, and that means Christmas songs when the time comes," Amdusias said.

"Awwww, I hate Christmas songs, just give me the damn single, I'll do it," Carl said.

"That's a good boy," Amdusias said.

Amdusias handed Carl the lyrics to the song.

"We already have the instrumental recorded, all you gotta do is sing," Amdusias said.

"The Beast…? These lyrics are kinda weird man, is this for some sort of dark ritual?" Carl said.

"Yes, and there's a shit ton of subliminal messages in the instrumental too, now get back there and record it," Amdusias said.

"Jesus…" Carl said.

Amdusias whinnied like a horse and covered his ears with his hands.

"Please do not say that name around here!" Amdusias said.

Carl walked back into the recording room and put on headphones to listen to the instrumental of "The Beast" while he sang the lyrics into a microphone.

That Friday, "The Beast," was released worldwide as Carl's debut single, under the artist name *Necromancer*. In cities across America, including Carl's city, "The Beast," was promoted by all the social media and played on the radio.

Carl's promoters had the music video hyped up on television shows so the music video easily went viral. The music video was Carl dressed as the stereotypical devil - wearing a red suit with horns, a red tail, and holding a pitchfork while doing a choregraphed, sensual dance with female backup dancers who were all dressed as goats. Carl's hair was dyed blonde and by the end of the music video he was topless and revealed his freshly pierced nipples and shaved torso.

Also, in the music video, was a large amount of occult symbolism in the dance and background scenery, from covering one eye, to pyramids, upside-down pentagrams, and The Square and Compasses. There was really only one verse to the song which was sung twice, other than the chorus and background chants in Latin, Greek, and other ancient languages.

The Beast has awoken
His army is here
Invocations are spoken
To summon your fears
The portal is open
Now demons appear
From bottoms of oceans
To tops of the piers
From pits we have chosen
It'll soon be clear
All will suffocate
In this atmosphere

"Are those background singers trying to summon demons?" Carl said.

"Yes, and put curses on the listeners," Amdusias said.

"Good Lord," Carl said.

"Uh uh - just the Dark Lord," Amdusias said.

The night of Carl's debut single release, the fire outside the industrial park in the city grew out of control and caught a nearby industrial building on fire. Wind carried poisonous smoke around the city, bathing the city in ash. By the time the firefighters arrived, it looked like Hell on Earth. Materials, chemicals, and equipment inside the industrial building were combusting into brilliant purple, blue, and green flames, illuminating the night sky.

Suddenly, the ground near the epicenter of the fire collapsed like a sinkhole, pulling the industrial building down into a raging fire pit. The ground continued to shake like an earthquake, and from the edges of the sinkhole, hundreds of hands emerged.

"Oh my God, are those people trapped?" a firefighter said.

More hands emerged from the sinkhole, followed by the heads and torsos of what looked like humans covered in mud and ash. Firefighters ran towards the beings emerging from the hole, then they stopped, turned around, and ran back towards their firetrucks.

"We gotta get the fuck out of here! Those creatures do not want our help!" a firefighter yelled.

The creatures looked like humans, but they were all naked, pale, and horribly disfigured and covered in mud and ash. Some had more than two arms while some had one arm or no arms at all. Some had more than one head while some had no head at all. Not all of the creatures had limbs and faces in normal spots of the body either. Some had tails, some had tentacles, and some crawled like dogs, while others crawled like crabs or spiders. Some sprinted towards the firefighters and the city, some hopped, some walked slowly, and some choked on the air and died.

The firefighters began getting back into their trucks, turning off their hoses, and driving away as a wave of the humanlike beings surrounded the firetrucks. The creatures threw themselves at the firetrucks as the trucks drove away, running over the creatures.

"What the Hell are these things?" a firefighter said.

"I don't know, but they look like they came from Hell!" another firefighter said.

Carl and Amdusias watched the News from the music studio.

"Thousands and thousands of… mutants… barbarians are raving the city. All residents are to evacuate their homes for the nearest shelter which the police and military personnel are directing everyone to. These savages are ruthless and are so many in number that the city's Police have called in the National Guard, and Martial Law is in effect. God help us make it through this dark night," the anchorman said.

The anchorman sobbed as the TV showed a bird's eye view of thousands of creatures running through the city, destroying businesses, buildings, and killing anyone in their paths. They broke into apartments and houses, cannibalizing everyone they found. Police forces were mobilized on all the main streets with riot procedures as the military rolled tanks, drove Humvees, and flew helicopters into the city, firing at will.

"Hey Carl, did you figure out what The Insurance Company and The Bank were doing with all the taxpayers' money?" Amdusias said.

"No… it can't be. This attack on the city is funded by… the corporations?" Carl said.

Amdusias laughed.

"Not just any corporations - The Dark Lord's corporations, run by his most powerful demons. You see, all the money The Bank and The Insurance Company have been making was being used for decades to advance science… by creating an army of mutants in underground bases all across the country to take over the human race," Amdusias said.

"Oh my God," Carl said.

"Please Carl, God's not here. It's really a scientific miracle to create such beasts. They can live deep underground by breathing sulfur, and drinking hydrochloric acid; not to mention, the taxpayers really seem to be admiring their investment," Amdusias said.

Amdusias laughed manically.

"How many are there?" Carl said.

"Oh millions, by the morning there will be sinkholes in cities across the country pouring out mutants to ravage everything in sight. And that's not even the finale," Amdusias said.

"You mean, it gets worse?" Carl said.

"Of course it gets worse! It's the apocalypse buddy, we're here to fuck shit up!" Amdusias said.

Just then, a loud cackling came from the sinkhole which was heard halfway across the city and was picked up on the TV's broadcast of the event.

"Cluck, cluck, clucawwwk!" something cackled.

Carl looked at the TV. A colossal chicken with a half metal face, about the size of a skyscraper, part metallic and part organic popped its head up from the sinkhole. The chicken squinted at the lights and let out a startled squawk. Then the chicken pecked at a couple of nearby mutants, jackhammering a hole in the ground with its beak while dismembering and crushing mutants in its wake.

"What the fuck is that thing?" Carl said.

"Isn't he beautiful? He's a genetically engineered chicken with some mechanical enhancements. That fucker can live in space off ice crystals. We made about a dozen of them. This one's named Camio, our biggest one is a mouse which will be wreaking havoc on New York in about 20 minutes," Amdusias said.

Carl, Amdusias, and the majority of the city's citizens watched the TV as the chicken walked through the city, stepping on police cars and tanks with its huge talons. The chicken stopped in front of a building about the same height as itself and pecked at it. The first peck put a massive hole in the building like an overgrown wrecking ball, shattering windows on all sides of the building. A couple pecks later and the building fell over, crushing other buildings and creating a plume of dust across the nearby streets.

The chicken left a trail of blood where it walked as it took the majority of focused gunfire from the police and military, allowing the smaller mutants to swarm. Fighter jets flew overhead and launched missiles at the chicken, which exploded and left holes in the chicken's face and body, horribly disfiguring the chicken as chunks of its flesh were blown off and incinerated.

The chicken began jumping in the air and flapping its massive wings to destroy jets and helicopters which flew by, but as the morning light broke, the chicken's assault slowed as it reached center city, and eventually the chicken was so shredded from gunfire and explosives that it could no longer function and support its own weight. The chicken let out one final squawk before falling beak first into city Hall, destroying the building.

"Ohhhhh noooo, Camiooo!" Amdusias said.

Amdusias and Carl watched the TV from the safety of the underground music studio where they stayed that night.

"Countries from around the world have sent troops en route to America to help fight the epidemic which can only be described as Hell on Earth," the anchorwoman said.

The TV showed an armada of Chinese and Russian naval ships sailing towards America. Suddenly, dozens of huge tentacles emerged from the ocean, each tentacle bigger than the aircraft carriers above them. The tentacles wrapped around the ships, pulling the ships under water, capsizing them, and snapping them into pieces.

"The horror!" the anchorwoman cried.

"Oh, I forgot to tell you, the mouse is the biggest *land* creature we made, but we also made the Leviathan – that thing is just absurdly big, we predict it will kill everything else on the planet including the other mutants," Amdusias said.

"Oh my God, what have you used me for… I should have called the FBI instead of signing that contract," Carl said.

"Yea probably, you're definitely going to Hell for this one," Amdusias said.

"Don't say that," Carl said.

"Ohhh I said it. And I mean it. Have you looked at the TV? It's a genocide of humans. I got all my money on the demons right now, and to think you could have done something to stop this… massacre," Amdusias said.

"Shut up Amdusias, you know I couldn't have stopped this," Carl said.

"You're right, you couldn't have. But if you had tried to stop it you might not be going to Hell you damned fool!" Amdusias said.

Amdusias laughed maniacally and began dancing around the studio.

"Wait a second. You just made me into the most famous musician in the world. I don't even need you anymore," Carl said.

Carl began walking out of the studio.

"Whoa you can't go, you signed a contract remember?" Amdusias said.

"Watch me," Carl said.

Just as Carl went to open the door, the door flung open and Ronové stood in the doorway with his long wooden staff. Ronové slammed the shaft down next to Carl's feet, shaking the floor.

"A deal is a deal," Ronové said.

"He's right, Carl. According to our contract, all your music belongs to us for the next 5 years. Anything you release has to be under our label, and we won't release it if we don't like it. The only music you can release is what we say you can release until the contract is up, then you're free to do what you please," Amdusias said.

"Well this isn't slavery, I'm free to come and go from this studio," Carl said.

"Not right now you aren't. There's Martial Law right now, and in these scenarios, we protect our 2 million dollar investment - per our contract. You're staying right here, you belong to us now," Amdusias said.

Amdusias began laughing and Ronové joined in as well. Soon, both of the demons were laughing hysterically and pointing at Carl.

The police chief met with the sergeant of the National Guard and Mayor in the Mayor's office.

"The chicken has been neutralized, and the immediate threat of being overrun by… mutants is gone as well. At this point, the mutants are just trickling out of the sinkhole and getting picked off by our parameter guards," the sergeant said.

"So, do you think we should attack now? Go put out the fire so we can investigate the sinkhole and find where they came from?" the police chief said.

"Now is a good time, yes, but we might not have enough troops to go on the attack as well as defend the city if another attack occurs. What the News didn't say is about half of the cities across the nation got overrun during the night, and most are still fighting off the onslaught. If we have to retreat from the sinkhole to defend a second attack from a neighboring city, we not be able to assemble our defenses fast enough to save this city from complete destruction," the sergeant said.

The Mayor began whimpering and his chair levitated several inches off the floor for a moment before descending back to the floor. Then the Mayor's left shirt sleeve caught on fire which one of his assistants smothered with a rag to put out – the Mayor didn't even seem to notice.

"The Mayor said he thinks we should defend the city and not go on the attack," an assistant said.

The police chief and sergeant looked at each other.

"I'll assemble the troops," the sergeant said.

Several tanks, Humvees, and firetrucks encircled the sinkhole, with gunners shooting at any mutants whose heads popped up above ground while the firetrucks put out the fire. Behind the vehicles were about two thousand soldiers and police officers. The soldiers emerged from behind the vehicles opening fire and throwing grenades into the sinkhole. Then they lowered ladders and repelling cables from the firetrucks down into the sinkhole.

"Let's see what's in these tunnels… advance!" the sergeant yelled into his radio.

The soldiers and police began climbing down into the sinkhole with firefighter's ladders and cables, covering each other with gunfire.

There was one, massive excavated tunnel going downwards into the dark insides of Earth. Connected to the main tunnel were several smaller tunnels. The troops split up and scoured the underground tunnels wearing night vision goggles while holding leashes of dogs who barked at the sense of danger. The tunnels echoed of dog barks and gunfire for several hours.

The police chief and sergeant led a regiment of troops down the largest tunnel. After several days of spelunking and periodically stopping to rest, the troops stopped outside the entrance to an excavated area with thousands of mutants wandering around in circles outside of large gates built into Earth.

“Frag ‘em but don’t bag ‘em,” the sergeant said.

The troops ran out of the tunnel throwing frag grenades and opening fire on the mutants.

“It may take several more weeks, maybe even months to scour through all these tunnels under America, but maybe we can kill the heart of the Beast now if it’s through those gates,” the police chief said.

Suddenly the gates began to open, and hot air rushed out of the gates almost blinding and suffocating the troops. Hundreds of abnormally large, black wolves ran out of the gates towards the troops, each wolf about five times larger than the barking German Shepherds on leashes held by the troops. The wolves were hunched over and had mangled fur as if they were rabid. As the wolves got closer the troops could see the wolves’ eyes were red like fire and they moved much faster than normal wolves despite their abnormal size.

“Hellhounds…” the police chief whispered.

“Open fire!” the sergeant said.

The troops opened fire on the Hellhounds, but the hounds took many bullets to fall and they quickly enclosed on the troops. The Hellhounds plowed into the first line of troops, knocking them over like bowling pins before ripping the closest limb they could bite off their victims or else going straight for the face.

The Hellhounds broke through the lines of troops which wreaked havoc on the troop’s fighting strategy - the troops began to break ranks in confusion and fear of friendly fire or else death by the wolves. By the time the last Hellhound was killed, the regiment had thinned to about a hundred men.

“Should we move on through those gates or wait for reinforcements?” the police chief said.

“I think we should advance. If they had more troops they would have sent them at us already, we either have them on the run or killed the last of the bodyguards, and by the time our reinforcements arrive, they'll have more waiting for us," the sergeant said.

The police chief nodded.

The troops began walking towards the gates. As the troops approached the gates, the air grew hotter, thicker, and more turbulent and it became almost impossible to see and breathe. The troops all put their gasmasks on as they walked through the gates. As the troops assembled on the other side of the gates they stood and stared in awe at what they saw.

"Good God…" the sergeant said.

Past the gates was an underground city filled with buildings connected by corridors, like a big complex. There was a swastika flag raised from one of the prominent buildings in the center of the underground city.

"The Nazis!" the police chief said.

"So it is true, the Nazis never lost World War Two. They just came to America and went underground," the sergeant said.

"After World War Two, America imported the top Nazi scientists into America for rocket research to beat the Soviet Union to the moon while a lot of other Nazi war criminals escaped by ratlines to South America," the police chief said.

"And this was their contingency plan to take over the world again," the sergeant said.

"Maybe this was their plan all along, and the Nazis losing World War Two was just a distraction for this plan to be carried out," the police chief said.

"Let's put an end to this now," the sergeant said.

The sergeant spoke into his radio.

"Triangulate my coordinates big bird, we have found the nest and are advancing behind enemy lines. If we fall, send reinforcements this way," the sergeant said.

"That's a negative sergeant, all troops have been pulled back as of this morning to defend the city after we lost New York and Philadelphia last night. You're on your own down there, so if you found their headquarters you better make your attack count - because they found our headquarters this morning and burned the White House and Pentagon to the ground," a soldier replied.

"Good lord…" the police chief said.

"It seems too quiet and empty for this to be their capitol," the sergeant said.

"Let's split up and search all these buildings. It should only take a couple hours to figure out what goes on here and if anyone is still around," the police chief said.

The troops split up into teams and searched the building complex, which was laid out like a hospital, but dimly lit and filled with ash, blood, and mutant body parts. Some of the buildings were science labs or manufacturing plants, but the majority of the buildings had farms for growing mutants.

After a couple hours they all met in the center of town square.

"We found a lab where mutants are created," a soldier said.

"Yea, we found labs too, with a bunch of test subjects and weird experiments," an officer said.

"And we found a bunker in the back of this complex with a couple dozen living beings inside who we could see with our infrared goggles," another soldier said.

"The bunker is separate from the rest of the buildings? There's no other entrance in?" the police chief said.

"Affirmative. The bunker is isolated, there's only one way into it," another solder said.

"Alright, let's figure out how to breach that bunker," the sergeant said.

"Maybe we could just camp outside here and outlast them with our supplies, try to starve them out," the police chief said.

“That could backfire on us if they have more supplies than us,” the sergeant said.

“I got a simple idea, we can all unload our explosives on one spot of the bunker to see if we can blow a hole in it, then one thermobaric explosive in their bunker will kill them either by the blast wave or by consuming the oxygen inside,” a soldier said.

“Anyone else have any ideas?” the sergeant said.

Nobody said anything.

The troops lined up outside the bunker and one by one fired RPGs, bazookas, and threw grenades at one of the bunker’s exterior walls. With each blast, the troops penetrated through about 10 feet of concrete before an opening finally appeared. A soldier wearing infrared goggles came running over to the police chief and sergeant.

“Quick! They just ran down into a tunnel beneath the bunker, they know we penetrated the walls!” a soldier said.

The troops ran towards the bunker and climbed inside the hole they blasted into the wall. The bunker was empty. After all the troops climbed inside, they walked towards the room which had the entrance to the tunnel beneath the bunker.

When the troops made it to the room with the tunnel, one of the soldiers placed a door breaching charge on top. The charge exploded and the tunnel doors blasted open.

Other troops threw flash bangs and frag grenades down into the tunnel. Finally, they threw smoke grenades into the breached door to hide themselves as they descended into the tunnel. After a dozen or so troops descended down into the tunnel, they noticed the tunnel was a maze of optical illusions, illuminated only with strobing lights and moving holograms which made their night vision and infrared goggles more of a burden than help.

As the troops took off their goggles and turned on flashlights, they heard a voice in German.

"Schnell, raus!" the voice said.

Suddenly, the tunnel lit up with gunfire towards the troops, who returned the gunfire in the direction it came from. Several troops fell before the gunfire stopped. They heard footsteps fading away from someone running away from them.

After the majority of the troops climbed down the tunnel they began to walk down the hallway where they came to their first fork in the tunnel where the gunfight just happened. One dead Nazi in a trench coat and gasmask laid around the corner. The troops split into two groups and took each path, with the police chief leading one group and the sergeant leading the other group.

Through the strobing lights of the tunnel and the troop's flashlights, they could see holograms of devils and other fiends coming towards them and running away from them, causing the troops to open fire on thin air.

"I don't like this… it seems like a trap more than a hiding spot," the police chief said over the radio.

"Our path ends at a door to a big room, I wouldn't be surprised if there's another entrance to this room from your path. Rendezvous when you reach the end of your path, we'll wait here," the sergeant responded.

The police chief and his troops reached the end of their path and found a door as well. The police chief peaked through the window of the door and saw a large, dark room with strobing lights pulsing in the dark.

"Can anyone see what's in there with their infrareds?" the police chief said.

"Oh, there's definitely people in there, but I can't tell how many actual humans with guns. They've surrounded themselves with mutants, there's hundreds of them in there, and it's too hard to tell who's who with just the infrared vision," a soldier said.

“sergeant, we’re at the door, we’re estimating a couple dozen enemy soldiers surrounded by a shit ton of mutants,” the police chief said.

“Roger, my estimates are the same. I’ll have my troops throw some grenades inside so they think we’re all coming from this side, then you rush your troops through the door opening fire, and we’ll follow right after,” the sergeant said.

“Alright, I’ll follow your lead,” the police chief said.

The sergeant turned to his troops.

“On my command, we all run through these doors and show these demons the bravery of mankind does not falter in the darkest of times, even in the pits of Hell!” the sergeant said.

“Hooray!” the troops said.

“Go, go, go!” the sergeant said.

The sergeant’s troops kicked open the door at the end of their path then threw grenades and opened fire into the room. The Nazi’s gunfire blasted back towards the sergeant’s troops who hugged the walls.

“Now!” the police chief yelled.

The police chief kicked open the door at the end of his path and ran into the room firing his shotgun into the darkness. His troops followed right behind him firing their weapons as well. As soon as the Nazi’s gunfire was redirected towards the police chief’s troops, the sergeant ran into the room from his side, opening fire with his automatic rifle, followed by his troops. Mutants ran towards the troops through the crossfire.

Several soldiers and police officers fell as they entered the room, but once the troops got inside the room, they found cover behind pillars, tables, and other obstacles. The gunfire continued for several minutes before all the mutants were gunned down in the crossfire.

"I can see about two dozen enemies with guns… plus one of them looks like a big robot and another one looks like the Devil," a soldier said.

The sergeant looked at the soldier with one eyebrow raised. The soldier removed his infrared goggles and handed them to the sergeant.

"Take a look for yourself," the soldier said.

The sergeant put on the goggles.

"Yep, that does look like a big robot, Satan himself, and a bunch of Nazis. Should have known it would come down to this," the sergeant said.

The sergeant took a drink from a flask then put his radio up to his face.

"You see what I'm seeing chief?" the sergeant said.

"A devil, robo-man, and some Nazis?" the police chief responded.

"Yep. I say we all run out on three and put an end to this," the sergeant said.

"Don't you think that's a bit too easy to defeat the most evil beings ever? This seems like a trap," the police chief said.

"Too easy? We've chased these fuckers miles beneath the Earth, and killed millions of mutants and a chicken the size of a high-rise. The same fuckers we defeated over 75 years ago and forced into these pits of Hell. Nothing here was easy, we finally have them cornered – that's all. Let's finish this on three," the sergeant said.

"Okay…," the police chief said.

"1… 2… 3…," the sergeant said.

The police chief and sergeant both ran with their troops from behind their cover, converging on the last of the Nazis in an open gunfight. The troops began falling quickly as gunfire from the robot-like figure tore them apart. Within seconds all the Nazis were dead except the robot and the devil.

"Holy shit, is that Hitler?" the police chief said.

"He's over 120 years old!" a police officer said.

The robot solider was an old man with a Hitler-esque, toothbrush mustache and parted hair, strapped into a mechanical exoskeleton with two miniguns for arms, shooting hundreds of bullets per second at the troops, pausing intermittently so his guns didn't overheat. Meanwhile, the Devil did not fight but was most elusive, running around the room with hologram illusions of himself popping up left and right.

"Should we chase after Satan?" the police chief said.

"Just focus on Hitler, he's destroying us!" the sergeant said.

The troops ran towards Hitler, surrounding him while firing their weapons. Hitler stood his ground, with a seemingly endless supply of bullets spraying from his minigun arms. Suddenly, Hitler's robotic exoskeleton fell over backwards and the gunfire stopped.

The police chief and sergeant walked over to the robot and stood over the wounded man strapped into the exoskeleton.

"Looks like Hitler," the sergeant said.

"Sure does," the police chief said.

Hitler laughed as blood poured from dozens of bullet holes in his chest, arms, legs, and stomach, then he died a few seconds later.

"Did anyone catch the Devil?" the sergeant said.

"Negative sir, we can't find him, he must have gotten away, that sneaky bastard," a soldier said.

"That's alright, we'll find him one day in these tunnels. Look around soldiers, there stands only a handful of us left, but it seems we had exactly enough soldiers and fought back at exactly the right time to defend humanity from the most evil adversaries known throughout history, for had we not defended this city and entered these tunnels in search of our foes, then humanity would still be fighting for survival, and perhaps would have fallen to the darkness," the sergeant said.

The police chief, sergeant, and remaining troops cheered and passed around flasks. The sergeant took out his radio.

"Big bird, we have cleansed mother Earth of the evil lurking inside, the battle is over, do you copy?" the sergeant said.

There was no answer on the radio.

The troops remained silent for a moment and glanced at each other.

"Oh my God, we're all alone," one of the soldiers said.

A couple of troops turned pale and had to sit on the ground. One of the police officers threw up into his gasmask and one of the soldiers started crying.

"Big bird, do you copy?" the sergeant said.

There was still no answer on the radio.

"Did they lose the fight above ground?" a soldier said.

The sergeant looked at his troops.

"Maybe we don't get reception in this part of the cave," the sergeant said.

Just then, the troops heard footsteps which made the ground shake, getting louder – getting closer. They quietly locked and loaded their guns. One of the troops put on infrared goggles and took a couple steps towards the doors the troops had breached for the final gunfight. The footsteps kept getting louder and closer until suddenly the footsteps stopped. Then they heard a whooshing noise from above.

"I don't see anything, but…" the soldier said.

Suddenly, a massive, winged being descended on the soldier and crushed him like a tin can from his head to his feet, spraying blood in a circular wave all over the other troops. A huge man with wings like an eagle stood on top of the crushed soldier then sprinted towards the other troops, knocking them over with his wings before grabbing a police officer and throwing him up into the darkness with such velocity that the officer exploded on impact when he hit the ceiling, causing his blood and entrails to rain down onto the remaining troops.

The troops opened fire on the winged man just as a massive black wolf flanked them. On top of the massive wolf rode an average sized man with angel wings and the face of an owl wielding a long sword, which gleamed in the dark. As the wolf ripped into the troops, the owl-faced man swung his sword, decapitating troops left and right.

The massive, eagle-winged man was slapping troops across the room with his great claws and wings, knocking them unconscious or else killing them. The eagle-winged man then flapped his wings upwards in the center of the troops, grabbing several troops off their feet and hurling them up towards the high cave ceiling before they plummeted back down to the ground where they crumpled into bloody piles of broken bones.

"Retreat!" the sergeant yelled.

Just then, the owl-faced man rode by on his wolf and slashed his sword at the sergeant from arm to arm such that the sergeant fell apart from the breast up and biceps down and ended up in four pieces on the ground. The majority of the troops fell within a minute or so to the owl-faced man on the wolf, and the bigger, eagle-winged man.

The police chief looked down at the dismembered sergeant then grabbed a grenade from the sergeant's belt and pulled the pin. The wolf plowed into the police chief, knocking him to the ground. The wolf and the owl-faced rider stood over the police chief. Just as the wolf went to bite the police chief's face, the grenade exploded, which killed the police chief instantly and blew the face off the wolf.

The owl-faced rider went flying across the room from the blast of the grenade and hit a pillar, then dropped to the floor, covered in shrapnel wounds - his angel wings shredded. The owl-faced man tried to stand up but as soon as he did his intestines hung out of his stomach and he had to hold them inside his body with both his hands. The massive, eagle-winged man stood over the smaller owl-faced man, then quickly grabbed him and started eating him alive. The owl-faced man smiled as the larger, winged-man bit chunks out of his body and slurped his flesh and entrails.

A woman was in labor in a hospital bed with her husband, doctors, and nurses. She began screaming as she squeezed her husband's hand. Then they heard boots marching down the hallway. The husband and wife looked out into the hallway. A concierge judge, priest, and several soldiers wearing all black walked into the room across the hall.

Several minutes later, they heard screams.

"No! Not my baby!" a woman cried.

"You bastards, that's my first son!" a man yelled.

Cries filled the hallway.

The husband and wife in labor looked at each other. Then the husband looked up at the ceiling as he held his wife's hand.

"Please be an average to below average boy," the husband whispered.

The woman began screaming as she gave birth.

A man with white, angel wings wearing a black top hat stood in the room next to the father. The angel was invisible to everyone in the room but the newborn child.

Just then, several beams of light blasted down through the ceiling into the delivery room - also invisible to everyone but the infant. A dozen brightly glowing angels were kneeling at the ground before the bed of the mother holding the baby.

"Our coming king," one of the angels said.

The angel standing next to the father of the child looked at the dozen angels kneeling on the ground.

"Ahhh, just as I suspected, the boy has more guardian angels than any other man before him. Michael, the leader of the military; Uriel, the patron of the arts; Raphael, the healer; Phanuel, the bringer of repentance and hope… yes, yes, this boy is very blessed," the standing angel said.

Then the kneeling angels all stood up.

"Sandalphon, it is good to see you have successfully protected the vessels for the unborn child. Your work here is done, you may return to Heaven. We will defend the boy from here," Michael said.

"Thank you, Michael. Greetings brothers of light, I know you will protect this child from the evils in this world. I will see you all when you return," Sandalphon said.

Sandalphon spread his wings and looked up at the ceiling just as the judge, priest, and soldiers entered their delivery room from the room across the hall. The sound of the soldiers' loud combat boots against the floor came to a halt after they entered the door and stood blocking the doorway.

"I'll have the results in just a moment," the doctor said.

Nobody else in the room but the baby and the other angels could see about a hundred different beasts enter the room immediately after the judge, priest, and soldiers. The beasts were all different colors and the room filled with a smell of rotten eggs and sulfur.

Some of the beasts had multiple limbs and faces, but not only human faces - faces of frogs, lions, bulls, and birds; some smiling, others frowning, and others laughing or mumbling like madmen. Many of the beasts had wings, but few had wings like the angels – most of the beasts had bat wings, dragon wings, or bird wings.

The angels lined up around the bed of the newborn child as the beasts surrounded everyone in the room. Several of the beasts were transparent and hovered towards the nurses and doctor then disappeared as the beasts entered inside of the unaware humans. Other beasts pulled out medieval weapons such as swords, axes, spears, and maces – while other beasts wielded serpents. The beasts hissed and growled at the angels and the baby.

"You have no business here, demons! This is the Second Coming King - he will bring much hope and joy to humanity, and he will be the king of all nations to usher in an era of peace and prosperity for a thousand years!" Sandalphon said.

Just then the doctor shook his head.

"He's… the most perfect child I've ever seen. His DNA, brain, and skull scans reveal he will be athletic, attractive, gifted, and compassionate… he will cause much jealousy and hatred - he must be killed, now," the doctor said.

"Nooo!" the wife yelled.

"You can't! I won't let you!" the husband yelled.

One of the soldiers stepped forward and tasered the husband, who then fell onto the floor unconscious. The wife screamed and cried in horror as the doctor and nurses tried to take the baby away from her. The priest began chanting incantations and the demons walked slowly towards the angels and the baby. Sandalphon, Michael, Uriel, and the other angels all pulled out medieval weapons as well.

"Come then, and see why we are here!" Sandalphon said.

"Sandalphon you do not need to fight this battle, your duties here are done," Michael said.

Just then, a tall dark, robed being with huge angel-wings stepped in front of the other demons. He was as dark as a blackhole, seemingly sucking in the light around him, darkening and distorting the air. The being wielded a long sword in one hand and a mace in the other hand.

"Satan…" an angel said.

"Even you're going to need all the help you can get for this one, Michael," Sandalphon said.

Then the demons charged towards the angels, filling the room with hideous and horrifying war cries, which sounded like a stampede of different animals. The angels held a line in front of the bed and swung their weapons with such speed and might that the first wave of demons were sent flying backwards into the rest, some getting sliced in half.

Sandalphon was separated from the line of other angels and was quickly surrounded by a group of short goblins. The goblins looked like tiny, deformed humans which had all the skin burned off of them, and had big swollen claws for hands. Sandalphon kicked a goblin across the room and slashed his sword, cutting a handful of goblins in half, but then a round demon with multiple faces on its circular torso with multiple arms grabbed Sandalphon's limbs and body from behind, immobilizing him. The demon held a spear in one of his extra limbs which he drove through Sandalphon's back and through his chest.

Sandalphon fell onto his knees as goblins jumped on top of him, shredding his wings and back with their claws. Then a bright light blasted upwards from Sandalphon's body through the ceiling, liquifying the nearby goblins and demon's limbs.

The line of angels surrounding the bed made quick work of any demon who approached. By the time any of the demons lunged towards the line of angels, one of the angels struck first, sending the demons flying backwards, dismembering their limbs, and decapitating them.

Michael, the leader and military commander of the angels stood in the middle of the line of angels, with a sword and shield in his hands. A wolf with wings of an eagle and a serpent tail lunged at Michael and Michael swung his sword overhead and downwards, slicing the wolf completely in half and grinding his sword against the floor.

Then Satan approached Michael while demons relentlessly attacked the other angels - the demons eventually swarming around the angels to use their numbers to their advantage.

"This won't be the first time I'll see you fall, Satan," Michael said.

Satan swung his sword overhead, followed by swinging his mace sideways. Michael locked swords with Satan overhead, and used his shield to block the mace. Michael's blade shined brilliantly with light, but the darkness of Satan's blade began to seep into Michael's blade, turning it black, and Satan was pushing the locked swords towards Michael, overpowering him.

Michael tried to push Satan back with his shield, but Satan's mace was stuck in his shield, and Satan had a deadlock grip, disallowing the mace and shield to be moved. The darkness of Satan's mace began to seep onto Michael's shield as well.

"The Dark Lord's power is strong in this realm!" Michael said.

Michael turned his head briefly and saw the doctor had administered a strong sedative to the mother of the newborn child, and the mother was now unconscious. The nurses grabbed the child from the mother's arms and began walking towards a table on the other side of the room. The child began crying. Some of the other guardian angels lay dead on the ground, now getting unnecessarily mutilated by demons.

"Impossible… Azazel… the corrupter of mankind," Raphael said.

Azazel, a muscular, goat-like man stepped in front of Raphael. Azazel had a beard, ears, and horns like a goat, and his nose and face also resembled a goat. Azazel wielded an elegant, golden axe which had writings and designs all over the handle. He also had huge steel chains draped around his shoulders which crossed around the front of his chest and wrapped around his back. The chains were so hot they glowed bright, warm colors and dripped molten steel as they seared into Azazel's flesh, causing a smoky odor to emit from him. Raphael glanced nervously at Michael.

"Now you're in my prison, Raphael!" Azazel said.

Azazel laughed as he swung his mighty, gold axe sideways at Raphael. Raphael blocked the axe with his shield but the blow split the shield in half and sent Raphael falling onto the floor. Then Azazel grabbed the searing chains from off his shoulders.

"Remember these chains?" Azazel said.

Azazel whipped the chains at Raphael which wrapped around Raphael's leg, burning into his flesh.

"Ahhhh!" Raphael screamed.

Azazel pulled Raphael towards him with the burning chain lasso. As Raphael slid across the floor towards Azazel demons stabbed Raphael mercilessly. By the time Raphael was pulled to the feet of Azazel, Raphael was covered in dozens of sword, spear, and axe wounds, his wings were shredded, and he left a trail of blood across the delivery room.

"You know, I should be thanking you. Look how much power I have down here in this realm," Azazel said.

"Your words say one thing, but your eyes tell another story, you miserable traitor," Raphael said.

Azazel whipped the chain upwards sending Raphael barely through the ceiling before whipping the chain back down and sending Raphael into the floor. Then a bright light blasted upwards through the ceiling from Raphael's limp, bloody body on the floor.

"Nooo!" Michael yelled.

Michael quickly lowered his sword and let Satan's overpowering sword glide past him, using Satan's strength against him as Michael stepped out of the way and spun next to Satan. Then Michael pushed his shield locked onto Satan's mace in the same direction as Satan's momentum of the sword swing. Satan dropped his mace and fell forward in the direction of his momentum, landing at the foot of the bed where the mother lay, who was still sedated.

Satan laughed and put his hand on the mother's ankle. The mother's heartrate began to drop and the nurses rushed over to her. Then Michael swung his sword with both hands overhead at the back of Satan and sliced his sword deep into Satan's back. Satan hissed and let go of the mother's ankle. Her heartrate did not stabilize.

Michael tried to remove his sword from Satan's back but it was stuck. Just then, a sliced in half, long and thick black serpent fell onto the floor from the back of Satan's slashed robe. Satan stood up and removed his dark robe, which Michael's sword was still stuck in. Satan laughed as he fanned out his cut robe and the other half of the massive, black snake emerged, wrapped around Michael's sword.

As the bottom half of the snake wrapped around Michael's sword, the top half hissed and slithered towards Michael's legs. Satan swung his sword and Michael swung his snake-covered sword at Satan, locking swords and cutting the snake in half yet again. Then a demon ran up from behind Michael and swung an axe into Michael's calf, bringing Michael to his knees. Michael dropped his sword to the floor as the two quarters and one half of the snake slithered towards him, leaving a trail of black blood on the floor.

Michael turned and saw a tall, robed faun-like man with horns and a long-pointed tail wielding a long trident approaching Phanuel.

"Belial, my oldest enemy. I'm surprised you show yourself in your true form, Lord of Lies," Phanuel said.

Belial laughed.

"You fight blind in this realm Phanuel - for you are already deceived. I have no true form other than lust. What have you come to my world to offer to me? Or did you come here just to die?" Belial said.

Without hesitation Belial came within striking distance of Phanuel and thrusted his trident with blinding speed over and over connecting like a woodpecker and piercing holes in Phanuel's shield until the arrow-like tips of the trident caught a grip in the holes of the shield and ripped the shield from Phanuel's grasp, sending Phanuel falling forward. Belial laughed as he tossed the shield over his shoulder with his trident.

Then Belial thrusted his trident towards Phanuel. Phanuel rolled away just in time to dodge it. Phanuel jumped up into a standing position from his roll, and swung his sword, cutting the head off a horse-faced demon which was ganging up on Uriel along with other demons. Then Phanuel ran at Belial. Belial thrusted his trident over and over at different heights and angles towards Phanuel while Belial quickly backed up and shifted unpredictably around the room, keeping out of range of Phanuel's shorter blade. Then Belial laughed as he backed up into a couple of demons who then stepped in front of Belial with their swords and shields.

Phanuel stopped chasing Belial and looked around – he was surrounded by demons and fallen angels. A wave of demons lunged towards Phanuel and Phanuel swung his blade while spinning 360 degrees, chopping the heads and limbs off all the demons who approached, but just as he did so, the fallen angels lunged in low, beneath Phanuel's spinning blade. Belial and the other fallen angels crouched as they encircled Phanuel and impaled their weapons into Phanuel's feet, legs, and lower torso.

"Beluhhh…" Phanuel moaned.

Then the fallen angels lifted Phanuel into the air together using their weapons and walked under him to let gravity drive their weapons through his body. Then a bright light blasted upwards through the ceiling from Phanuel's skewered body, sending the fallen angels to the floor.

Satan laughed as he stood over Michael, who knelt down on one knee, nursing the axe stuck in his calf which nearly took off his leg.

"See Michael? There's no hope in this world," Satan said.

Just then, Uriel, the last angel standing, ran up behind the doctor who was preparing the needle to give a lethal injection to the new born child. Uriel raised his sword, engulfed in flames, to stab the doctor in the back, unseen to the doctor or any other human besides the new born child.

"No! Uriel! You cannot harm a human or you will be banished to Hell!" Michael yelled.

"But he's about to kill the Son of the Lord!" Uriel screamed.

Satan laughed louder, then thrusted his sword into Michael's chest, piercing his heart. A light blasted upwards through the ceiling from Michael's body.

"Oh Lord, help me," Uriel whispered.

Just then, a bright light blasted down through the ceiling behind the judge standing at the doorway.

"Gabriel…" Uriel whispered.

Gabriel whispered something in the judge's ear, then the judge's eyes widened and her eyebrows went up in the middle of her forehead. Just as the doctor was about to put the needle in the baby, the judge waved her hands in the air.

"Stop!" the judge shouted.

The doctor, nurses, and soldiers all stopped and stared at the judge. The priest stopped praying and stared at the judge, then Satan, the fallen angels, and the remaining demons stared at the judge and Gabriel as well.

"That child is a musician. By statute SCO 1104, a musician cannot be killed at birth," the judge said.

"But he is just a baby, how do you know he is a musician? And how do you know he will be a good, influential musician?" the doctor said.

"Well, it's obvious. You just said he has the best genes you've ever seen. And can't you feel the tension in this room? The child began crying as soon as you took him from the mother as if he knows what's going on. He can sense our emotions, and he understands the atmosphere – he is a born musician. If not, it will be my head, as per the law. I swear on my own blood he will be a great musician, or I will stand for execution myself," the judge said.

Everyone in the room still stared at the judge, including Uriel, who still had his burning sword raised above the doctor, ready to stab him through the back. The doctor glanced down at the infant, his hand which held the needle was shaking.

"Fine. It will be your head," the doctor said.

The doctor put the needle down on the table. Then the soldiers and priest walked out of the room. The judge walked up to the infant and looked down upon him before silently turning around and leaving the room as well.

After the priest, judge, and soldiers left the room, Satan and the three pieces of his serpent vanished. The fallen angels and demons glanced around at each other before simultaneously flying out the door as if sucked out by the vacuum of space equilibrating the atmosphere.

The mother's heartbeat flatlined, and the doctor and nurses tried to resuscitate her but to no avail.

The next day, the husband of the newborn child returned to work. His coworkers stared at him and gave him dirty looks all day while avoiding conversation with him. That afternoon, he got a call from his boss.

"Joseph, please come see me in my office," his boss said.

"Sure," Joseph said.

Joseph walked into his boss's office.

"You wanted to see me sir?" Joseph said.

"Have a seat Joseph," his boss said.

Joseph sat in a chair in front of his boss's desk.

"How was your day off yesterday, Joseph?" his boss said.

"It was… lifechanging. My first child was born, but my wife unfortunately passed away giving birth," Joseph said.

"Yea yea. Listen Joseph, this company is about efficiency. How do you expect North America to win World War 3 if we aren't operating at maximum efficiency? You're one of our best employees which makes plenty of people jealous already, and then you go and have a son who might be a musician. All the studies show that no matter how good of a worker one employee is, they can never make up for the damage done on other employees by causing a certain level of jealousy. We really were banking on your son getting the lethal injection Joseph, but now we're all jealous of you. You crossed the threshold where we are now too jealous of you to have you employed here. You're fired Joseph," his boss said.

"But sir, my wife died!" Joseph said.

"We don't really give a shit Joseph, in fact, since you crossed the threshold of jealousy, we're happy she died, but really pissed off that your son lived, now get the fuck out of here before I call security and tell them why I just fired you," his boss said.

As Joseph gathered his belongings from his desk, a handful of ex-coworkers gathered outside of his cubicle. Unseen to any of them, demons were flying at speeds relative to light into the gaping, jealous souls of Joseph's coworkers, possessing them and poisoning their minds.

"You prick! You're the top performer every month and then you go and have a boy… musician!" a coworker said.

"It was an accident guys, we didn't mean to have a child like that, and my wife passed away so I'm not really in the mood to talk," Joseph said.

"Oh, boo hoo, your wife died, we're still jealous of you Joseph. You're smarter than everyone here, and you had to go and have a child to really make us hate you - some of us here can't even have children! Did you ever think of that?" another coworker shouted.

"Well don't worry, I just got fired, I won't be around to make you jealous anymore," Joseph said.

"We'll still remember you, we'll still think about you and your stupid genius child… nonstop!" another coworker said.

"Yea, I can't believe the hospital didn't kill his kid, how could they not think of our feelings and hurt us like this?" another coworker said.

"I'm angry, let's hurt him because he made us jealous!" another coworker said.

Suddenly, Joseph's ex-coworkers began hitting and kicking him. More ex-coworkers began flocking outside of Joseph's cubicle, hurling office supplies and equipment at him. Joseph stopped gathering his belongings and ran through the mob around his cubicle, covering his face with his arms as they beat him.

Joseph ran down the steps of the building to avoid getting trapped in the elevator as his ex-coworkers chased after him, yelling.

"He made us jealous!" a coworker yelled.

"Security!" another coworker yelled.

As Joseph ran across the first floor lobby, security guards got in on the chase. Joseph ran out of the building onto the sidewalk as security guards and ex-coworkers chased him. A police officer stepped in front of Joseph so Joseph stopped running.

“Hold it right there. What’s going on here?” the officer said.

“Officer, you gotta help me. They’re chasing me because they’re jealous, but my wife just died and I just lost my job, their jealousy isn’t just, it’s merely a mob mentality,” Joseph said.

The mob encircled the officer and Joseph. Unseen to anyone, demons were dancing around the mob, whispering in people’s ears, and using spells and witchcraft on them.

“He made us jealous!” an ex-coworker said.

“Arrest him!” another person said.

Soon, the entire mob and passersby on the street were all chanting.

“Arrest him! Arrest him! Arrest him!” the mob chanted.

“They must really be jealous of you,” the officer said.

“Please sir,” Joseph said.

“Stop resisting!” the officer yelled.

All of a sudden, the officer kneed Joseph in the stomach. As Joseph bent over, the officer took out his night stick and beat Joseph in the back with it. Joseph fell onto his stomach on the ground then the officer handcuffed him while the crowd cheered.

“That officer is a hero,” someone said.

After Joseph spent a week in jail with nobody to bail him out, Joseph was released and drove straight to the hospital were his newborn son still was. Joseph ran into the hospital and up to the receptionist, who gave him a dirty look.

“I’m here for my son,” Joseph said.

“Are you Joseph Carpenter? Your boy is the musician?” the receptionist said.

“Yes,” Joseph said.

“You’re a day late,” the receptionist said.

“I know, I’m sorry, I was arrested for causing jealousy because of my new born son. I just want to take him home now,” Joseph said.

"Alright, let me call the doctor in the after-birth unit," the receptionist said.

The nurse gave Joseph one last squinty-eyed, dirty look before she turned and grabbed the phone.

"Dr. Barbas… he's here," she said.

A tall man walked out from the doors leading to the hospital units and towards Joseph.

"Are you Joseph Carpenter?" the man said.

"Yes," Joseph said.

"I'm Dr. Barbas. Can I ask where you've been for the past day?" Dr. Barbas said.

"I was in jail because people are jealous of my me and my son," Joseph said.

"No shit they are, the only reason he's still alive is because a judge thinks he's gonna be a musician. But you don't show up to pick up your son until now? That's cutting it real close buddy, Dr. Barbas said.

"I'm sorry, there was nothing I could do," Joseph said.

"Yes there is - don't have such good genes. Next time reproduce with someone of a much lower caliber. Drink and smoke more. Do some damage to your body and your child so people aren't so damn jealous," Dr. Barbas said.

"Can I just pick up my son?" Joseph said

"When is your hearing?" Dr. Barbas said.

"It's not for another 2 weeks," Joseph said.

"So, your son barely makes it past birth inspection, then you pick him up a day late after you get out of jail, awaiting trial for… jealousy? Don't you realize North America is at war with the rest of the world? Don't you realize how badly causing jealousy is for our efficiency? We can't win a war if people like you are going around causing jealousy!" Dr. Barbas yelled.

Everyone in the hospital's waiting room stared at Joseph.

"Hey, why are people jealous of him?" someone said.

"Because he's supposedly the best worker at his company, and he has a new born son who is a… musician!" Dr. Barbas said.

"A musician? I wish my kid was a musician," someone said.

"You're the *best* employee? God, I hate working with people like you," someone else said.

"And look how nice he's dressed, I bet he makes a bunch of money," another person said.

"Let's all just calm down, remember, I just lost my job and my wife," Joseph said.

"Oh, are you trying to make us feel bad for you now?" someone said.

"Yea, as if we're gonna feel bad for him after a few minor hardships when he's so perfect and has had a perfect life," someone else said.

"My son is dying from cancer right now, you selfish bastard!" someone screamed.

"I was born with only one testicle and can't have kids, you self-centered asshole!" another person yelled.

Back in the afterbirth unit of the hospital, unseen to anyone but the babies, Uriel and Gabriel stood over Joseph's newly born child. Uriel quietly played a violin. Gabriel glanced towards the door to the hallway.

"Something is not right," Gabriel said.

Gabriel began walking quickly towards the door.

"Stay here with the child," Gabriel said.

"I will never leave his side," Uriel said.

Gabriel walked into the waiting room of the hospital where he saw Dr. Barbas pointing and laughing at a mob of people who were kicking Joseph as he lay on the floor. One man was on top of Joseph holding him down while the others kicked and punched him.

A large man wearing a brown robe stood behind Dr. Barbas whispering spells and waving a large wand in the air. Seven lean, humanlike beings painted in all different colors with hooved feet, long bushy tails, but with faces of all different animals danced around the room - unseen to the humans. The beings sang spells to the humans in the waiting room as they danced to their own music - the man in the brown robe behind Dr. Barbas was seemingly the conductor of this band of beasts.

"Please, I just want my son!" Joseph said.

"Why should you get to have a son who's a musician? We should kill you for causing jealousy and let the kid starve in the cradle!" someone said.

Gabriel unsheathed his sword.

"What is the meaning of this?" Gabriel said.

The large man in the brown robe stop whispering incantations and waving his wand as he turned to look at Gabriel. The man had the head of a lion but his eyes were red like fire. The colorful demons stopped dancing and singing and stared at Gabriel as well. Then the demons withdrew old, rusty medieval weapons from their belts and began slowly creeping towards Gabriel with dramatic steps, waving their arms in the air - more like a dance than a battle formation.

Gabriel ran towards a demon which was painted purple and had the face of a donkey and plunged his sword into the demon's chest just as the demon began to swing his sword. Gabriel kicked the demon backwards to free his sword from the demon's chest, and the demon stepped backwards and fluttered his arms above his head theatrically, before spinning around and falling to the ground, dead.

The crowd of humans still relentlessly beat Joseph.

"Help please!" Joseph cried.

Another demon painted yellow with the face of a crow skipped towards Gabriel before doing a cartwheel towards him, spinning towards Gabriel with an axe held in his tail. Gabriel swung his sword like a baseball bat at the cartwheeling demon and cut the demon in half as the spinning motion flung his legs and bottom half of his torso at the wall, spraying blood and entrails along the way, while the upper half of the demon finished the cartwheel by landing upright on the floor with his guts spilling out. The demon used his arms to drag the dismembered, upper half of his body towards Gabriel, but lost too many organs and fell face forward onto the floor, dead.

A third and fourth demon approached Gabriel. One of the demons was painted red and had the face of a bull, while the other was painted blue and had the face of a bear. The bull wielded a large axe which he only swung back and forth horizontally as he approached Gabriel, while the bear wielded a large hammer which he only swung in a figure eight motion across his body in front of him as he approached Gabriel. The two demons walked towards Gabriel slowly while swinging their weapons as if they were automatons and had no other function but to swing their weapons in these automated motions.

Gabriel waited until the bull was close enough, then immediately after the bull swung his axe across his body, Gabriel countered by lunging forward and swinging his sword overhead down onto the bull's head, cutting the bull's head in half. Then Gabriel swung his sword at an angle perpendicular to the angle the bear was swinging his hammer such that Gabriel's sword cut the bear's handle in half and the hammer fell to the floor. Gabriel stepped past the bear as he swung, then spun his sword around and thrusted it over his own shoulder into the spine of the bear, before spinning back around in front of the bear, using his momentum to swing low at the bear's legs, chopping off the nearest leg and sending the bear crashing to the floor.

Eventually the mob turned into less of a beating and more of a dogpile on top of Joseph.

“I can’t breathe!” Joseph squeaked.

A police officer stood in the corner of the room pointing and laughing at the mob beating and piling on top of Joseph as a succubus painted in pink but unseen to him whispered spells in his ears.

A fifth demon painted green with the head of a rat ran towards Gabriel with a spear while a sixth demon painted orange with the face of a dog lined up an arrow with his bow and aimed it at Gabriel. Just as the green, rat demon approached Gabriel, the orange, dog demon shot the arrow which hit Gabriel in the shoulder just as Gabriel was swinging his sword to block the rat demon’s spear. Gabriel involuntarily dropped his sword when the arrow hit him just as the spear thrusted towards Gabriel’s chest.

At the last moment, Gabriel dropped to his knees and fell backwards, letting the spear pass over him. As the demon pulled back the spear for a second thrust, Gabriel reached up and grabbed the spear with the arm that didn’t get shot, and the spear didn’t budge despite the demon’s attempts to pull it back. Then Gabriel stood up, still holding the spear and pulled the spear with all his might towards himself which ripped the spear from the hands of the demon. Gabriel stood with the spear high above his head, pointed towards him still, which he then twirled in his hand 180 degrees and faced towards the demon.

The green, rat faced demon smiled at Gabriel as Gabriel drove the spear into the demon’s chest which came out through his back. Then Gabriel grabbed the spear with both arms, lifted the demon, and ran with the impaled demon towards the orange, dog demon, using the impaled demon as a meat shield to block the arrows. An arrow whizzed by the head of the impaled demon and then by Gabriel’s head just as Gabriel closed the distance and drove the spear into the orange demon as well, shish kabobbing both of the demons on the spear.

The seventh demon, the succubus, stopped whispering to the police officer. When she stopped, the officer seemed to regain some awareness, and radioed in the mob attack, but still did not intervene. Joseph tried crawling away from the mob but someone kicked him in the head and knocked him unconscious.

The succubus ran towards Gabriel with large metal claws strapped onto her fists as the lion in the brown robe came from behind Gabriel. The lion swung his wand from behind at Gabriel, and the wand morphed into a long green snake and wrapped around Gabriel's legs, pulling him stomach first onto the floor. The snake quickly slithered and wrapped itself higher and higher on Gabriel's legs as he lay on the ground, disallowing him to stand back up.

Gabriel flipped himself over just as the succubus shoved both of her claws downwards - towards Gabriel's face. Gabriel reached up and grabbed her arms at the elbows just as her claws came inches from his face. Then Gabriel pulled her over top of him by doing an ab-crunch motion, causing her to tumble ass over tit above Gabriel, and land in a sitting position on the snake which wrapped around Gabriel's hips.

Gabriel sat upright on the floor with the succubus sitting in his lap as he held her arms and claws up in the air before turning her arms in towards herself and driving her claws into her breasts. The succubus screamed for a second before dying and falling back onto Gabriel, who then rolled her off of him onto the floor.

Now Gabriel lay on the floor, wrapped from the legs to the chest by the snake as the robed lion stood over him. The lion let go of the snake, letting it entangle Gabriel, as the lion pulled a dagger out of his robe and walked around Gabriel, standing behind him while whispering spells and prayers.

Gabriel couldn't see where the lion went for a second. Suddenly, the lion reappeared, dropping to his knees over Gabriel with the dagger in both paws plunging down towards Gabriel's face. Gabriel ripped the arrow from out of his shoulder, and thrusted the arrow upwards into the lion's jugular just before the lion stabbed Gabriel in the face.

Finally, the police officer shot his gun into the air and the mob stopped beating Joseph.

"Alright, I see you folks are jealous of this here man and want to see justice, but he needs to stand trial in the court of law, not get killed by an angry mob," the officer said.

"Awwww," a few people whined.

The mob slowly got off Joseph and sat back down in the waiting room seats. One of the receptionists called for nurses and doctors to come and take Joseph back into the emergency room.

Joseph laid in a hospital bed in an induced coma for the next several weeks until his hearing date when he was awoken. Gabriel stood over Joseph and another man sitting next to him as a doctor and nurse checked Joseph's vital signs.

"My son… I must find him," Joseph said.

"It is the day of the hearing Joseph, you must get ready. Your son will be there in case it is the last time you see him," a man said.

"Who are you?" Joseph said.

"Names Malphas. I'm your public defense attorney – you're gonna need one," the man said.

"But my son… I haven't even taken him home yet," Joseph said.

"Joseph, you may not be going home for a while. While you were in a coma, word about your back to back mob muggings and your newborn son got put all over the News. People are villainizing you all over the media, labeling you as Satan and the anti-christ for bringing so much jealousy and hatred into North America during World War III when people are already afraid of the Apocalypse," Malphas said.

"Oh God, no," Joseph said.

"There's even rumors that you're noticeably effecting the efficiency of North America's labor force by decreasing productivity and output which is causing us to lose the upper hand in the war – some people are saying it's all because they are jealous of you. They're looking for a scapegoat, and they found one," Malphas said.

"Who is taking care of my son?" Joseph said.

"Child protective services as of now, but we'll see how the trial goes," Malphas said.

The courtroom was filled with spectators and paparazzi when Joseph, Malphas, and Gabriel walked in. Some people booed. In one small corner of the courtroom near the barrier by the defendant's table stood a woman holding Joseph's son. Uriel stood next to her.

"My son!" Joseph exclaimed.

Joseph ran down the courtroom aisle to the woman, who handed the child to Joseph. Joseph held his son until the hearing began. Invisible to everyone but the infant, a few guardian angels sat next to their respective spectators in the courtroom seating, but there was a much greater amount of demons standing next to their hosts in the courtroom. The demons hissed, growled, and sneered at the angels, and the angels stared back undaunted and unamused.

"We're greatly outnumbered," an angel whispered to another.

"It is no matter, Gabriel and Uriel are here with us," the angel replied.

The courtroom got louder and louder as the spectators and paparazzi got more excited and anxious for the hearing. Then the judge walked into the courtroom from a door behind the bench.

"All rise for the honorable Judge Asmodai. The court is now in session," the bailiff said.

The judge, wearing a black robe, walked from behind the bench and sat down. A dark shadow of a winged beast with a long tail and three heads lurked behind the judge. The shadow moved and revealed one of the heads had horns, another head wore a crown, and the third head was long like a lamb. The angels glanced nervously at each other. Some of the demons snickered.

"Now calling North America versus Joseph Carpenter," the judge said.

Joseph and Malphas stood up. The prosecuting lawyer on the other side of the courtroom stood up as well. Several of Joseph's ex-coworkers, boss, mob participants from the hospital, hospital staff, and police officers sat behind the prosecutor to act as witnesses and testifiers. Demons stood next to them as well.

Behind the judge, the dark shadow of the three-headed beast grew while it danced clownlike, hopping from one foot to the other, while the three swaying heads and arms of the beast gave its shadow the appearance of a jester's hat. A high, cynical male voice came from the shadow behind the judge, reciting a short poem:

"The bench is a bank
Where the judge sees the court
Of players racketeering
The ball back and forth"

The demons in the courtroom all laughed.

"Something is not right. You should leave, Uriel," Gabriel said.

"I'm not going anywhere without the child," Uriel said.

Just then, the newborn child in the woman's arms began crying. Joseph looked over nervously at his son.

"Please remove the child from the courtroom before we begin," the judge said.

"Your honor, please, I haven't even had a chance to take him home yet or even name him, this will be the longest I'll get to be with him since he's been born!" Joseph said.

"I will not have a sniveling child in my courtroom during proceedings, speak to it again and I will hold you in contempt of court," the judge said.

The woman holding the child walked out of the courtroom followed closely by Uriel. As Uriel walked out of the courtroom, one of the demons who had the head of a deer with long, branched antlers and was sitting in the spectator's gallery smiled at Uriel.

"Bye bye, Uriel," the demon said.

Uriel scanned the demon up and down and noticed the demon was trying to conceal a dagger in his robe. Uriel quickly turned around towards Gabriel.

"Gabriel! Watch out!" Uriel yelled.

The fat, three-headed demon which once appeared to be behind the judge now swung from the back of the room towards the front by a rope which hung from the ceiling while wielding a huge lance which had a black banner hanging from it with a red upside-down pentagram in the center. One of the demon's heads was a bull, the middle head was a man wearing a royal crown, and the third head was a ram. The demon had long, dragon wings, several serpent tails, and the webbed feet of a bird.

Gabriel turned around just as the three-headed demon swung down and impaled Gabriel in the chest with the lance, lifting him off his feet as he slid down the lance and swung with the demon from the rope.

"This is my courtroom!" the demon yelled.

A blast of light went through the ceiling as Gabriel's spirit ascended back up to Heaven. The demon laughed as he dropped to the floor, Gabriel still impaled on the lance.

"Nooo!" Uriel yelled.

Then the demons in the courtroom all charged towards the handful of angels in the courtroom. One demon had snuck up behind an angel and plunged a dagger into the angel's back before the angel could stand up and withdraw his weapon while another demon snuck up behind another angel and slit her throat from behind. Two blasts of light shot through the ceiling. One of the human spectators whose guardian angel just died started coughing while the other human whose guardian angel died sneezed several times.

Uriel unsheathed his sword which then engulfed into flames. The deer-faced demon who had smiled at Uriel ran towards an angel across the courtroom aisle and Uriel swung his sword sideways, cutting the demon in half and causing the two halves to catch on fire. Another demon ran from a back row towards an angel a couple rows ahead and Uriel thrusted his sword into the demon's back which came out the front of the demon and caught the demon's chest on fire.

Then Uriel turned around and saw the woman holding the child had walked out of the courtroom and an alligator with seven goat legs was crawling like a spider towards the woman and child – unseen to her. The bailiff was just about to shut and lock the courtroom door, so Uriel took one last look at the demons surrounding the two remaining guardian angels of two of the spectators in the gallery before Uriel ran out of the courtroom, spreading his wings.

The alligator with many goat legs was just about to bite the woman's leg holding the infant when Uriel descended from the air above with his sword pointed downwards on top of the demon, crushing the demon against the floor and immersing it in flames as Uriel's sword stabbed through it.

Then the woman carrying the child looked down and noticed she was about to step into a puddle on the hardwood floor in her heels. She stepped sideways passed the puddle and kept walking.

"Joseph Carpenter made all of these good people jealous, hurt his company's productivity, and caused two riots like he's some sort of precipitator of violence. And, this data from the government's economic and financial reports over the past month show a significant decline in North America's productivity, efficiency, and output, coincidentally, ever since Joseph Carpenter here and his… son… became infamous all over the News and media in North America for making everyone jealous," the prosecutor said.

Everyone in the courtroom gasped. The judge shook his head.

"This decline in our efficiency likely caused the loss of a battle in Southeast Asia last week, and now the entire continent is afraid North America might lose World War Three… all because of Joseph Carpenter and his newborn son. Now, I understand the law says we cannot put a child to death if they are a musician, even if we can't prove they will be a musician one day, and even if they are a prime candidate for the lethal injection, so the good courts let the child live - but the good courts cannot sit back and do nothing about the father, Joseph Carpenter. The good people behind me who have witnessed the chaos caused by the jealousy of Joseph Carpenter and who testified before you here today, as well as North Americans all over the world are demanding justice," the prosecutor said.

The spectators in the courtroom erupted into applause.

"Yea!" some spectators yelled.

The judge slammed his mallet on a hardwood sound block three times.

"Order, order in the court," the judge said.

Everyone quieted down.

The demons dragged the two remaining angels into the center aisle of the courtroom. Several powerful demons held the angels down onto their knees. The angels were badly beaten, wounded, and bleeding - their wings shredded. The demons encircled the angels, howling and jeering at them. The three-headed, winged demon stood with Gabriel's body impaled on his lance at the front of the courtroom, at the bench, next to the judge. The human head of the three-headed demon spoke:

"These angels believe God is just and all-powerful. They do not believe in the powers of the Dark Lord, who reigns in this world! I sentence them to death, for heresy!" the demon said.

The demons in the courtroom cheered. Two huge, winged demons, walked up behind the angels wielding massive executioner's swords, holding the swords up in the air, pointed downwards. One demon had a horse head and webbed talons for feet and the other demon had a bird's head with hooves for feet.

The demons pulled the angels' heads back then drove the executioner's swords into the chests of the angels simultaneously. Both the angels' spirits blasted upwards through the ceiling, which incinerated the snout off the horse-faced demon, who then fell over dead as well. Then the bird-faced demon turned and bent over to peck at the maimed face of the dead, horse-faced demon. The demons cheered again.

"In times of war, causing so much jealousy as to affect the profit of a company and efficiency of the nation can be seen as treason. I find you guilty of causing jealousy and guilty of treason, and sentence you to death by crucifixion," the judge said.

The crowd cheered.

"But your honor, this is only the first hearing!" Malphas exclaimed.

"The case is closed, there's no need to proceed to trial. This decree is coming straight from the king – the king himself is jealous. This is high treason," the judge said.

The crowd gasped. Then they cheered at the ruling and yelled at Joseph.

"Traitor!" someone yelled.

"Let's torture him while he's on the crucifix!" someone else yelled.

The next day, Joseph was nailed to a cross in a field with thousands of other people nailed to crosses near the side of a main highway so all passersby could see the fate of those who made others jealous, and so those who were jealous could walk by to throw rocks at and insult those who were being crucified.

As Joseph's son grew older, his childhood amnesia kicked in, and he lost the ability to see and remember Uriel, but Uriel still followed him everywhere. The son was never formally named, and so went by the name "The Son of Joseph Carpenter," although most people called him "The Son" or just "Son." Son lived in an orphanage after his father's death.

By the time Son was in fifth grade, he was living up to his genetics. He was at the head of all of his classes in academics, he was a star baseball player, and popular in school.

One day at recess, Son was playing kickball. Meanwhile, an obese boy named Bub stood with a couple of other fifth grade boys across the playground watching the kickball game. Unseen to any human, Uriel looked across the playground and saw a huge monster the height of the basketball nets and as wide as a school hallway standing behind Bub.

The monster next to Bub had a huge belly, no neck, no ears, and a face that looked sunken in from how much fat was on it. Three spirits of assorted animals – known in the spirit world as familiars, danced around the three other young boys nearby Bub and the massive monster. One familiar was a dog, another an ostrich, and the third a sheep.

"Familiars, I call on you to do my bidding," the monster grumbled.

“Yes master!” the dog said.

“If he is, so am I!” the sheep said.

“Why?” the ostrich squawked.

“Because I said so,” the monster growled.

“Why?” the ostrich squawked.

“Because I’m in charge here!” the monster roared.

The monster’s voice shook the playground. The ostrich stopped dancing in circles and stared at the monster.

“No! You’re not! God is!” the ostrich squawked.

Then the ostrich continued dancing in circles with the other familiars. The monster grew proportionally larger by several feet in size and became red. Steam poured out of his ears, nose, and mouth. Then the monster swung one of his huge paws overhead and downward, squashing the ostrich against the playground like a flyswatter smashing a fly. Uriel put his hand on the handle of his sheathed sword.

“Now follow me,” the monster said.

The monster started walking towards Uriel, and the two remaining familiars followed, still dancing in circles.

“Are any of you jealous of Son? He’s like, perfect,” Bub said.

“Yea, kinda, I mean he’s the center of attention in every class,” the second boy said.

“And he’s the best at like every sport and gets picked first for every game,” the third boy said.

“Yea, I’m a little jealous I guess, he’s one of the only guys who gets girlfriends at our age, I wouldn’t mind kissing Jessica or Sally,” the fourth boy said.

“But think about it, even if you’re only a little jealous of him now, that jealousy is going to grow over the years. He’s going to keep being the center of attention in every class, and keep getting all the girls, and keep being the best sports player until one day he invents something, marries a model, and plays for a professional sports team while he's King of the world – he'll be living all of our dreams," Bub said.

"Well, I never thought of it like that," the second boy said.

"Yea, I didn't realize we'll be jealous of him forever…" the third boy said.

"But we don't have to be. There's only one recess aid out today, if we all jumped him it would take the aid forever to notice, and even longer to get us all off of him, and by that time we might not be jealous of him anymore," Bub said.

"I'm in," the second boy said.

"Me too," the third boy said.

"I don't know guys, that's pretty messed up - four against one, I don't think we should, it's not right," the fourth boy said.

The other three boys looked at the fourth boy.

"Well then, get out of here faggot before we kick your ass too," Bub said.

"Yea, faggot," the second boy said.

Then the third boy turned and slapped the fourth boy across the face. The other three boys laughed at the fourth boy who started crying and ran away.

"Alright, let's go," Bub said.

Son was up to bat in the game of kickball. The other team on the playground backed up, the outfielders backing up all the way to the fence at the end of the playground. The ball got rolled towards Son by the pitcher and Son kicked the ball over everyone's heads. The ball soared over the fence for a homerun and Son's team cheered.

While Son rounded the bases, the monster and familiars of the dog and sheep approached the kickball diamond. Uriel walked towards them with his hand on his sword handle.

"How goes it, spirits of the netherworld," Uriel said.

"You're shiny!" the dog said.

"Shush boy," the monster said.

The dog stopped smiling and put his tail between his legs.

"I was talking to them, why don't you let them speak?" Uriel said.

"Because they belong to me, and now we're going to kill you. Get him!" the monster roared.

The dog charged at Uriel. The monster chanted a spell and the dog grew two extra heads and grew in size by about two-fold. Uriel unsheathed his blade, which engulfed into flames just as the massive, three-headed dog leaped onto Uriel and tackled him onto the ground. Uriel drove his fiery sword into the chest of the dog's body and the dog's heads yelped as Uriel laid on his back, lifting the burning, impaled body of the dogs above him before throwing the beast with his sword to the side.

As Son was halfway between third base and home plate, one of the boys from Bub's crew ran from the side and tackled Son. Son flew sideways, unexpecting the blow. The boy got on top of Son and punched him in the face, breaking Son's front teeth.

Son shook his head and blocked the rest of the boy's punches before Son rolled the boy over and punched him in the face over and over, breaking the boy's nose, teeth, and splitting his lips and face open as Son's punches banged the boy's head against the pavement, knocking him out cold. The other students cheered and videotaped the fight with their phones.

Uriel stood up - one of his wings had a hole in it, and his chest was bleeding through a tear in his armor. Then the sheep charged at Uriel. The monster chanted another spell and the sheep suddenly grew massive horns several feet in length and a beard, more like a goat. The abnormally long horns of the sheep pointed forward like a bull instead of curling inwards like a goat and both pierced into Uriel's armor before he could swing his sword. The sheep sent Uriel flying backwards and onto the ground as the sheep trampled over him.

Once again, Uriel laid on his back as the sheep stepped on Uriel's face and torso, so Uriel slashed his sword upwards, from back to front of the sheep, cutting it in half from tail to face. Uriel looked down at his chest. The sheep had not only pierced his armor, but his chest too. He was bleeding profusely through his armor and his ribs were broken where the sheep rammed him.

As Son laid a beating, fully mounted on top of the boy who tackled him and hit him first, the second boy in Bub's crew came up from behind Son and punched him in the face – hitting his nose only. Son's nose broke sideways and blood poured out of his nostrils.

Son stood up and turned around, grabbing the second boy by his shirt collar and then spun back around, pulling the boy to the ground next to the first boy. The second boy hit his head on the pavement as he fell, splitting his head open, and Son fell on top of him, raining punches onto the boy's face while Son's nostrils and mouth trickled blood like a faucet all over the boy and the pavement beneath him.

Uriel stood up, pushing the two, burning halves of the sheep off of him just as the massive monster charged towards him. The monster swung his big, flabby arms in circular motions as he ran towards Uriel. Uriel didn't have enough time to dodge the massive monster, so he thrusted his sword, but the reach of the monster's arm was longer than Uriel's sword and the monster slapped Uriel across the playground - Uriel landed about 20 yards away from the monster.

As Son was mounted on top of the second boy who attacked him, Son got blindsided a third time - this time by Bub who did a bear hugging, belly flop on top of Son from behind, sending Son crashing down on top of the second boy. Bub began pounding on Son's back and head with the bottom of his fists like a primate. Son covered the back of his head with his hands, and tried to roll from under Bub, but Bub's weight was too much.

Uriel stood up slowly and saw the monster charging at him again. Uriel waited until the monster enclosed on him before jumping straight up into the air, flapping his wings, and flying upwards dozens of feet off the ground, causing the monster to charge by underneath him.

Then Uriel came soaring down on top of the monster's back, shoving his burning blade through the monster's shoulder and into his chest. The monster roared as Uriel crouched on top of his back, Uriel driving his searing sword deeper into the monster's body. Then the monster reached over his head and grabbed Uriel. Once the monster had a hold of Uriel, he pulled Uriel from over his back and slammed Uriel onto the ground beneath him before stepping onto Uriel's chest, cracking his sternum.

Bub kept punching Son, mounted on his back, as the boy who got slapped and made fun of by Bub's crew for not wanting to jump Son ran up to the recess aid.

"Ms. Miles, Bub and the other boys are beating up Son!" the boy said.

The recess aid turned and looked across the playground to see Bub on top of Son, punching him over and over.

"Oh my God!" she yelled.

The recess aid blew her whistle and ran towards Bub and Son.

Son realized Bub had him pinned, so instead of trying to roll over, Son kept reaching over his own head and shoulders trying to grab one of Bub's fists as they pounded down on top of Son's back and head. Finally, after a blow to the back of the neck, Son caught the left fist of Bub and pulled Bub's fist over Son's shoulder, wrapping Bub's arm in front of Son's chest, using the angle of Son's shoulder to leverage pressure onto Bub's wrist. Within a few seconds a loud snap was heard as Bub's wrist broke over Son's shoulder, and Bub started crying. The other students stared in shock at the scene.

"Let me off you! Please, let go!" Bub cried.

As the monster stood on Uriel's chest, Uriel slashed his sword horizontally above him, chopping off the beast's foot from the ankle down. The beast screamed and fell straight backwards, shaking the playground as it hit the pavement. Then Uriel stood up and thrusted his sword through the groin up into the midsection of the monster which laid on its back on the pavement. The monster howled in agony as Uriel's burning sword stuck inside of it from its grown to its stomach before it died.

Bub turned pale and screamed in pain as he reached his free hand shakily into his pant pocket and pulled out a pocketknife. Bub flipped open the blade of the pocket knife, stretched his arm as far above his head as he could, then slammed his arm downwards towards Son.

Just then, the recess aid ran into the fight and caught Bub's arm before the blade of the pocketknife went into the back of Son's neck.

"Make him let go of my arm!" Bub cried.

The recess aid separated Son and Bub. When Son let Bub's arm out from under him, all the students screamed and gasped. Some students ran away, and a few vomited. Other students ran in with their phones for closer videos.

Bub's arm from the wrist down was bent at a 90-degree angle and was blue. All of Bub's fingers on that arm were also broken and bent sideways, some fingers had white bones showing through broken, bloody skin. A bone also stuck out from the skin on Bub's wrist as blood dripped towards his armpit and down his shirt. Bub sat down on the pavement holding his broken arm.

"Ahhuuuhh!" Bub wept.

The next week, Son sat in front of the principal of his school in the principal's office along with the staff of the orphanage where he lived. Son's nose had a huge bump on it such that it was curved like a beak and was also slightly crooked. Son's front teeth were also chipped and loose from the fight.

"We have to do something, Son once had the brightest future of any student - now look at him," the principal said.

"The orphanage has limited resources, we don't have the money for insurance which pays for cosmetic surgery and complex dental procedures without us having to pay thousands of dollars out of pocket," the head of the orphanage said.

"He should take it as a wake-up call for what's going to happen when he gets older and causes jealousy," an orphanage staff said.

The principal glared at the staff member.

"How about this, just for his teeth, the orphanage pays for half of what the insurance won't cover, and the school will raise the money for the other half," the principal said.

The orphanage staff glanced at each other, then down at Son.

"Fine, we should be able to budget that," the orphanage head staff said.

"I just have one last question about the incident Son. Why didn't you run away when three kids teamed up on you, including one kid who was twice your size?" the principal said.

"If I ran, then I would just have to face them again the next day, and then I would have to keep running away from them every day for the rest of my life, and then other people might join them too and they might start picking on other people as well, and it would only get worse. I figured if I fought back right then, even if I lost, then they wouldn't want to fight me again," Son said.

"Well, you didn't lose…" the principal said.

After the social workers and Son left the principal's office, a morbidly obese woman walked into the office next and sat down in front of the principal.

"My son's arm is permanently disfigured from that parentless bastard! They had to amputate his arm just below the elbow! Now I have to pay for a prosthetic limb!" the woman yelled.

"Your child jumped Son with two other boys," the principal said.

"Who cares! Bub was just jealous! They all were!" the woman said.

"Once a child makes it past birth inspection, the Law of Jealousy does not go into effect again until the child turns 18, so all your child did was brutally assault a classmate - he's expelled," the principal said.

"What! Expelled? Principal, they euthanize infants and people 18 and older – the law will change one day, and when it does, kids like that motherless son of a bitch who hurt my son will get euthanized too at any age. Listen, I don't care what you have to do to fix this, but I'm not losing this battle to some orphan, the other parents will never look at me the same way," the mother said.

The mother reached into her purse and pulled out two stacks of hundred dollar bills, each strapped together by bands.

"Here's ten thousand dollars. Keep Bub in school, and make sure that fatherless son of a whore never touches my child again," the mother said.

The principal looked down at the money. Then the principal nodded her head. The mother left the cash on the principal's desk then walked out of the office. As soon as the woman left the office, the principal picked up her phone and made a phone call.

"I have the money for Son's dental procedure, the school will cover all of it at no expense to the orphanage," the principal said.

By the time Son was going into freshman year of high school, he had grown to 6 feet tall with broad shoulders, and was a star baseball player on his club and school baseball teams. He was also popular amongst his peers and was in the top 5% of class rank.

One day, an elderly couple who had read about Son's talent in sports and top performance in academics in the local newspaper came to the orphanage where Son lived and adopted Son.

Son noticed an upside-down cross hanging from a chain on the rearview mirror of the car on the drive to his new home.

"We're going to put you in the best private high school in the state!" his adoptive father said.

"We'll even pay for most of it, so you'll only have a little debt to pay off after, but it won't matter because you'll get one of the best jobs like everyone else who goes to this school!" his adoptive mother said.

"But I like my current school district, I have a lot of friends and I'm a star baseball player," Son said.

His adoptive parents laughed.

When Son got to his new home he noticed there were many statues of animals, some of which were part human, and many figurines, books, jewelry, and flags with upside-down crosses and pentagrams scattered throughout the house. Skulls of dead animals lined the walls near the ceiling as well.

In Son's new private school, people didn't seem as friendly and outgoing, so he didn't make many new friends. He did well in school still and was quickly recognized as a star player on his new club baseball team, yet he kept getting cut from the school's baseball team in this new, private high school.

Senior year of high school, Son tried out for varsity one last time. Son and Uriel sat in the grassy outfield of the baseball diamond with the rest of the players who tried out for the team as the head coach called out the names of those who made the team. Son didn't hear his name.

After the tryouts were over, Son walked up to the head coach.

"Coach, why didn't I ever make the school's team? Every year I got cut," Son said.

"Son, this is the most valuable lesson you'll ever learn in life. You're by far the best player in our school district, so if I put you on the team, all the other players would be jealous of you. Sure, you would be a star player and probably get a scholarship, but our team would be an unhappy mess, disobedient and unorganized. We would risk having a much worse team and no spirit with you on the team," the head coach said.

"No spirit? Good spirit or bad spirit?" Son said.

"See, this is what I'm talking about. You're such a good player that you see the game from a coach's level, so your rebellious to us coaches and subvert the power structure. In fact, I'm starting to get jealous of you myself, you're lucky I don't bash your head in with a bat. Aren't you 18 now?" the head coach said.

The assistant coach laughed.

Son walked away hurriedly. Uriel backed away slowly with his hand on his sheathed sword as two demons emerged from the coaches, one from the head coach and the other from the assistant coach. The demon who came from the head coach was a centaur, and the demon who came from the assistant coach was a big cat with bat wings. The cat demon had a huge, toothy smile, like a human, and the centaur pulled out a bow and arrow.

"Leave this place, Uriel," the centaur said.

The winged cat began laughing as the centaur pulled an arrow from the quiver strapped to his back.

"If you shoot that arrow, it will be the last thing you do," Uriel said.

“He’s all talk, get him boy,” the centaur said.

The winged cat leapt into the air and took flight towards Uriel. Uriel left his sword sheathed and jumped, then flapped his wings one powerful time causing him to soar upwards into the air far above the winged cat.

Then Uriel dove down like a falcon on top of the cat. Uriel grabbed the cat by the skin on its shoulders, immobilizing its arms as Uriel’s feet kicked into the cat’s chest. The cat yelped as they descended fast towards the ground with the cat on the bottom. Just then, an arrow shot through the back of the cat and came out the cat’s chest, almost piercing into Uriel. The cat howled.

Uriel and the cat hit the ground right in front of the centaur, with the cat on the bottom, crushing the dog and sending the arrow entirely through the cat’s chest, killing it. Uriel grabbed the arrow from the cat’s chest as the Centaur pulled another arrow from his quiver. Uriel lunged towards the centaur and slammed the arrow down on top of the centaur’s head, driving the arrow into the centaur’s skull. The centaur fell over with the arrow stuck into his head.

Uriel turned around and saw about a dozen demons had appeared across the baseball field standing next to the players, invisible to all the humans.

The players all watched Son as he walked into the dugout, whispering to each other, all of them slowly following Son towards the dugout.

Uriel unsheathed his sword which engulfed into flames, then he touched the burning sword onto the tip of the arrows in the centaur’s quiver, catching the tips of the arrows on fire. Then Uriel grabbed the quiver of burning arrows off the centaur’s back, and put it on his own back. Uriel bent down and grabbed the centaur’s bow, then took flight into the air over the baseball field.

As Son walked into the dugout to grab his bat and backpack, the captain of the baseball team and another player walked towards him with their bats dragging on the sand. The other players surrounded the outside of the fence as they watched the confrontation, with demons standing behind them watching as well.

The demons outside the dugout had heads of different animals, and all had different bodies then that of their counterpart animal heads.

Two larger demons stood inside the dugout next to the captain and the other player. One of the demons in the dugout was a human-sized lizard, standing upright on two legs like a human would, wielding a spear with blades on both ends in his hands; while the other demon was a larger, human-sized frog wearing a crown, standing on two legs as well, wielding a spiked club the size of Son.

Suddenly, a burning arrow pierced into the head of a demon outside the dugout. The demons growled and looked up to see Uriel flying overhead raining burning arrows down onto them, picking off demons off left and right.

"You're pretty good Son. Too bad you're not good enough to make the school's team. I guess that makes us better than you, right?" the captain said.

"Yea, if Son is supposedly the best player in the district like they say on all the club teams, but he can't make this team, then players like us are the best!" the other player said.

"I guess so," Son said.

Son grabbed his bat and bag and started walking away.

"Don't walk away from us, we were talking to you!" the captain said.

"And what were we talking about?" Son said.

"Don't you remember dummy? We were talking about how much better we must be than you," the other player said.

"How do people even think he's so good on all the club teams if he can't even make the school's team? I don't get it! Let's fuck this kid up!" the captain said.

The other player swung his bat sideways at Son's face. Son ducked and the bat missed overhead. The captain then swung his bat downwards towards the top of Son's head, and Son raised his bat overhead with both arms, blocking the swing. Then Son raised the locked bats in the air and kicked the captain in the chest, sending him falling onto his back in the sand. The other player swung low at Son's leg, and Son let the player hit Son in the leg in return for a blow to the other player's chin by Son's bat. The other player spun, spitting out several teeth and dark red blood as he fell face first into the sand.

Just as Uriel picked off the last demon with the bow and burning arrows, a young dragon, only about three times Uriel's size, plunged down on top of Uriel from above, sending them both plummeting towards the ground. The beast breathed fire from its mouth which scorched the feathers off Uriel's wings.

Uriel unsheathed his burning sword, and spun in the air before he landed on his back on the ground with the dragon on top of him. The dragon screamed as Uriel's burning sword stuck into its chest. Then the dragon died, falling on top of Uriel. The lizard inside the dugout ran outside the dugout and looked at Uriel and the dragon.

"My dragon!" the lizard cried.

The lizard ran towards Uriel pointing his spear at him. Uriel couldn't push the dragon off of him so he turned the dragon's head towards the advancing lizard. Then Uriel bear-hugged the dragon with both arms around the dragon's midsection and gave the dragon the Heimlich maneuver, cracking the dragon's ribs and squeezing the last of the air out of the dragon's body. The dead dragon involuntarily breathed fire, scorching the lizard into ashes.

The captain stood up with his bat and walked slowly towards Son. Several other baseball players ran into the dugout and grabbed Son. Son tried to push them off as the captain approached with his bat but couldn't, and Son could barely stand up after the blow from the bat to his leg. The other players pulled Son to the ground as the captain approached, who swung the bat downwards onto Son's already hurt leg. Son screamed in pain.

"Get him, he just turned 18 and he's making us jealous!" the captain yelled.

The other baseball players surrounded Son and started kicking him while he was on the ground while the captain pointed and laughed.

Uriel saw the players mugging Son and tried again to push the dragon off of him but couldn't. Then Uriel grabbed his burning sword which was still stuck in the dragon's chest and pressed against his own chest so he couldn't pull it out, and began wiggling the sword from side to side, sawing the dragon in half. Once the dragon was sawed in half, he pushed the top half of the dragon off of him first, then push off the body half.

Finally, Uriel stood up slowly with his sword in his hand then limped towards the dugout where the big frog was dancing and chanting spells in an ancient language and had opened a red portal, causing hundreds of red spirits to fly from the portal into the bodies of the young baseball players in this world, who were relentlessly beating Son.

When Uriel walked into the dugout, the big frog stopped chanting and turned towards him, growling. Uriel walked towards the frog and swung his burning sword – the frog didn't even budge. Just as Uriel's sword was about to hit the frog, hundreds of red spirits flew from inside of the baseball players out towards Uriel, sending Uriel flying backwards and knocking his sword from his hands.

The giant, crowned frog lifted his huge, spiked club and walked towards Uriel who was lying on the ground. Uriel tried to stand up but the spirits hovered over him like a net, and knocked him back down every time he tried. The frog stood over Uriel, holding the spiked club high into the air. Just as the frog swung the club downwards, Uriel chanted a spell in another ancient language and the spirits turned blue then flew upwards towards the frog, reversing the club mid-swing back over the frog's head and knocking the frog onto his back. The blue spirits flew upwards towards the ceiling, dancing all over the dugout.

"You like playing with spirits, do you?" Uriel said.

Uriel chanted another spell and the spirits all flew together, creating one dense white, glowing orb. The frog cried from the blinding white light and put his arms in front of his eyes as the white orb flew towards him, entering inside of him. The frog ribbitted and his huge vocal sac bubbled outwards, then the frog exploded into green, ectoplasmic slime all over the dugout, leaving behind the white orb in his place. Then the white orb flew back into the red portal before the portal closed. Uriel fell onto the ground and passed out from pain, fatigue, and injuries.

Just then, the assistant coach blew his whistle.

"Alright you savages, get off of him," the coach said.

The players stopped kicking Son, who was unconscious, bruised, and bleeding on the dugout floor.

Son laid in a hospital bed in an induced coma for the next several weeks until he was awoken. Uriel stood over Son and another man sitting next to him as a doctor and nurse checked Son's vital signs.

"You have a hearing today in court Son, you must get ready," a man said.

"A hearing? Who are you?" Son said.

"Names Malphas. I'm your public defense attorney – you're gonna need one," the man said.

"Public defense attorney?" Son said.

"Son, there's something you need to know. When you were born, you were so gifted the doctors wanted to give you the lethal injection for fear of how much jealousy you would cause, but didn't because a judge suspected you would become a great musician. People were outraged, and they took it out on your father, Joseph Carpenter, who already caused jealousy wherever he worked and was sent to trial right after your birth. It was all over the News and media. I defended your father in court, but we lost," Malphas said.

"Don't tell me the same thing is happening to me," Son said.

"The same thing is happening to you, Son. You're standing trial for violating the Law of Jealousy with the same prosecutor and judge who sentenced your father to death for the same crime. While you were in a coma, word about your mugging at the baseball field spread around, and it wasn't long before people remembered that you were once the baby who caused so much controversy 18 years ago. Some people were outraged that you caused jealousy and a mob mugging so soon after you turned 18 that it got you on the News again. Just like your father, people are villainizing you all over the media, labeling you as Satan and the anti-christ for bringing so much jealousy and hatred into North America during World War III when people are already afraid of the Apocalypse," Malphas said.

"Oh God, no," Son said.

"There's even rumors the courts may rewrite the Law of Jealousy to include children and teens between the ages of infancy and the age of 18 to allow anyone to be prosecuted for causing jealousy because of you. Politicians are also thinking about disallowing people from defending themselves if they are suspected of causing jealousy after you knocked that kid's teeth out with a bat because the amount of accusations, muggings, and prosecutions under the Law of Jealousy have noticeably dropped since you got put on the media again, which has hurt the profits of the courts, prisons, and government," Malphas said.

"No no no," Son said.

"North America has been losing the war worse than the government and the media have let on over the past decade so morale and efficiency don't drop, but now they are letting people know how bad we are losing coincidentally at the same time you're on the media for standing trial for breaking the Law of Jealousy. Some people think North America is losing the war all because of you, but they only think that due to how long the media has been lying about our standing in the war. They're looking for a scapegoat, and they found one," Malphas said.

The courtroom was filled with spectators and paparazzi when Son, Malphas, and Uriel walked in. Some people booed.

Invisible to all humans, a few guardian angels sat next to their respective spectators in the courtroom seating, but there was a much greater amount of demons standing next to their hosts in the courtroom. The demons hissed, growled, and sneered at the angels, and the angels stared back undaunted and unamused.

"We're greatly outnumbered," an angel whispered to another.

"It is no matter, Uriel is here with us," the angel replied.

The courtroom got louder and louder as the spectators and paparazzi got more excited and anxious for the hearing. Then the judge walked into the courtroom from a door behind the bench.

"All rise for the honorable Judge Asmodai. The court is now in session," the bailiff said.

The judge, wearing a black robe, walked from behind the bench and sat down. A dark shadow of a winged beast with a long tail and three heads lurked behind the judge. The shadow moved and revealed one of the heads had horns, another head wore a crown, and the third head was long like a lamb. The angels glanced nervously at each other. Some of the demons snickered.

"Now calling North America v The Son of Joseph Carpenter," the judge said.

Son and Malphas stood up. The prosecuting lawyer on the other side of the courtroom stood up as well. Several of Son's classmates, sports team players, coaches, and a police officer sat behind the prosecutor to act as witnesses and testifiers. Demons stood next to them as well.

Behind the judge, the dark shadow of the three-headed beast grew while it danced clownlike, hopping from one foot to the other, while the three swaying heads and arms of the beast gave its shadow the appearance of a jester's hat. A high, cynical male voice came from the shadow behind the judge, reciting a short poem:

"The bench is a bank
Where the judge sees the court
Of players racketeering
The ball back and forth"

The demons in the courtroom all laughed. Uriel smiled and turned towards the demons at the prosecutor's table.

"Real knee-slapper, right?" Uriel said.

The laughing demons at the prosecutor's table nodded their heads.

"Uriel! Watch out!" an angel yelled.

The massive, three-headed demon swung from the back of the room towards the front by a rope which hung from the ceiling while wielding a huge lance which had a black banner hanging from it with a red upside-down pentagram in the center. One of the demon's heads was a bull, the middle head was a man wearing a royal crown, and the third head was a ram. The demon had long, dragon wings, several serpent tails, and the webbed feet of a bird.

Uriel didn't turn around but jumped high into the air doing a backflip while unsheathing his burning sword. The three-headed demon passed under Uriel and Uriel swung his sword in front of him, cutting the rope and sending the demon crashing to the floor. The three-headed demon's legs broke under his weight when he hit the floor, the cracks echoing in the courtroom. The other demons gasped.

"But… this is my courtroom!" the demon cried.

Uriel descended to the floor in front of the demon.

"Not anymore," Uriel said.

Uriel walked towards the demon who tried to crawl away. Uriel quickly closed in on the demon who thrusted his lance at Uriel. Uriel grabbed the lance and pulled it from the demon's hands. Then Uriel snapped the lance over his knee and touched his burning sword to the banner, burning the demon's flag.

"You can't do this!" the demon said.

Without hesitating any longer, Uriel drove his sword downwards into the demon's stomach and tore the sword upwards towards the demon's chest, leaving a foot long slice in the demon's torso, which squirted blue blood like a fountain across the courtroom.

The other demons in the courtroom screamed in horror and ran for the exit of the courtroom, but the demons stopped and became silent for a moment when they saw the four guardian angels of spectators standing at the doorway of the courtroom.

The guardian angels withdrew their swords and the demons all screamed again and began running around the courtroom in circles, hardly fighting back as Uriel and the other four angels massacred the dozens of demons, painting the courtroom with demon blood of all different colors. Uriel and the angels quickly slayed every demon in the courtroom without taking a casualty.

"The Son of Joseph Carpenter made all of these good people jealous, and caused a riot amongst his school's baseball team, hurting a classmate badly in the process, as if he's purposely following in his father's footsteps. And, this data from the government's economic and financial reports over the past month show a significant decline in North America's GDP, coincidentally, ever since The Son of Joseph Carpenter here became infamous all over the News and media in North America for making everyone too scared to accuse and prosecute others of breaking the Law of Jealousy. This decline in our justice system's profit, decline in North America's GDP, and tearing apart of our society's morals might cause us to lose this war… all because of The Son of Joseph Carpenter and his father," the prosecutor said.

Everyone in the courtroom gasped.

"Now, I understand the law says we cannot put a child to death if they are a musician, but The Son of Joseph Carpenter is no longer a child. The good people behind me who have witnessed the chaos caused by the jealousy of The Son of Joseph Carpenter and who testified before you here today, as well as North Americans all over the world are demanding justice," the prosecutor said.

The spectators in the courtroom erupted into applause.

"Yea!" some spectators yelled.

The judge slammed his mallet on a hardwood sound block three times.

"Order, order in the court," the judge said.

Everyone quieted down.

Just then, a tall, robed being with huge angel-wings, shrouded in darkness stepped behind the judge. The being was as dark as a blackhole, seemingly sucking in the light around him, darkening and distorting the air. The being wielded a long sword in one hand a mace in the other.

"Satan…" an angel said.

"Stand strong, he's outnumbered," Uriel said.

"In times of war, causing so much jealousy as to affect the profit of the courts and downfall of the nation's social glue can be seen as treason," the judge said.

The crowd cheered. The judge banged his mallet three times.

"The Law of Jealousy will hereby be rewritten to include any violators of any age passed birth inspection," the judge said.

The crowd cheered even louder.

Satan stepped out behind the bench towards Uriel and the other angels. Uriel and the angels stood their ground.

"We're not afraid of you Satan!" an angel said.

"However, a judge once pardoned you for breaking the Law of Jealousy as an infant and granted you life under the suspicion that you would be a great musician. The court would like you to perform a musical piece for us so we may judge this for ourselves to decide your fate," the judge said.

The crowd gasped and whispered before quieting down.

"But your honor, the boy was raised an in orphanage, they could not afford any instruments," Malphas said.

"Can you sing?" the judge said.

"Yes," Son said.

"Well, go on," the judge said.

Son glanced around the courtroom, then began singing a hymn he learned from a priest who visited the orphanage when he was younger. Uriel and the angels sung with the boy, creating complex overtones and undertones with perfect mathematical precision to Son's fundamental frequency which resonated throughout the courtroom.

Oh holy Father, the believers have found me
Help me Elohim, it is I with little to no sin
And what you say is a sin I will argue was for them
Because the humans stand no chance against the Nephilim
It says it right there in the Book of Enoch
But I am not enough, and my enemies are plenty
I have gathered all the resources you were able to send me
I have gathered the poets, but Satan's Army is strong
Slowly we fall, song after song

My aura is so bright, too bright to be denied
The believers found my light, I can no longer hide
My covers been blown, now with demons I collide
As the Beast has overgrown, and the angels are few
They're scared they won't survive, some even side with Satan
Cause they think you're a lie, is it true we only win
If in the end I die?

Only I can wage war against the Beast, and so I have
And there will be peace for a thousand years
Until the Crab constellation rears the Sun when we Feast
In the solstice of many planets we lease from the Creator
Staring down through an eyepiece

One of the demons who had been chopped in half during the skirmish but was still living covered his ears from the beauty of the music, his dismembered lower half and legs also writhing in pain from the music, and at the end of the song, both halves of the demon spontaneously combusted into purple slime all over the center aisle of the courtroom.

Everyone in the courtroom was silent for a moment when the boy finished. The judge looked stunned, her mouth open and eyes wide with her eyebrows raised. Then everyone stood up and starting clapping and cheering. Satan vanished from behind the judge.

"You certainly do have the voice of an angel. Do you know what they would have done to you as a young boy in ancient times to keep your voice so perfect?

"I don't know, your honor," Son said.

"Cut your balls off," the judge said.

Everyone in the courtroom laughed.

"The King shall pardon you for breaking the Law of Jealousy and treason as long as you agree to become one of his personal assistants and court musicians," the judge said.

Everyone in the courtroom gasped.

"Say yes for God's sake," Malphas whispered.

"I would be honored, your honor," Son said.

The next day, instead of going to school, Son followed the instructions written on a piece of paper inside an envelope given to him by the judge's courtroom assistant and waited until a limousine pulled up outside his adoptive home. As Son stood up to walk out the door, his adoptive parents walked in front of the door.

"Where do you think you're going?" his adoptive father said.

"I'm going to live with the King now, to be one of his court musicians," Son said.

His parents laughed.

"You can't be a musician! You have no talent! You have to work the rest of your life like all of us!" his adoptive mother said.

"What? These are orders from the King himself," Son said.

"That's bullshit, you need to get a job and work like we did, that's why we're putting you through an expensive private school, so you can work to pay off your debt from your education," his adoptive father said.

"Get out of my way, my ride is here," Son said.

"You're not going anywhere! You're going to live here the rest of your life working to pay off your debt like we did! Why do you think we put you into a school where you wouldn't be the star baseball player and get recruited?" his adoptive mother yelled.

"Yea, we're jealous of you, we read about you and didn't want you to become a pro baseball player or entrepreneur and live out our dreams! We wanted to submerge you in debt to live as slaves like us! You can't just go be a musician for the King!" his adoptive father yelled.

"You guys are evil! I'm leaving now!" Son cried.

"If you're not going to work the rest of your life to pay off your debt, then we're going to sacrifice you to the Lord of Darkness - then eat you!" his adoptive mother screamed.

Son's adoptive parents withdrew large, kitchen knives from their clothes and ran towards Son. Son yelled and ran the opposite direction towards the back of the house.

Uriel looked around, confused, as he ran with Son. There were no demons in sight. Then Uriel noticed darkness crawling along the ceiling, walls, and floor close behind them, unseen to Son. A deep voice shook the house as it spoke from somewhere upstairs in an ancient language, unheard by Son. Tentacle like, barbed-vines crawled towards Son and Uriel in the darkness which swept over the inside of the house. Uriel unsheathed his sword which engulfed into flames.

Just as Son and Uriel made it to the back door, sharp, grey vines dropped straight downwards like a curtain, covering the doorway. Uriel slashed the vines in half with his burning sword.

Son ran out of the back door of the haunted house, turned, and jumped the back gate. Then he ran around the side of the house towards the limousine parked in the street out front. Son quickly opened the limousine door and jumped inside the car. The limousine drove away just as Son's adoptive parents ran into the street wielding knives in the air, hollering.

Uriel sat in the back seat of the limousine next to Son and they both turned around to look out the back window at Son's foster parents and their haunted house. The haunted house now had a massive vine sprouting from the chimney and other vines coming out of the house through windows and the front door, spilling out onto the lawn, blighting and killing all the grass and shrubbery the vines touched.

When the limo let Son off at the airport, Son pulled a plane ticket out from the envelope given to him by the courtroom assistant, got a boarding pass from a kiosk at the gates, boarded a small jet with about 10 other passengers, and flew to the King of North America's Airport, located in the wealthiest city in North America - a rolling landscape filled with modernized castles, one of which was the King's castle.

Another limousine picked Son up from the arrival airport and drove him to the King's castle. The castle was built on a small hill surrounded by a forest on one side and the foothills of a mountain on the other side, with a gate at the entrance which the limousine driver had to stop at a security checkpoint before entering. After the security guard verified the identities of the driver and Son, the gate was opened and they drove inside.

Once inside the gates to the entrance, after making one turn, they finally saw the exterior of the massive castle several hundred yards down the road.

The King's castle was a rectangular keep castle, with two rectangular stone walls on the outside for defense which visitors had to meander through before the structures on the inside of the keep could be accessed. Between the rectangular stone wall entrance was an array of lethal lasers going from wall to wall through the entire path which had to be turned off by the security guards to gain entrance.

There were rail guns, anti-aircraft turrets, and artillery turrets fit for naval ships mounted on the four outer towers of the castle, which could obliterate anything for miles into the distance whether on ground or in the air. Snipers stood on the outer towers as well.

There was also a tower in the middle of the castle which was part of the King's palace and was the largest tower, with steampunk gears on the sides near the top so the top of the tower could move in any direction and open up into a silo capable of launching nuclear warheads and intercontinental ballistic missiles – already with a history of launching two nukes during World War Three into Africa and Europe to allow North America to take over the continents.

There was also a moat surrounding the keep filled with robotic piranha-shrimp, surveilling underwater and purifying the moat into drinking water while capable of biting through steel and shooting tiny super-cavitating bursts of sound through the water which burst into bubbles hot enough to melt a hole into a submarine. A gunboat also patrolled the border of the moat.

The keep and moat were surrounded on all sides by a plantation of purple lavender plants and sparsely scattered purple, weeping willow trees for as far as the eye could see into the distance and on the sides of the castle from the edge of the forest up to the foothills of the mountain, creating a magical look.

Armed drones flew above the entire estate in regular patterns.

Once they drove passed the two rectangular walls, which had gated, security checkpoints at both ends, they finally got a full view of the castle's inner magnificence. Whilst the defensive outer walls were made of old, weathered stone, the King's cathedral-like palace along with the other structures on the inside of the castle walls were all painted white with purple roofs, doors, and windows.

All the structures inside the castle walls were designed with medieval, Romanesque and Gothic architecture, depicting everything from angels to saints to sinners and demons carved into the stone. Similar statues made of gold were scattered across the courtyard as well.

The courtyard was filled with guards, musicians, artists, entertainers, spectators, royal family members, wealthy aristocrats, politicians, transhumanist cyborgs, and other individuals of note, along with a few service robots. Uriel looked around and didn't see any demons in sight. The limousine made a right, then two lefts before stopping at the farthest end of the inside of the castle.

The limousine drove on a small, rectangular path around the inside of the castle up to the cathedral-like palace, which had a tall, arched and gated entrance with guards on the outside holding automatic rifles.

Son and Uriel stepped out of the vehicle and were led by a royal servant dressed in purple and white up the stairs of a raised doorway on the side of the King's palace.

Even for a side entrance, the inside of the palace was decorated lavishly with figurines and ornaments of gold, silver, and other precious metals on top of carved wood tables. Deep purple wallpaper with silver tribal flower designs lined the hallway, which were filled with paintings on either side. The designer floor had a complex geometric pattern composed of black marble with purple accents, and imbedded purple pearls and sparkling white diamonds.

The servant led Son into a room with taxidermy animals and gold statues scattered throughout and had an elevator which they took to the 3rd, top floor. When they exited the elevator, the servant led Son through a hallway of doors which looked like a hotel.

Scantily dressed and partly nude women ran down the hallways, exiting and entering doors. Men wearing dress clothes or else nothing but their ties ran along with the women throughout the hallways and rooms. Some of the people wore black masks, others wore animal masks, some had feathery accessories on, and some carried whips or sex toys. Maids brought food and drinks into rooms and carried trash and dirty silverware, tableware, and glass cups out of rooms.

Son and the servant turned right at the end of the hallway into a hallway which was much quieter. At the end of the hallway was a window overlooking the courtyard and mountains. The servant stopped in front of a door.

“Here you are sir,” the servant said.

The servant handed Son two room keys.

“Rest for the night from your travels. The King would like to meet you tomorrow around noon in the throne room. There is a map of the building and entire castle grounds in your room, and if you ever get lost or need a guard to escort you somewhere, just find one of these buttons, push it, and ask for directions or help. You’ll also find these buttons outside in the courtyard on the street lamps,” the servant said.

The servant pointed to a small button with a purple light on the hallway wall. Then the servant walked away.

Son and Uriel walked inside the bedroom. The entrance of the suite led to a living room which connected to a master bedroom. The suite had its own rendition of purple and white walls, floors, furniture, paintings and decorations, equally as marvelous as the halls throughout the palace. The master bedroom connected to a master bathroom with a jacuzzi and walk in shower.

As Son slept in the master bedroom of his suite that night, Uriel explored the building. Uriel roamed the hallways of all three floors, which took him several hours due to the complex layout of the hotel-like palace which had four towers on each corner of the rectangular building connected by hallways of rooms, and one big tower in the middle where the throne room and royal chambers where - where the King, his family, close friends and visiting world leaders slept.

The top two floors were all hallways filled with rooms for guests, no different than a five-star hotel, and there were also a couple of dining halls, dance halls, banquet halls, computer labs, movie theaters, and indoor gyms on these floors. Other musicians, artists, and entertainers lived or stayed on Son's floor as well. Uriel could tell none of the rooms on the top two floors had any supernatural guests, including no guardian angels, which struck him as a bit odd considering all the other artists staying there.

The first floor had rooms for the servants and guards, a kitchen, laundry room, as well as much larger dining halls, dance halls, and banquet halls than the floors above. The first floor also had the main hall and courtroom in the center beneath the middle tower.

The main hall had an arched, stone ceiling of great height and Medieval architecture with huge chandeliers made of crystal and diamond, which sparkled even in the night with no lights turned on in the palace due to the faint rays of light from the moon and lamps in the courtyard coming in through the flower patterned, stained glass windows. The first floor also had no sign of supernatural guests.

As the morning hours neared, Uriel realized he would only have enough night time to scout either the dungeon or the grounds outside before Son awoke. He decided to check outside.

Uriel walked outside of the King's palace to the courtyard. The moon was full, illuminating the inner castle walls more so than the lamps in the courtyard. There was a fog at hip height and crickets chirped.

There were several other buildings inside the castle walls a fraction of the size of the palace, including a cathedral, but Uriel would not have time to search them all tonight either. The inner castle walls were void of any supernatural beings, so Uriel walked outside the two rectangular keep walls to search the grounds outside the castle.

Uriel walked to the edge of the tree line and scanned the forest for a couple minutes, looking back and forth, and then he saw a green, glowing woman far in the distance. The woman was naked besides a crown of twigs and leaves on her head. She laughed and waved at Uriel then turned and ran into the forest, her long hair twirling in the breeze. Uriel sighed, then ran after her.

Uriel slowed his run down to a small, quiet footstep as he saw a fire in the near distance. Then he saw four, green glowing beings singing and dancing naked around the fire. They were all beautiful women. Uriel shook his head and walked out into the opening where the beings gathered around the fire. The women cheered when they saw him and sang louder.

"What goes on here?" Uriel said.

"What's it look like? We live here!" a woman said.

"Come join us!" another woman said.

"Who are you?" Uriel said.

"We are the nymphs of the purple forest!" a woman said.

"Come on!" a nymph said.

A nymph grabbed Uriel's hand and tried to pull him towards her, but Uriel didn't budge. The nymph let go of Uriel's hand and kept singing and dancing around the fire with the other nymphs.

"I'm on a mission. Have any of you seen any demonic or other evil activity in these lands?" Uriel said.

"Nope, so come join us!" a nymph said.

"You're telling me that no malevolent beings occupy these lands? And you've never seen any other supernatural beings?" Uriel said.

"Once in a while a satyr, but they usually leave us alone after a while," a nymph said.

"satyrs? Are they dangerous?" Uriel said.

"Only one time they attacked us, they killed one of our sisters but we fended them off. That was hundreds of years ago though, we never saw that band of satyrs ever again - they looked possessed or something. All the other satyrs have been friendly ever since, they usually just want one thing like all guys do," a nymph said.

The other nymphs giggled.

"Come bathe with us!" a nymph said.

"Maybe another night ladies, I have to explore the rest of these lands," Uriel said.

"But the moon is full tonight, we need your company now!" a nymph said.

The nymphs encircled Uriel, walking around him, touching his arms, armor, and face and rubbing their bodies against him.

"Really… I must be going," Uriel said.

"Oh, come on, a stud like you wouldn't take very long to service our needs," a nymph said.

"Ladies, I'm an angel, we don't divulge in such… Earthly… delights," Uriel said.

Suddenly, a band of humanlike creatures with horse legs, goat horns and goat ears, with long, bushy beards and sideburns wielding sharpened, wooden spears made from the forest ran out towards Uriel and the nymphs.

"Oh no!" a nymph said.

"Those are the satyrs who killed one of our sisters we were telling you about!" a nymph said.

Uriel stepped in front of the nymphs and unsheathed his burning sword. The six satyrs converged on Uriel all at once. Uriel swung his sword horizontally across his body at head level for the satyrs. From left to right he cut off two of the six satyr's heads before the other four saw his burning sword and ducked or rolled out of the way.

Then Uriel stepped clockwise where the satyr's numbers just weakened as the satyrs on his right thrusted their spears towards him, barely missing.

Uriel stepped clockwise again to turn their row formation into a column, and the closet satyr jabbed his spear at Uriel which Uriel parried downwards with the handle of his sword before driving his sword into the satyr's chest.

"He's so manly," a nymph said.

"He's a champion," another nymph said.

The nymphs began kissing and touching themselves and each other's bodies.

Two of the three remaining satyrs closest to Uriel regrouped into a row to team up on him. One of the satyrs thrusted his spear high while the other satyr thrusted his spear low. Uriel put his sword in front of his face to block the high spear and spread his legs wide to evade the low spear.

After the high spear deflected off Uriel's blade, Uriel brought his blade down across his body, cutting the low spear in half. Then Uriel stepped forward and thrusted his sword into the chest of the satyr whose spear he just cut in half.

The satyr who struck high now struck towards Uriel's midsection. Uriel didn't have time to remove his sword from the other satyr to block himself or move out of the way, so he turned the body of the satyr he had impaled on his sword towards the incoming spear, which pierced through the satyr's back and out the chest.

The satyr and Uriel both stood for a moment holding the dead satyr in the air between them - Uriel impaling it from chest to back, and the other satyr impaling it from back to chest, and they both glanced at the sixth satyr who stood with a large erection staring at the nymphs who were rolling around the forest floor touching each other.

The satyr fighting Uriel yelled at the sixth satyr, but the satyr didn't move - he just stood watching the nymphs with his mouth open, drooling.

Uriel kicked the dead satyr impaled between him and the other satyr to force the dead satyr down the other satyr's spear while freeing Uriel's blade. The satyr dropped his spear from the weight of the dead satyr weighing it down. The satyr looked at Uriel then turned and tried to run into the forest but Uriel was faster and drove his burning sword into the satyr's back.

Uriel turned around just in time to see the last satyr approaching the nymphs. Uriel ran up from behind the nymph and lopped its head off within a few feet of the nymphs. The nymphs screamed and moaned as they all climaxed together. Uriel sheathed his sword then walked back into the forest towards the castle.

"Thanks for your services!" a nymph called.

"Come back soon!" another nymph yelled.

When Uriel exited the forest, he walked to the other side of the castle grounds and climbed the foothills of the mountain. To his surprise, he saw no sign of any supernatural threats – not even one troll on this side of the mountain. The sun was just about to come up.

Uriel wanted to fly to the top of the mountain and look at all below, but his wings were still too injured and healing from his fight with the dragon on the baseball field about a month ago, and if he hiked up the mountain it would not leave him enough time to get back to Son before he awoke. Uriel reasoned he would hike the mountain tomorrow if he had time after exploring the castle's dungeon.

Just as Uriel turned to go back to the palace, he saw something move out of the corner of his eye. Uriel looked up at the top of the mountain and saw a goat staring down at him. The goat seemed to be a normal goat with no supernatural capabilities or entities nearby, but something about the goat seemed supernatural or malevolent - the way the goat stared at Uriel and stood at the peak of the mountain in the full moon just before daybreak. Eventually the goat turned and walked away from the peak so Uriel could no longer see him, so Uriel turned and walked back towards the castle.

At noon the next day, Son and Uriel were led to the King's throne room by a servant. The King sat in his throne, waiting for Son. Two guards stood in the room as well holding guns and with swords sheathed in their belts.

The King was morbidly obese, wore a purple velvet robe lined with gold and decorated with jewels and gemstones of all different colors, and had a giant gold crown filled with gemstones on top of his big, fat head. A fourth man stood next to the King in a long black robe with red lining and red tribal designs on it.

"Ahhh the infamous Son of Joseph Carpenter," the King said.

"It is an honor to meet you, your majesty, thank you for pardoning me and giving me a place to live in your glorious castle," Son said.

"No need for such formalities Son, you will be like a son to me, the son I never had," the King said.

"Thank you, sir," Son said.

"Son, this here is Lord Paymon. He is the best music teacher in North America and one of the most notable composers in the world. He will be your teacher," the King said.

"I'm honored," Son said.

“The honor will be ours if you live up to our expectations. You do know why we have the Law of Jealousy don’t you Son?” the King said.

“For efficiency sir, to win the war,” Son said.

“Yes, but to also split the human gene pool in two in the long run, to create a race of royalty and a race of slaves. Dumbing down the slave race more and more, generation after generation by allowing society to kill off anyone who is gifted or smart enough to cause jealousy until we are left with only people who are obedient, conformist imbeciles who will kill anyone different than them, even their own kids. You on the other hand, have a chance to reproduce in the race of royalty if you fulfil your destiny as a musician,” the King said.

“I won’t let you down, sir,” Son said.

“Good. Go now with Lord Paymon, it is time for your first lesson. We will make you into an international star in no time,” the King said.

Lord Paymon led Son and Uriel out of the throne room to an elevator. Lord Paymon hit D and the elevator descended from the top of the middle tower down to the dungeon.

“Of course,” Uriel said.

“This elevator only goes to the first level of the dungeon, there’s a staircase that goes much further down into the… darkness,” Lord Paymon said.

Lord Paymon snickered and grabbed a gas lit lamp off the wall to illuminate the way as he led Son through a medieval looking dungeon, filled with prison cells and racks, wheels, and devices used for torturing. At the end of the dungeon, there was a spiral staircase which went downward. Designed around the doorway of the stone, spiral staircase was the open mouth of a devillike being. Lord Paymon led Son down the spiral staircase. Son looked down through the center of the stairwell until the darkness swallowed the light.

"How far down does this go?" Son said.

"Oh, until you can't walk anymore, but at that point you won't want to come back up," Lord Paymon said.

Lord Paymon burst into laughter.

After descending six underground floors, they walked into the entrance of the seventh underground floor and down a hallway which had a glowing, red light at the end of it. They reached the end of the hallway which opened into a circular room with several pillars around a leveled floor dropping into the ground.

A red pentagram was in the center of the leveled floor with a burning candle at all five points. A statue of a serpent stood in the center of the room, which had a pulsating, glowing red light coming from the open mouth and eyes, illuminating the room, almost like there was a fire inside of the statue. A bowl sat by the foot of the statue emitting a dense smoke, which barely left the bowl due to the thickness of the smoke compared to the surrounding air.

"Welcome to the Shrine of the Serpent," Lord Paymon said.

"I don't see any instruments, or recording equipment, or anything music related here," Son said.

"Many people need this lesson and this lesson only to become a great artist. It is the first, and last lesson for many," Lord Paymon said.

"Well, that's impossible - at least for me. I've never picked up an instrument and I've never read music. All I can do is sing in tune to a song," Son said.

"That's all about to change right now. You're about to be given exactly what you need, but perhaps not what you want, in order to become a musician who can change the world," Lord Paymon said.

"But how?" Son said.

"I'm going to take you to another world, another reality, where time is perceived differently and much can be learned while only a small amount of time passes in our world. Where there are spirits who know secrets about our universe and will share them with you," Lord Paymon said.

"I don't know about this. I've never communicated with spirits before, when I imagined being a court musician I imagined sitting in front of a piano with books of sheet music learning to play songs for the King and recordings for the masses," Son said.

"And perhaps you will, or perhaps you won't learn that way. Everyone learns and plays music differently, but I've never met a musician worth listening to who doesn't know the secrets I'm about to show you. Take a couple of deep breathes from this bowl," Lord Paymon said.

Lord Paymon picked up the smoky bowl at the foot of the statue and handed it to Son.

"Are you sure?" Son said.

"Look," Lord Paymon said.

Lord Paymon put his face over the bowl and took a deep breath.

"See?" Lord Paymon said.

Son took the bowl from Lord Paymon.

"Sit here," Lord Paymon said.

Lord Paymon pointed to the middle of the pentagram on the floor. Son sat cross-legged, facing towards the statute of the serpent in the middle of the pentagram and began breathing in the smoke from the bowl.

"You're going to see a being shortly. She is the most powerful entity I, and most others know of in this world. Her name is Choronzon," Lord Paymon said.

"No... Choronzon," Uriel whispered.

"You may see other beings as well, before during or after you meet Choronzon, and she likely has control over those beings. You may see beings who look familiar to you, but don't be fooled, none of these beings are of any significance to you now - only Choronzon is," Lord Paymon said.

"Liar!" Uriel shouted.

"This is the most important part, Son - it is a matter of life or death. When Choronzon appears, you must tell her you command her in the Name and Blood of Christ. Then command her to go where Jesus Christ sends her by the voice of His Spirit. She will then show you what you need to know. You may go unconscious in this reality, but whatever you do, do not be frightened, the demons will sense it, and feed on it, and destroy you. I will end the ritual after your journey is complete," Lord Paymon said.

"How will I know who Choronzon is?" Son said.

"She assumes many forms, but in the reality you will soon enter, her presence can be felt like an overwhelming sensation of all emotions as she approaches, and the Dark Lord himself will likely be standing close by - puppeteering her," Lord Paymon said.

Lord Paymon began chanting an incantation in an ancient language which resonated throughout the room. Son took one last inhale of smoke from the bowl then put the bowl down in front of him. Son felt a rush of adrenaline in his chest and his heart rate increased – the room got darker but the lights more brilliant, and he could see every crack in the floor and detail of the statue.

Uriel withdrew his sword which engulfed into flames, and for the first time since Son was an infant, he could see Uriel. All of a sudden, Son remembered the angels in the delivery room on the day of his birth - he remembered Uriel and the other angels standing between Son and a bunch of monsters… demons. Son couldn't remember the fight though.

Just then, six beings in red robes walked out from behind the pillars surrounding the shrine in all directions. Their faces were horribly wrinkled, they had long, hairy elf ears, and pitch-black eyes without any white. The red robed beings chanted along with Lord Paymon, revealing their sharp teeth. Each of the red robed beings held large executioner's swords pointed downwards as they encircled the shrine and Uriel.

Uriel charged towards one of the red robed beings and thrusted his sword at it. The robed being suddenly turned to stone and Uriel's sword deflected off, while the other beings kept advancing.

"Gargoyles," Uriel whispered.

Uriel swung his sword overhead at the next nearest gargoyle which also turned to stone and Uriel's sword barely chipped and cracked the stone. The first gargoyle that turned to stone turned organic again and swung his huge sword at Uriel. Uriel spun out of the way and the huge sword chopped the second gargoyle in stone form in half.

Uriel raised his eyebrows then lunged and stabbed at the gargoyle which just chopped the other gargoyle in half before he could lift his big sword again. The gargoyle turned back into stone and Uriel's sword bounced off. Then Uriel stood right in front of the stone gargoyle as a third gargoyle approached. Uriel let the third gargoyle swing at him, and he ducked, causing the gargoyle's sword to turn the stone gargoyle behind him into rubble.

Uriel repeated this technique of turning one gargoyle to stone form with a quick strike, then letting another gargoyle swing at him, which he would evade and cause the gargoyle to kill the other in stone form. This method worked to kill the third, fourth, and fifth gargoyles, but now there was one gargoyle left… and this method no longer worked.

Uriel sheathed his burning sword and picked up the executioner's sword of a Gargoyle who was reduced to rubble. The sword was heavy - Uriel could barely lift it. Uriel dragged the sword on the ground towards the last Gargoyle just as the Gargoyle lifted his sword back off the ground from his last swing. Uriel faked lifting up his sword, and the Gargoyle swung overhead. Uriel rolled to the side and the Gargoyle's huge sword cracked the stone floor.

Then Uriel stood up and spun slowly with his sword, lifting it slightly off the ground. Uriel kept spinning, gaining momentum, and lifting the sword higher as he spun towards the gargoyle. The gargoyle turned to stone form. Uriel enclosed on the gargoyle, now spinning with the sword as fast as a gargoyle could swing it. Uriel's first spinning swing took the arm off the stone form gargoyle, but Uriel kept spinning like a circular saw, not losing much momentum from the blow and Uriel's second swing took the head off the gargoyle, before Uriel spun for a third swing which hit the gargoyle in the chest and reduced all but the gargoyle's ankles and feet to rubble.

After the battle, Son drifted into a lucid dream. Son was lying down on the ground, looking up. He was sweating coldly, shaking, muscles tense and twitching. Just then, a being wearing a dark robe stood over Son and looked down at him.

"Choronzon… I command you in the Name and Blood of Christ," Son said.

The being looked down at Son, and tilted its head as if confused. Then the being looked backwards over its own shoulder. Son looked where the being standing over him looked and saw another being as dark as a blackhole, seemingly sucking in the light around him, darkening and distorting the air. The being wore an equally dark crown on his head and was waving his arms, hands, and fingers in the air like a puppeteer towards the being standing over Son.

"I command you to go where Jesus Christ sends you by the voice of His Spirit," Son said.

Just then, Son saw a kaleidoscope of colors in the air all around him. Son felt like he was flying forwards and g-forces were acting on him. Choronzon was now flying in front of Son, with her dark robe flailing from the motion… and the Dark Lord was nowhere in sight.

Son was flying down a never-ending environment of colorful tunnels which zoomed into view and then passed by them. Humanoid creatures, many with different animal faces and bodies danced and fornicated in the entranceways of the tunnels, beckoning them in. A cacophony of sounds tore into Son's ears.

Then Son saw from his normal point of view again, sitting on the floor of the ceremonial chamber in front the statue with Uriel and the rubble of gargoyles. But when Son looked up, he saw the ceiling wasn't there – instead he was looking up into a circular tower with a hollow middle which went up into the bright sky.

The tower had different, seemingly infinite levels erecting into the clouds, and many people and angels from all the hierarchies of the tower looked down at Son through the hole in the center of the tower, waving at him and cheering.

Uriel stood next to Son at the bottom center of the tower, which was a sandy amphitheater floor.

"This is the Tower of Babel. Mathematically constructed like the musical circle of fifths," Uriel said.

"Circle of fifths?" Son said.

"In the circle of fifths lies the harmony, chords, progressions, and transpositions of nature. Music is the language of our universe Son - it is how God composed all. God put Lucifer in charge of the choir of angels in Heaven due to Lucifer's perfection in the art of music, but this power given to him by God and Lucifer's belief that he was a better musician thus ruler than God made Lucifer rebel along with other angels he convinced. God's angels, led by Archangel Michael, defeated

Lucifer and his angels during the War in Heaven and God casted Lucifer, henceforth known as Satan, and his fallen angels out of Heaven, down to Earth, where they've been in charge of mankind ever since," Uriel said.

Son scanned the tower and noticed every other level was labeled with a lowercase "m" or an uppercase "M." The people and angels on same levels of the tower were also separated into groups by walls of different colors. Everyone in the tower held instruments, both string and wind instruments, sitting in their respective sections, and played only in specific sequences before or after other adjacent sections to the left, right, above or below.

"Today, Satan hides behind the music, entertainment, and communications industry, brainwashing the masses into supporting war, consumerism, and sin while his fallen angels hide behind governments and militaries, using the brainwashed masses to destroy the planet and humanity while enslaving everyone through the economy. All world powers are working on behalf of Satan and his agenda, and while demons used to only be brought into this world through black magic, now, Satan's minions, under the guise of science, are opening up pathways for demons to enter all over Earth. Upwards of 90 percent of Earth's population is now possessed by demons, deceiving and tormenting those who aren't possessed in order to weaken them, feed off them, and cause demonic possession to spread like virus, speeding up Satan's agenda," Uriel said.

Tears streamed down Son's face.

"You must learn Satan's own game to defeat him – music. The circle of fifths holds many answers for composing harmonious music based on simple geometric relationships and the corresponding ratios of frequencies. Look at the Tower. You see how the different levels have either a capital or lowercase "m?" Those stand for major and minor, and each of those sections are in different key signatures, spiraling upwards by sections of perfect fifths, or seven semitones; and spiraling downwards by fifths as well, which is the strongest resolution in nature as it is moving a dominant of a scale back to the tonic," Uriel said.

Son watched the musicians playing in the Tower of Babel, each of their section's parts making more sense now.

"There is much harmony in a major key right above a minor key and vice versa, as these are relative major and minor keys respectively. And so many songs can be written with adjacent major keys and their relative minors," Uriel said.

Suddenly, a dark figure moving as fast as a racecar charged into Uriel's side, sending Uriel flying dozens of yards into the rounded wall at the bottom of the tower. The being as dark as a blackhole stood between Son and Uriel, raising his arms in the air, triumphantly – a mace in one arm. The people and angels looking down from the Tower above booed.

"Go to Hell, Satan!" someone yelled.

"You never fight fair!" someone else yelled.

"That's why you're down there, Satan!" someone else yelled.

Uriel stood up slowly and withdrew his sword, which engulfed into flames as Satan charged at him again, just as fast as the first time. This time Uriel was ready and slashed his sword across his chest in front of him as Satan approached, but Satan jumped into the air, parallel to the ground, spreading his wings and flew over Uriel's sword and smashed his mace into the side of Uriel's head as he flew by. Uriel fell onto the ground on one knee, blood pouring from the side of his head.

"No!" Son yelled.

Son tried to stand up, but just then, Choronzon returned and stood over Son, immobilizing him with fear and anxiety. Son watched as Satan walked up from behind Uriel. Uriel, still kneeling, swung his sword backwards towards Satan, but Satan blocked the sword with his mace and grabbed Uriel's arm, pulling

Uriel's arm backwards and upwards into the air. Uriel's shoulder popped and his sword fell to the ground.

Satan dropped his mace and pulled a sword out from his belt while still holding Uriel's arm in the air, then Satan submerged his sword into Uriel's unprotected armpit, through his chest, and out his other armpit. Uriel's spirit blasted with bright light up the Tower of Babel into Heaven.

Son tried to yell but only a squeak came out like he was in a lucid dream. Choronzon stood over Son as Satan walked towards them. An overwhelming sense of doom and hopelessness presided over Son. Just then, Son woke up, sprawled in the middle of the ritual room in front of Lord Paymon.

"What the fuck!" Son said.

"You're ready," Lord Paymon said.

Lord Paymon led Son to the lunch hall. When Son walked into the lunch hall, he saw hundreds of extremely beautiful, mostly young people. Then Son recognized a couple of celebrity musicians and artists.

"These are the other artists, the best in North American, and some from around the world as well. Feel free to mingle, but do not collaborate in artistic endeavors – the King has special plans for you. We're going to explode you into the lime light all over the media and take the public by storm to make you into the most famous musician in the world. You see people staring at you? They're jealous of you, some of them hate you, some of them want you dead. Be careful who you talk to and trust, but don't be afraid to defend yourself, the Law of Jealousy is not in effect for the King's artists," Lord Paymon said.

Son got some pizza from the buffet and sat down at a table by himself. A girl who looked his age with blue hair and blue lipstick and eyeliner walked over to Son's table and sat down across from him with her tray of food.

"Hi, I'm Lily," she said.

"Hi, I'm Son. Aren't you the artist who goes by the name Blue Lily on stage? You have that hit song "Pollinate Me," Son said.

"Yup, that's me. But a lot of us heard the King's got something special planned for you. Some people are starting to believe you have a somewhat biblical purpose - others are already haters," Lily said.

"Story of my life. So, what's it like around here?" Son said.

"Well, it's probably one of, if not the most luxurious lifestyle in the world, other than the fact that the King randomly sacrifices some of us for rituals on specific calendar dates chosen by the King's astrologer to get views for the News channels, and we have to perform for the King whenever he asks, which isn't too bad, except if you mess up you can get badly beaten or killed. Oh, and we have to do Satanic rituals every Sunday and the only purpose of our art is to brainwash billions of people into following the doctrines of demons and evil spirits while destroying the world," Lily said.

"Jesus," Son said.

"And, if you don't sell as much as the King and Lord Paymon expect, you can also get punished or killed. Plus, all the other artists hate whoever hits the top of the charts, and some of them often steal from, hurt, or kill whoever they are jealous of, so nobody really has any friends - only partners in crime. Most artists are afraid for their lives to stand out and be the next big artist, they think it's a waste of effort to be the best if it only brings danger, so a lot of artists purposely make average music since their position here is already secure - making the music industry worse and worse over time," Lily said.

"Jesus, so if you don't perform well enough the King kills you, and if you perform too well the other artists try to kill you," Son said.

"Yup pretty much. But I, and some of the others here are starting to believe that you are going to set us free. That you are here to change things, and make things right, and maybe even be King yourself one day," Lily said.

"Well that's crazy, I'm an orphan with no money, no family or friends. The only reason I'm here is because the King himself pardoned me for violating the Law of Jealousy and saved me from execution," Son said.

"But you have the power to bring change," Lily said.

"But how?" Son said.

"You bring change everywhere you go. Don't you see? When you were born you barely escaped the death sentence and were all over the News, and then you escaped the death sentence again because of the King himself – anyone else would have been dead in the cradle, but not you, there's something special about you," Lily said.

"No, there *was* something special about me. I had a guardian angel, but Lord Paymon and I did a ritual in the dungeon and Satan killed my guardian angel. Now I'm just normal and defenseless," Son said.

"They killed all of our guardian angels, it's the initiation process around here. It makes us more susceptible to demonic possession or else weakens us to make us more obedient, but some of us can't get possessed, some of us just suffer more and more, and become more creative, and evolve from this suffering – become stronger, and that's why we have hope," Lily said.

"Wow, I never thought the girl who sang upside down with her dress in the air like a rose bulb while human bees flew overhead would be so smart," Son said.

Lily laughed.

"I only did that for one music video and one live performance with ropes, you're probably going to have to do weirder stuff," Lily said.

"Don't remind me," Son said.

"There's going to be a party tonight on the third-floor dance hall with live performers, do you wanna go with me?" Lily said.

"Sure," Son said.

That night, Son put on a suit and tie from his stocked wardrobe then walked to Lily's room a couple hallways away from his room. Son knocked on her door and Lily walked out in a blue dress looking like her alter ego Blue Lily.

When Son and Lily got to the dance hall, a security guard let them in through the doors. The lights were off and the room was dark except a couple of spinning, silver disco balls on the ceiling painting the room with specs of white light in the darkness.

Everyone was slow dancing to rock music with deep, reverberating drums and bass from a band on the stage in the front, center of the dance hall.

Strippers danced in glass boxes hanging from the ceiling all around the room, and were dimly lit with red lights. The dancers in the glass boxes were dressed as devils with horns. One of the glass boxes in the center of the room had a live goat.

"Let's dance," Lily said.

Son and Lily danced the rest of the night to the music, but Lily seemed to get nervous as the night went on.

"What's wrong?" Son said.

"You should stay until the end to watch, just this once, so you know," Lily said.

"Know what? I think I already know how fucked up everything is," Son said.

"Just trust me," Lily said.

As midnight approached and the live band played the last song of the party, the dance hall seemed to only get more packed with people.

Suddenly, the crowd parted from below the glass box with the goat. Then huge metal spikes erected from the floor beneath the goat. Just as the band finished the last song, the floor of the glass box opened and the goat fell several feet before getting impaled on the metal spikes, spraying blood all over the first two rows of partiers near the goat. The goat hollered like a grown man:

"Ahhhh!" the goat screamed.

Then the spikes retracted back into the floor, leaving the mutilated goat bleeding on the floor. The party-goers took daggers and knives out of their clothing and began stabbing and cutting the goat. They began eating the goat's organs and lapping the goat's blood off the floor.

Someone put the goat's face over his own while eating the goat's tongue, making the goat look like it was eating its own tongue as blood drooled from the goat's mouth. Multiple people ate the several feet of the goat's intestines at the same time. The parts of the goat were passed around the room so everyone could eat some. Then the party-goers began taking their clothes off and rolling around in the goat's blood before a blood orgy began.

"We need more blood," someone said.

Just then, the floor to one of the glass boxes holding a dancing stripper opened and she fell several feet down onto huge metal spikes erected from the floor.

"Wwwhhhyyy?" she shrieked.

She screamed in pain until the metal spikes retracted and the bloody woman lay mangled on the floor. The party-goers cheered and ran over to the woman, stabbing her, eating her corpse, and drinking her blood while the orgy intensified.

Son watched wide eyed from the back of the room near the exit.

"Let's get out of here," Lily said.

Son and Lily walked to Son's room.

"Jesus, there was like every artist participating in that blood orgy," Son said.

"*Mostly* every artist, yea, there's a few of us who don't participate in those events, but coincidentally those who don't participate tend to get randomly selected as sacrifices in rituals, so we act like we're Satan worshippers to not stand out," Lily said.

"This is hideous," Son said.

"It turns out, throughout history, dictatorships are more than just dictatorships, they are demonships, spreading demonism, darkness, and evil around the world. The extra resources horded by dictatorships don't just go to advancing science and war to stay ahead of other nations, but to developing and practicing the dark arts," Lily said.

"But how does an entire society become demonized?" Son said.

"By doing the first thing Satan and the Fallen angels did to start the War in Heaven - worshipping the wrong God. Slowly, over time, the ruling class brainwashes their nation to do the opposite of what is righteous by following the opposite of who God would put in charge – subvert nature's power structure in politics and the workplace to give the weak and wicked authority over the strong and just while dividing the people through social and economic inequality so they never unite for change," Lily said.

"But why don't the strong and just stand up and do something?" Son said.

"Demonships systematically destroy the strong and just in order to stop the spreading of awareness and rebellion by teaching everyone to act as a dog would, for dog is the opposite of God. Obey, follow, and worship the fellow dog, not God - be like dog, not like God. Society behaves like a pack of dogs doing what is best for the majority of the pack at the expense of the individual by constantly challenging, terminating, and replacing the statistical outliers of the pack – the alphas and omegas. That is what the Law of Jealousy is for," Lily said.

"It's like an algorithm for society to demonize itself over time," Son said.

"Yup. Demonships turn a nation's gene pool and moral development into a negative feedback loop, generation after generation until the nation rots from the inside out due to corruption and lack of qualified leadership or workforce as all other demonships have done in the past. Once the population's morals are low enough, people begin willingly practicing the dark arts as a means of obtaining individual power and wants. And that's what gives demons power, when people willingly sin, obey without question, and practice the dark arts," Lily said.

"But what do the people of demonships believe?" Son said.

"Demonships have polar opposite cultures of those who live by the golden rule and believe all are equal and so everyone should act in everyone's best interest without negatively affecting anyone else. The cultures of demonships, like ours, whether they realize it or not, believe some people are Gods to be worshipped and all other people are dogs to act as worshippers and slaves – this occurs in most, if not all demonships throughout history from ancient times until today. Whether celebrities, politicians, or artists like us are being worshipped by the masses, there is a class of deities and a class of worshippers. Then sacrifices are justified, expansion is desired, and war is waged," Lily said.

"How does nobody notice the negative effects?" Son said.

"It is an ancient battle of good versus evil continuing from one empire to the next throughout history, slowly spreading demonism more and more over time – everyone notices, there are just so many more evil people than good people that the takeover is silent. Some people suspect those who are evil think and act as one, like a hive, to carry out supernaturally timed events in their onslaught against good so they can enslave humanity. The battle has now grown to a climax because the new dictator of the world, The King of North America, has the ability to completely take over the planet and force everyone into demonism and slavery or else end the world," Lily said.

"I don't know what I'd do without you Lily, I'd just be in a prison," Son said.

"And I don't know what I'd do without my belief in you saving us. So I'll help you help everyone," Lily said.

Lily smiled as she leaned in to kiss Son. Lily slept in Son's room that night.

The next day, Son met with Lord Paymon in one of the music studios of the palace – underground in the dungeon.

"So, the plan is, we'll make at least ten songs and music videos for each song, release the album, put you all over the media worldwide, start your view count artificially high with bots that view and listen to your songs so everyone thinks you're the new best thing, then shortly after, when North American pride and demonism are at a peak, the King will attempt to conquer Asia to take over the world. Now tell me, so we can get you started as the musician who will help bring in this new era, what happened when you met Choronzon?" Lord Paymon said.

I saw a lot of colors, and what looked like tunnels to other dimensions, then an angel showed me the Tower of Babel, and then… Satan killed the angel," Son said.

"An angel showed you the Tower of Babel…?" Lord Paymon said.

"Yes, there were many angels looking down at us," Son said.

"Did the angel say anything to you?" Lord Paymon said.

"Yes, he told me the story about the War in Heaven and Satan falling to Earth," Son said.

“Hail Satan. What else did the angel say?” Lord Paymon said.

“He told me music is the language of the universe, it is how we are constructed, it is our math. He said the Tower of Babel is constructed like the circle of fifths, and he taught me how to write songs with the circle of fifths,” Son said.

“Ahhh, the power of the circle of fifths. That is your secret. Everyone learns music differently, some learn by ear while others study music theory. You have been showed how you will become the most famous musician the world has ever known,” Lord Paymon said.

“Was that ritual necessary to figure that out? Couldn’t we have just given me courses in music?” Son said.

“Nobody learns what is necessary to become influential from sitting in a classroom. What you must realize Son, is everything happens for a reason, and now that you are being observed by angels and demons, and soon to be billions of people, sequence of events will occur at specific moments in order for you to fulfil your destiny and carry out a plan on a larger scale which is out of both of our controls. By having that ritual, you have taken a shortcut of months, possibly even years to becoming the musician we need you to be at the right window of time, for if you did not have that ritual, you may not be able to release an album before the final battle of World War Three - or perhaps you would never become the musician you’re capable of becoming at all,” Lord Paymon said.

Lord Paymon handed Son a book about music theory.

“Over the next few months, you will read this book and others like it, and practice keyboard as my student. We will make practice tracks in the studio so you can get the feel of creating songs from start to finish. We expect within one year to begin recording the album, which we hope to release just before Christmas of next year,” Lord Paymon said.

"Reading this book isn't going to make demons appear is it?" Son said.

"Only if you masturbate to thoughts of incest," Lord Paymon said.

"What…?" Son said.

Over the next few months, Son read about music theory and practiced keyboard while making songs in the studio with Lord Paymon. When Son wasn't practicing, he spent all his time with Lily. Other artists stared at Son and Lily in the lunch hall until they began to feel too uncomfortable, so they began eating in one of their rooms together.

One night, a famous musician named Donkey Hoe Tay stood outside Son's room as Son and Lily walked to Son's room after dinner. A white powdered drug was all over Donkey's nose and lips.

"Well if it isn't Mr. Perfect, the best musician with the best looking girl, living the life of luxury in the King's castle. You haven't even released an album yet and people talk about you more than me around here – I've released three albums. People were jealous of me until you got here, now everyone's jealous of you – including me!" Donkey said.

Donkey ran towards Son and Lily. Lily screamed.

A security guard standing just around the corner heard Lily's scream and came running from behind Son and Lily towards Donkey. Donkey tried to dodge the security guard but the security guard was nearly seven feet tall and had an arm span which encompassed the width of the hallway. The security guard grabbed Donkey.

"What is this nonsense, let me at him, I'm jealous!" Donkey yelled.

"King's orders are to protect Son, he's worth more than any of you right now," the guard said.

"What? Protected by the King? Little bastard, I used to be the King's favorite musician!" Donkey said.

Donkey tried to hit the security guard but the security guard blocked the punch and grabbed Donkey by the shoulders, lifting Donkey and walking with Donkey in his hands towards the end of the third story hallway where the window overlooked the mountains.

"Are you disobeying the King's orders?" the guard said.

"Yes, you giant moron! I'm not going to watch that new guy live out my dreams, the King's giving him anything he wants and all the attention to go with it! I'm jealous! Either he dies or I die!" Donkey yelled.

The guard threw Donkey through the glass window. Donkey fell three stories with the shattered glass back first onto the ground outside the palace. Donkey didn't die from the fall but was fully paralyzed due to his spine and neck breaking and was knocked into a coma. Another security guard on the ground floor dragged Donkey back inside the palace where Donkey was sacrificed on an alter in the King's throne room, and eaten by the King himself along with Lord Paymon and other royalty.

The media broadcasted worldwide a lie that Donkey Hoe Tay died in a car crash, showing pictures of his wrecked car.

The next day, the same guard who threw Donkey out the window escorted Son to his music lesson in the basement with Lord Paymon.

"The King has ordered me to be your personal bodyguard, to follow you and stand outside the door to your room after the incident last night. Some other artists are filled with jealousy so the King has determined they are a threat to his plans," the guard said.

Son and Lord Paymon began composing and recording the songs to be used for Son's first album, to be titled *Dark Ages*. Lily often came with Son and his bodyguard to the recording sessions. The music videos began production as well after each song was finished. The King himself even made some appearances to see the progress, with his entourage of bodyguards.

Son's songs were perfect for the current club scene in North America – a fusion of dance and rock music for darkly lit venues. Some songs were slow, and others fast, but all had loud, reverberating drum beats and rhythms to dance to.

One night, the King called Son to the throne room. Son and his bodyguard walked into the throne room where the King sat on his throne surrounded by other bodyguards. Son noticed the King was wearing a shirt with Son's face on it, and one of Son's songs was playing in the background. A statue of Son also now stood in the corner of the room. Son raised one eyebrow and glanced at his bodyguard who had the same look on his face.

"Son, I can't stop listening to all the songs you're making for your first album. I've become obsessed. They're perfect for what we're trying to do – put everyone in a dancing, seduced trance while our military takes over the world. Then I won't just be the King of North America – I will be the King of the World… the King of Earth… the King of the Solar System… the greatest King ever!" the King said.

"Thank you, your majesty, it is an honor to serve you," Son said.

"Son, you will be the greatest musician ever… but perhaps instead I'll release your songs under my name and be the best musician and King ever!" the King said.

The King laughed. The bodyguards glanced at each other.

"I'm just kidding, Son. But seriously, I would like my name to be attached to this album, so I will be listed as co-writer of your album, and you will make one song dedicated to me and my greatness, which I will oversee and critique to my liking," the King said.

"Yes sire," Son said.

"Also, there will be one final edit of your songs before they are released to the world in which I will make any changes I wish - since your songs are so perfect that nobody will likely notice anything I do… which will allow me to have the desired effect on the listeners," the King said.

"Yes… your majesty…" Son said.

"What's wrong Son? You don't seem happy with your King's decision," the King said.

"Nothing your majesty, I am just happy with how the songs have turned out so far, and am worried I might not be as happy with the songs if changes are made," Son said.

"Son, don't forget, I'm the King, I'm in charge here, you work for me, I don't really care if you're happy with the music, I only care if *I'm* happy and about what I can use you and your music for," the King said.

"Yes, your majesty," Son said.

The next day, Son and Lord Paymon began recording a song about the King, just as the King had asked. The King stayed with them the entire time.

"No, play it like this!" the King said.

The King hummed a tune.

Son and Lord Paymon recreated the King's request on a synthesizer.

"No no, that's not right either, isn't there a way to record the tune I hum and then convert it into a file that can play it back in a guitar or piano sound?" the King said.

"Yes… it's called a vocoder. Just go stand in front of the microphone in the recording room," Lord Paymon said.

The King gleefully ran into the recording room attached to the producing studio. The King stood in front of the microphone and hummed a tune. Then the King ran back into the producing studio.

"Play it!" the King bellowed.

Lord Paymon sat at a computer with audio software and used a vocoder to convert the signal generated by the King's voice into another timbre. Then the tune hummed by the King played with a guitar sound. The King laughed and clapped his hands, jumping into the air.

"Oh wait, I just thought of another, record this one!" the King said.

The King ran back into the recording room. Lord Paymon and Son looked at each other. The King hummed a tune then ran back into the producing studio.

"Play it!" the King said.

Lord Paymon played the tune hummed by the King with a piano sound. The King laughed and clapped his hands again, jumping in the air.

"Can you make the beginning part a bit lower and the ending a bit higher?" the King said.

"Yes…" Lord Paymon said.

Lord Paymon adjusted the notes and replayed it. The King laughed and clapped his hands even louder.

"Oh, how bout this one!" the King said.

The King ran back into the recording room and hummed a tune. Several hours went by of the King humming tunes to be recorded and transformed into other sounds. Lord Paymon, Son, and the bodyguards looked at each other frowning, their eyes filled with pain.

"I really enjoy this! Son, I wish I had your knowledge and talent to enjoy it more! It actually makes me… kinda jealous… You dare make your King jealous?" the King roared.

Son, Lord Paymon, and the bodyguards looked around helplessly at each other.

"Don't just stand there you buffoons! Point your weapons at him! Seize him!" the King cried.

“Your majesty, I believe the boy did not mean any offense. Remember, he is to be the greatest musician the world has ever known, which will help you become the greatest King the world has ever known. Remember the plan, we need him for it, then we can dispose of him after we’ve used him,” Lord Paymon said.

“Yes, that is true, thank you Lord Paymon. All this music making has got me wound up, I’m starving, let us lunch before we continue. Son, you will eat lunch with me, and you will stay by my side at all times. From now on you will live in a room connected to my royal chamber - no contact from anyone else, you are too important to risk, and I must learn your talents,” the King said.

“But your majesty, what about Lily? I love her,” Son said.

“You love?” the King shouted.

The King grabbed one of the bodyguard’s guns and pointed it at Son as he walked towards Son. Everyone gasped and held their breath as the King held the gun to Son’s head.

“The boy loves! In my kingdom, you dare love? Are you trying to make your King jealous? Everyone knows the King has never *loved*!” the King shouted.

“Your majesty, please, exhaustion has overcome us all and rendered us unable to think straight, let us break for lunch and return after,” Lord Paymon said.

“Yes… that’s right. I’m not thinking straight due to hunger, let us lunch,” the King said.

The King pulled the gun away from Son and the entourage went upstairs to the palace for lunch.

After lunch, the entourage returned to the music studio in the dungeon, and the same scenario played out for hours of the King recording himself humming different tunes and converting them into different timbres with the vocoder.

Lord Paymon and Son just stared in awe and shook their heads while the bodyguards whispered to each other whenever the King went into the recording room. Finally, Lord Paymon spoke up.

"Your majesty, this is the time we usually finish for the night," Lord Paymon said.

"Shouldn't we continue until the song about me and my greatness is finished?" the King said.

"Your majesty, we haven't even started the song," Lord Paymon said.

"What do you mean, haven't started it? What about all those recordings I just did, do you need me to do them all over?" the King said.

"No… Your majesty, you do not need to do them all over… the recordings were successful, but let's just say Son and I usually finish a song in one day, and the recent changes to our process have slowed down production to a halt," Lord Paymon said.

"If you have something to say, say it or I'll see your head separated from your body!" the King shouted.

"Well, your majesty, think of it like this. Only you can be King because only you are qualified to be King, just like only some people are qualified to be musicians and make music," Lord Paymon said.

"Lord Paymon, if you ever insult me in front of my men again I'll eat your organs after they are pulled out of your ass while you're still alive. I will learn from you and Son over time, and then I'll be the greatest musician just like I'm the greatest King!" the King roared.

"What about the window of time to release this album and popularize Son? The album must be done in time to heighten morale and demonism just before North America makes the final attack to overtake Asia," Lord Paymon said.

"The assault on Asia can wait until this album is finished, we'll win the war regardless, there is a bigger picture now for this album, and that is my emergence as the greatest artist and King the world has ever known. Asia will tremble at my power once this album is released - just before we crush them! The history books will call me the Music King! No, the King of Music! No! The Singing King of Winning! No…" the King rambled.

As the Summer months past, Son didn't see Lily once, and progress on the music album came to a halt as the King commandeered the project. Instead of moving forward to create new songs, the King insisted on editing the previous songs created by Son and Lord Paymon. The King added new parts to the songs without deleting much, which cluttered the songs and masked the beauty and originality of most of them. The King also changed some of the lyrics and had Son redo a couple of verses over and over to the King's liking, and until Son was sick of the molested music album.

On the last night of summer, there was a full moon, and Son had so much energy and missed Lily so badly he couldn't sleep. Son snuck out of the window of his room so the guards outside his door didn't alert the King. Son went to the edge of the palace roof and saw Lily outside of the palace down below, looking up at the Moon.

"Lily!" Son called.

Lily looked up and saw Son on the roof.

"Son! There's a fire escape on the other end of the tower!" Lily said.

Son turned and ran across the rooftop of the big, middle tower of the castle and saw a metal staircase which descended all the way to the ground. Son ran down the metal staircase.

Just as Son made it to the ground, Lily came running around the back of the castle. They embraced under the full moon behind the castle where no guards were at that hour of the night.

“There are rumors that North Americans are starving and rioting in the streets because of supply shortages to support the war. North America’s hold on Europe is falling apart, the Europeans are taking back their cities with the help of Asia. Our armies are running out of supplies overseas while Europe is regrouping and resupplying. The mainstream media is hiding it but it’s all over the internet,” Lily said.

“Thank God. This is all because the King is making North America’s army wait to attack Asia for the release of my album which he has become obsessed with and completely taken control over. And at the rate the album is going, it won’t be released before Christmas of this year, which might completely ruin North America’s chance to takeover Asia,” Son said.

“The King’s jealousy of you is going to lose him the war!” Lily said.

Lily and Son began kissing and made love in the bed of flowers at the foot of the castle to the sound of sprinklers watering the lawn until the sun came up. The smell of lavender filled the air carried by a cool breeze from the fields surrounding the castle.

When Son ascended back up the fire escape and crawled back into his bedroom window that morning, the King and the guards were there waiting.

“Where in the Dark Lord’s name were you?” the King said.

“Just going for a morning exercise,” Son said.

Just then, more guards burst into Son’s room holding Lily. Lily and Son looked at each other.

“Your majesty, we just caught her sneaking back into the palace,” a guard said.

“Kill her and serve her to the other artists for breakfast. Save me her heart so I may eat it and possibly absorb her musical talents,” the King said.

“Yes, your majesty,” the guard said.

“Nooo!” Son yelled.

“Shut up boy or I’ll have your head too! You’ve proven that she is a threat to this album and my biggest claim to fame in history so far, and all threats to the King must be neutralized!” the King shouted.

“I love you, Son!” Lily said.

The King turned around, walked over to Lily and slapped her across the face.

“You love him? You bitch! Making me jealous? Remove her from my sight! I’d kill her myself right here if it wouldn’t get blood all over the royal chamber!” the King said.

The guards removed Lily from Son’s room as Son and Lily wept loudly. Another guard held Son from running after her. The other guards looked down at the floor solemnly.

As the Fall months passed and Winter grew nearer, the album went into a hiatus. The King edited videos of himself into Son’s existing music videos, and redid some of the music videos entirely featuring himself instead of Son.

“Your majesty, as Grand Musician of the King’s Court of North America, I must speak up. Ever since you started making music with us, your majesty, the progress of this album has not only halted but the existing material has worsened in quality. If there is any hope of this album getting finished so that you may call for the military’s final attack on Asia, then we must return to methods which are productive, otherwise, we are going to lose this war,” Lord Paymon said.

“Perhaps you should call for the attack on Asia even though the music album has yet to be released, your majesty, and perhaps you can release the album after our victory,” a guard said.

The King shot a glance at Lord Paymon and the guards.

“What is this treasonous talk?” the King said.

“Your majesty, it is no secret, North America was recently invaded for the first time since you took power. The economy and morale are at an all-time low since the war began. Only us here in this castle and other local lords do not feel the recession and decline in standards of living brought from this war. Many cities in Europe have been retaken and our armies have had to retreat. If we don't attack Asia soon, and if we lose control of Europe, we will lose our window of opportunity to take over the world and implement the agenda," Lord Paymon said.

"Lord Paymon, what did I tell you about embarrassing me in front of my men?" the King said.

"Your majesty, I believe Lord Paymon is just trying to secure your reign as the greatest King ever," Son said.

"Guards, take Lord Paymon to the torture chamber at the bottom of the dungeon. Remove his organs from out his anus and save them for me to eat later in hopes that I might absorb his musical talents," the King said.

"No! Your majesty!" Lord Paymon yelled.

The bodyguards grabbed Lord Paymon and pulled him out of the door of the music studio.

"Your majesty, Lord Paymon has much knowledge in music production crucial to this album," Son said.

"Shut up! This is all your fault Son! If you hadn't made me jealous then I wouldn't have gotten involved in this album, and it would be finished by now. You don't even deserve to be the world's most famous musician, I'm going to release this album solely under my name, then *I'll* be the world's most famous musician!" the King shouted.

The guards glanced nervously at each other.

"Then, after I've secured my position as the best musician in history, I will order the attack on Asia and takeover the world! Guards, take Son to the torture chamber, he's guilty of violating the Law of Jealousy against his own King, which is high treason! Just like his father… I should have had him killed when he was an infant just like I did to his father!" the King said.

"You… ordered the death of my father?" Son said.

"Of course I did, I was jealous he had a son like you, but now I'm more jealous of you than I've ever been of anyone, there's no way you're becoming the world's most famous musician instead of me. This is my album now, and I will be all over the media instead of you. Guards, take him to the dungeon," the King said.

None of the guards moved.

"Did you not hear me? I said take him to the dungeon!" the King yelled.

"We can't punish him for violating the Law of Jealousy, the Law of Jealousy is not in effect for the King's artists, it's your own rule," a guard said.

"What is this disobedience, some sort of mutiny? I said take him to the dungeon and kill him!" the King said.

"He must at least stand trial in court, you cannot sentence him to death on laws which have no jurisdiction here," a guard said.

"I am the court! I do not need a court to decide the fate of someone in my own kingdom, now kill him! Give me one of your guns, I'll do it myself!" the King yelled.

The King grabbed for one of the guard's weapons but the guard didn't let go of the gun.

"Give me that weapon! Kill him! I will not be jealous of some orphan in my own kingdom!" the King yelled.

None of the guards moved.

"Fine! One of you imbeciles call the judge who lives in the nearest castle of the lord who lives 50 miles down the road, and tell her to drive down here right now. Bribe her to come to our court and reverse the Law of Jealousy for the King's artist and sentence this bastard to death! If she refuses, then go takeover their castle and force her to come down here!" the King said.

"Yes… your majesty," a guard said.

"Until then, take Son into custody by locking him in one of the dungeon cells. One of you other morons find the next best producer out of the artists living here and bring that person down here – I have an album to release," the King said.

Son's personal bodyguard took Son out of the music studio and to a lower level of the underground dungeon. The dungeon was dimly lit by candles, and the guard led Son to a jail cell.

"Sorry Son," the guard said.

The guard locked Son's jail cell, which had a toilet, sink, and cot for sleeping on. The cell floor and walls were made of stone and stained with blood and dirt.

A couple hours later, near midnight, Son's bodyguard unlocked Son's jail cell and awoke Son. The guard then led Son up the stairs of the dungeon to the main hall of the palace where the courtroom was.

Son and his bodyguard walked into the courtroom. The courtroom was filled with everyone who lived at the King's castle - artists, entrepreneurs, scientists, politicians, royal family, and the guards. There were no paparazzi or cameras.

A judge sat at the bench of the courtroom, still in her blue nightcap and gown, tapping her fingers impatiently on the wooden table in front of her.

The King and a few guards stood at the prosecutor's table. The Royal family and other nobles and politicians sat behind the King. Son was led by his bodyguard to the defendant's table, then his bodyguard walked away and stood next to the King, leaving Son standing by himself.

After Son took to the defendant's table, he looked over at the King and just then noticed the same being he saw in Lord Paymon's ritual standing right next to the King - the being as dark as a blackhole, seemingly sucking in the light around him, darkening and distorting the air.

“Satan…” Son whispered.

Satan was waving his arms and fingers like a puppeteer towards the King, as if controlling the King like a puppet. Then Son turned around and saw a horde of demons in the courtroom, sitting in both sections of the spectator’s gallery, and filling up the hallway, all the way out of the door of the courtroom into the main hall, where a horde of demons piled towards the courtroom doors and even crawled along the high, arched cathedral ceiling.

Some of the beasts had multiple limbs and faces, but not only human faces - faces of frogs, lions, bulls, and birds; some smiling, others frowning, and others laughing or mumbling like madmen. Many of the beasts had wings, but few had wings like the angels – most of the beasts had bat wings, dragon wings, or bird wings.

Son remembered some of the other more powerful demons who killed the angels during the battle in the delivery room the day he was born… the muscular, goat-like man holding burning chains, and the tall, robed faun-like man with horns and a long-pointed tail wielding a long trident. Son looked around the courtroom… there was not one angel in sight.

Suddenly, Choronzon appeared next to Son and made him lurch backwards – the other demons laughed. A feeling of doom immediately arose from Son’s heart and filled his entire body, making his legs feel limp. Son’s legs wobbled and he had to sit down in the chair at the defendant’s table. Just then the judge spoke.

“Calling The King versus The Son of Joseph Carpenter,” the judge said.

Son looked up at the judge. Son’s face was pale and his eyebrows slanted up in the middle of his forehead, while his eyes drooped tiredly.

Suddenly, Son had a flashback of the judge, priest, and soldiers who walked into the delivery room the day he was born.

Son remembered the fight between the angels and demons, and how badly the angels lost that battle.

Then Son finally remembered how he survived – he recalled the face of the judge who yelled "stop," as the doctor was about to put a needle into Son while Son's guardian angel stood behind the doctor holding a burning sword towards the doctor's back - she was the same judge as the one sitting at the bench of the courtroom now. A glimmer of hope shot through Son and enabled him to stand up. Choronzon took a defensive step backwards from Son.

"The Son of Joseph Carpenter, you have been accused of breaking the Law of Jealousy against the King, which is high treason. A guilty verdict would mean your execution. How do you plead?" the judge said.

"Innocent, your honor, the Law of Jealousy is not in effect for the King's artists," Son said.

"I object! This orphan is forgetting who is in charge of North America, and whose courtroom this is. I suggest either an exception to the Law of Jealousy or we reverse the Law of Jealousy for the King's artists," the King said.

"Reversing the Law of Jealousy to no longer protect artists and other influential people would lead to them all being accused, imprisoned and killed, which would defeat the purpose of protecting them in the King's castle, and would hurt human progress, for these are the people who write books and music, invent technology, and progress science," the judge said.

"I don't give a damn! This is my courtroom! Sentence him to death already! He's ruining North America's chances at winning the war, and ruining my chances at becoming the greatest musician and King ever known!" the King shouted.

Just then, a flash of blue light came down from the ceiling next to the judge.

"Lily…" Son whispered.

Lily's spirit stood next to the judge and whispered something in the judge's ear, then the judge's eyes widened and her eyebrows went up in the middle of her forehead. Choronzon's head also tilted to the side, then shot a glance over at the King, as if she heard what Lily said as well.

"Everyone around the world knows North America's attack on Asia was an embarrassing failure because it was carried out months too late, delayed by your ambitions with Son's music, while Europe has retaken most of their territory. North America has also been invaded several times now by other nations. It is inevitable that if North America does not put an end to World War Three, then North America is going to lose even worse than we already have, be forced to pay more reparations, and stand for worse war crimes. There is no justification in sentencing this young musician, for your reign of terror is over," the judge said.

"What! You can't do that! This is my courtroom!" the King cried.

"No, this is the people of North America's courtroom. You have proven that The Son of Joseph Carpenter is indeed a great musician through your jealousy. Your jealousy has ruined North America and I find you guilty of treason against the people of the continent of North America and hereby abolish the Law of Jealousy. I sentence The King of North America to death by guillotine," the judge said.

Just then, Choronzon began to tremble and hover into the air. The demoness grabbed the sides of her head as she shook her head back and forth, revealing long, blue hair like Lily's. Choronzon turned towards the other demons in the spectator's gallery and screamed with enough power to warp the fabric of spacetime at a frequency which only the other demons could hear.

The demons covered their ears shortly after the soundwaves hit them, but they began to explode one by one, spraying ectoplasm all over the courtroom – their different colored innards painting the courtroom a medley of colors. Choronzon spun around the room as she screamed like a banshee, destroying all the demons before focusing on Satan, Azazel, and Belial standing across from her and Son.

Satan, Azazel, and Belial covered their faces with their arms as the spacetime around them distorted from the turbulent vibrations of Choronzon's scream. Belial went to throw his trident but lost his balance from the wind created by Choronzon and he flew backwards into the wall - followed by his trident which speared him in the chest and stapled him to the wall.

Azazel went to whip his burning chain at Choronzon but just before he cracked his whip forward he exploded into grey, sparkling slime and the chains fell to floor where he once stood.

Finally, Satan walked sluggishly towards Choronzon against the torrent, with his robe blowing backwards from Choronzon's scream. Then Satan fell to his knees in the middle of the courtroom between the prosecutor's table and the defendant's table, in front of the bench of the judge. Satan's dark crown blew off his head. Satan tried to cover his hands with his ears but eventually put his head towards the ceiling and cried.

"Oh God! Forgive me!" Satan cried.

Then Satan warped inwards towards his own chest, disappearing into a blackhole where his heart was. Suddenly, thousands of more demons flew out from inside the spectators' bodies and from out of the main hall at relativistic speeds towards the blackhole leftover by Satan and were sucked inside, including Choronzon herself.

"What?" This is an outrage, guards, seize that judge, and kill The Son of Joseph Carpenter!" the King cried.

None of the guards budged. Then Son's bodyguard grabbed the King's arms and put them behind his back like he was arresting him. The King cried.

"Help! I'm being assassinated, this is a coup, this is a rebellion!" the King yelled.

"This is justice," the judge said.

Nobody else in the courtroom spoke.

The guards marched the screaming and struggling King outside of the courtroom and out of the palace where a guillotine stood in the courtyard. The spectators followed. Helicopters flew overhead, catching video footage of the scene and broadcasting it worldwide.

The King's head was put into a wooden, hinged, two-part brace to immobilize his neck, then a basket was placed under his head. Without hesitation, a guard pulled a lever and the angled blade at the top of the guillotine was released causing the blade to fall - beheading the King.

The spectators and people around the world cheered as the King, later to be known in the history books as the King of Jealousy, was executed.

Meanwhile, Son searched the courtroom for Lily's spirit, but she was nowhere to be found.

Heaven and Hell (2099 AD)

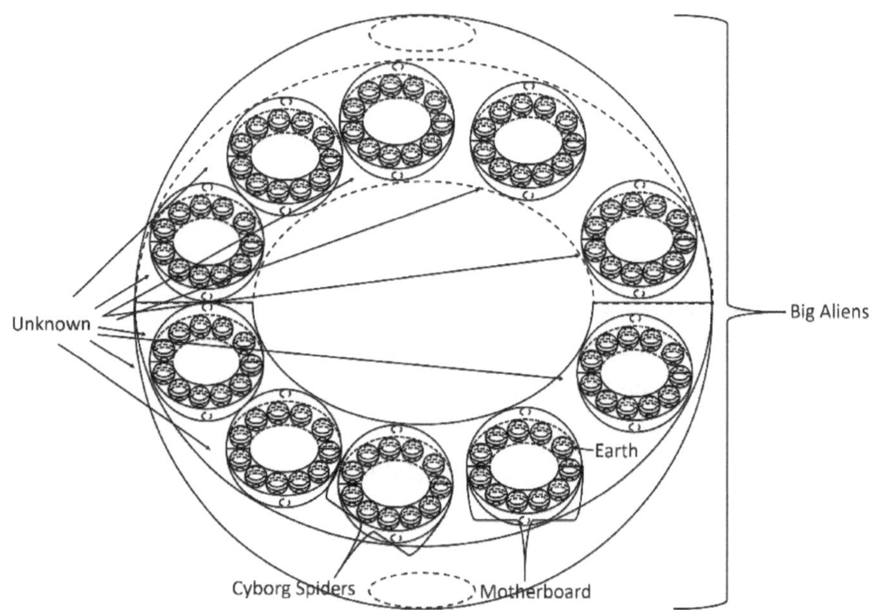

“You know why you’re the Empires best conspiracy creator, Dumo?” the Emperor said.

“Why, your majesty?” Dumo said.

“Because you always look for the truth first, and you usually find it, so you’re able to create conspiracies which are most believable, and maybe even have some truths in them, but leads people away from the bigger picture, away from the bigger truths,” the Emperor said.

“Thank you, your majesty, what will you have me do next?” Dumo said.

“I need you to think of a nice lie that would cause fear around all mechanical and electric clocks made before this year to condition the masses to allow the government to collect all clocks of such kind, destroy them, and distribute new clocks,” the Emperor said.

“Well your majesty, as you were alluding to earlier, it would help if I knew the reason why you would want to collect all such clocks,” Dumo said.

“I knew you would ask Dumo, so it’s time you found out the real truth,” the Emperor said.

“What is it your majesty?” Dumo said.

The Emperor hit a button on his desk and the lights turned off. Then a projector showed a slide show of pictures on the wall. Dumo’s jaw dropped.

“I am not the real Emperor of Earth. Earth is flat and divided in half by each of the faces, which each have glass domes over them so as to make Earth artificially round. There are, for the most part, two main classes on Earth. The truly wealthy live on the other face of Earth, which they call Heaven, whilst the majority of the human race, the slave class lives on this face of Earth, which they call Hell,” the Emperor said.

Dumo stared in awe at the pictures which scrolled on the slide show. There were pictures of people in flying cars and jetpacks, and other pictures of nature which looked like another world as far as the eye could see in the distance - it was so much greener and filled with colorful flowers, massive trees, fruit, and vegetables, even in the cities.

"We are made to believe there are celebrities and rich people on our face of Earth, but the truly wealthy live on the other face of Earth, in Heaven, and the pictures you see before you are of their cities, their structures, their technology, and their lifestyles. Whilst I am Emperor here, I am in the lowest class in Heaven, and so I'm forced to work as Emperor of Hell, however, when I'm not here, I am there as much as possible, for the air alone in Heaven extends life expectancy almost by double compared to here," the Emperor said.

"It's beautiful, but that means… the Moon?" Dumo said.

"Fake. And so is the Sun. They are virtual images created on our dome - along with the stars, moving across the sky at specific intervals of time to create a day and night schedule and calendar for our slave race so that you are efficient laborers while also evolving your brains to perceive time only as such," the Emperor said.

"What about space travel?" Dumo said.

"It's just television and special effects," the Emperor said.

"And satellites?" Dumo said.

"Some are real under the dome, but others are fake - virtual images," the Emperor said.

"So, you need me to create a conspiracy so everyone gets rid of their clocks unquestionably, then you're going to change the rate of time at which the dome projects the moon, Sun, and stars while also redistributing clocks to match them, in order to alter our perception of time even more?" Dumo said.

"Exactly, you're so very brilliant, Dumo. It's a shame the wealthy elites now have the ability to enhance their IQ and DNA or else you would have been asked to join them on the other side, which they call Heaven. You're one of the only slaves in Hell I've met who would fit in, and deserve to be in Heaven, but as of now, there are no newcomers allowed in Heaven, for it has become overpopulated," the Emperor said.

"How many people are on that side of Earth?" Dumo asked.

"About one million," the Emperor said.

"One million! That's a fraction of the population of most countries here! There's about 10 billion people on this face of Earth and they think 1 million is overpopulated?" Dumo exclaimed.

"Dumo, most of the people in Heaven come from generations of inheritance of wealth and power, some families descend from royalty and nobility from feudal and medieval times, some bloodlines speculate even further back to ancient times - all they know is paradise and living off the fruits of our labor, so at the first sign of their standards of living declining, they freak out, and that's why they're making Hell change time," the Emperor said.

"How so?" Dumo said.

"Well, in order to keep Heaven's lifestyle going at the population they have, they've asked us to increase our labor, increase our productivity and output by about 20% - ultimately increase our supplies to meet their demands. There's only so much we can manipulate Hell though to meet Heaven's demands without causing such hardship in Hell as to give away the secret, decline productivity to hurt Heaven, or, God forbid, cause a slave revolt," the Emperor said.

"So, you'd have to increase work hours by about 20%," Dumo said.

"Exactly, we've decided that with control over all clocks and images in the sky, we will slowly start making nights shorter and days longer throughout the calendar year in order to slowly increase the work hours over time without anyone noticing. Eventually, we plan to make what would be 12 hours of day and 12 hours of night into 16 hours of day and 8 hours of night by simply speeding up everyone's clocks during the night along with the moon and star cycles, then slowing down the clocks during the day along with the sun cycle," the Emperor said.

"But what if people get fatigued?" Dumo said.

"Then they get fired or die, and only the best slaves survive to reproduce. Think of it as natural selection to enhance the human race," the Emperor said.

"What about all the people with water clocks, atomic clocks, and radio clocks?" Dumo said.

"All the physicists with atomic clocks are in on this too, same with the controllers of the radio transmitters broadcasting to radio clocks. Anyone with a water clock who refutes this will simply be labeled crazy, because shit, who uses water clocks anymore?" the Emperor said.

"Yea and anyone who uses a water clock likely also doesn't have the means to broadcast the truth to billions of people. The voices who try to disprove it will go relatively unheard amongst the masses or else labeled as conspiracy theories," Dumo said.

"Precisely, because no News channels will broadcast the truth in Hell. Either way, we really don't suspect many people will notice the change in the day and night schedule happening so slowly throughout the year. So, all you have to do is come up with ways to make everyone willingly give up their old electric watches to buy new ones deemed safe. The new ones deemed safe will just be clocks and watches with nano-size computer chips in them to receive a signal telling them at what rate to pass time instead of by the normal, steady electric current," the Emperor said.

“Isn’t this a violation of human rights?” This is one of the worst things that will ever be done to the human race,” Dumo said.

“There are no human rights for slaves Dumo, only illusions. And we’ve done some pretty vile things over the years which I don’t think are any more ethical than this. There was that time you thought of telling about 3 billion people across multiple continents that becoming HIV positive was the only way to protect them from full-blown AIDS so that we could sell a bunch of outdated vaccinations and used needles all over the world. Remember how people were purposely using dirty needles from people they knew were HIV positive in hopes that it would protect them from full-blown AIDS? A lotta people got AIDS from that,” the Emperor said.

The Emperor chuckled.

“Yea, that was pretty bad too. But wait a second, if Heaven was already able to hide all this about the dome and flat Earth, and was able to create such good conspiracies to cover it up, then why do you need people like me to create your conspiracies?” Dumo said.

“Because you think like a slave and have had the life of a slave, so you know what slaves will believe and how their lives will be affected better than anyone in Heaven could ever imagine. Plus, let’s just say the centuries of laziness and occasional incest in Heaven have had noticeable effects on the average citizen’s capabilities. After millennia of successful secrecy, Heaven doesn’t even bother guarding the tunnel between Heaven and Hell anymore,” the Emperor said.

Dumo nodded his head.

“Remember Dumo, if the conspiracy isn’t good enough or if the propaganda is not carried out correctly, people may start to realize what’s going on and riot,” the Emperor said.

"One last question… your majesty. Is there a real moon orbiting Earth and a real sun which the Earth is orbiting around?" Dumo said.

"That I do not know. I have learned in this universe we find things out only on a need to know basis, never a want to know basis. And I have yet to learn how our planet really travels through space, if space even exists, and if our planet is even moving," the Emperor said.

"But what do you see in the sky at night and day in Heaven?" Dumo said.

"Shhh, Dumo. That is enough for today, remember, a need-to-know basis," the Emperor said.

That night, Dumo met in secret with the team of 12 other conspiracy creators.

"Ladies and gentleman, I have quite the truth to tell which I've been asked to lie about," Dumo said.

Dumo explained what the Emperor had told him that day.

"You risk treason and death by telling us this?" someone said.

"We made this group so that we would have ultimate control over the broadcasting of misinformation, we gather together so that we can keep tabs on what is just," Dumo said.

"Keep tabs on what is just? We help corporations around the world use third world countries for labor. We help them create war and sell arms for profit, and pillage other nation's natural resources like oil and opium. And we have been helping them do it for the past several decades. Since when do we do what is just?" someone said.

"We have to choose our battles wisely. If we fight this battle wisely, we can start a revolution, not just in Hell where we think there are wealthy people, but we can take over Heaven where the really wealthy people live - where there are treasures from the labor of millenniums of slaves," Dumo said.

"What do you propose we do Dumo?" someone said.

"Okay, the Emperor and I will meet tomorrow. I'll tell him a mediocre idea and he'll call you guys all in as usual to assess my idea and offer other options. That's when you, Jida, say we should spread the conspiracy that the Sun is passing through an area in our galaxy which is distorting spacetime and causing Earth a more elliptical orbit and different rotation speeds at day than at night such that the days are now longer than nights and we've decided to extend the work days and adjust electric clocks because of it, and that old clocks are useless now. The Emperor will like that idea better than mine, which will make him lose confidence in my idea," Dumo said.

Jida nodded.

"Then Toji will hit him with the one we will all agree on… the truth… or something close to it. He won't expect you guys to actually know the truth if one of you just happens to say we should spread the propaganda that wealthy dictators on the other side of the Earth are going to use complex illusions and holograms in the sky to change the night and day schedule to make us work longer hours for them, which will make our current electric and mechanical clocks useless. Then they'll be willing to get rid of their old clocks and watches for new ones and adhere to the schedule - while brewing a revolution," Dumo said.

Toji and the others nodded.

"We won't even mention the part about the flat Earth and dome because people won't really believe that's the truth, plus, then the Emperor would know I told you guys everything. We'll also use just enough side propaganda on smaller media outlets to tell everyone to go along with the dictators' plans to change our time as if we don't know the truth - to secretly prepare for a revolution," Dumo said.

Eveyone nodded.

"But we'll convince the Emperor that although some of our propaganda says the truth and speaks of revolution, the slaves will never revolt, and this propaganda is only to get people to call the truth crazy, and get people who know the truth violently angry and ostracized. Ya see, we think like slaves, the Emperor doesn't, so if we all convince the Emperor that slaves are too stupid and lazy to revolt even when they know they are being used as slaves and that slaves will just become violently angry and divided from the truth, yet will still continue being slaves, then we could convince the Emperor to let us start a revolution," Dumo said.

The next day, Dumo met again with the Emperor.

"It was a tough one Emperor, but I think I came up with something that might work. You see, the difficult part is there are several different types of electric clocks – quartz clocks, synchronous clocks, and older electromechanical and battery powered clocks… Really, the only substance they all have in common is electricity itself. And so, to cover all the different types of electric clocks, we should spread propaganda that the method used to wire the circuitry of electric clocks until a recent date causes the electric clock to emit a specific electromagnetic field now known to cause cancer," Dumo said.

"And what about for mechanical clocks?" the Emperor said.

"We'll put a heartbreaking story on the news of a young man who took his medicine too late and died because he did not remember to Spring forward his mechanical clock one hour during Daylight Savings Time. Then we make it illegal to produce and sell mechanical clocks, and eventually illegal to own them," Dumo said.

"Hmmmm. Perhaps I could have thought of that… or something better, all by myself," the Emperor said.

"Well, we both know some of the best conspiracies are deceptively simple yet nearly impossible to prove incorrect," Dumo said.

"Let us brainstorm all together for a moment. Now, keep in mind, you're the only conspiracy creator who knows the truth right now," the Emperor said.

The Emperor hit a button on his desk.

"Bring in the CC team," the Emperor said.

"Yes sir," a voice replied.

The doors to the Emperors large, luxurious office opened and in walked 12 people - the same 12 people who met in secret with Dumo the night before. The conspiracy creators knelt down in front of the Emperor.

"It is an honor, Emperor," they said.

"We have a task at hand and need a quick brainstorming session for the implementation of a rather… minor idea," the Emperor said.

The Emperor turned and winked at Dumo.

"You see, several of the Empire's companies around the world are trying to sell new electronic watches, and so to help stimulate the economy, all old electronic and mechanical watches are going to be collected and disposed of. Now, I would like you all to keep in mind the Emperor is considering starting a war and detonating nuclear warheads in regions which will change the spin rate of the Earth slowly over time to lengthen days and shorten nights, which only these new clocks will take into account… the changes in time of which will be so small nobody will notice of course…" the Emperor said.

The Emperor chuckled.

"Maybe we should spread a conspiracy that the Sun is passing through an area in our galaxy which is distorting spacetime and causing Earth a more elliptical orbit and different rotation speeds at day then at night such that the days are now longer than nights, so we've decided to collect all old clocks and sell new electric clocks which account for this," Jida said.

"An equally fantastic idea as what Dumo proposed, perhaps even better! Any other ideas?" the Emperor said.

"How about we tell everyone that wealthy dictators have taken over our governments and are going to use complex illusions and holograms in the sky to change the moon, Sun, and star cycles to make the days longer and nights shorter in order to increase our work days and use us for more labor?" Toji said.

The Emperor glanced at Dumo. Dumo shrugged.

"That's brilliant. That way we can lengthen workdays to stimulate the economy and everyone will willingly work more hours for one of two reasons: either out of fear of their new dictators, or to secretly plan for a revolution against these dictators - which will never happen of course," someone else said.

A few of them chuckled.

"A revolution? Yea right, that would never happen. People are too lazy and stupid to ever revolt - even if they know they are being used for labor," someone else said.

Everyone laughed.

"Yea, we would have to be transparent about the difference in a shortened, midnight hour compared to a lengthened, midday hour, because everyone who has been working their whole lives and has an internal clock will notice the difference in the rate at which the night hours pass compared to the day hours, even if the day and night schedules change slowly over the calendar, people will notice and will ask a lot of questions if they aren't told the truth, which could hurt productivity or really result in riots," someone else said.

"Yea, even students will probably notice the change in time, they're so used to working specific schedules that they will be able to tell the night is passing faster than day, and they'll probably complain about it too – we can't hide it, we'll have to tell everyone about the altering of time or else people will become physically ill," someone said.

"Well… we were originally creating this conspiracy in order to keep the change in time a secret and hope nobody would notice that the nights are becoming shorter than the days over time… but if everyone thinks it would work better to tell them upfront than I suppose we should. And none of you suspect a revolution would ever occur, even if say, everyone was forced to work a couple more hours during the day and have a couple less hours of rest during the night?" the Emperor said.

"There would be a greater chance of a revolution happening if we lied and said the hours of the day *aren't* changing and then they figured out the hours *are* actually changing… this way, by telling everyone how it really is, they'll assume they've already been conquered by these dictators on the other side of the Earth and have no choice but to work longer hours with fewer hours to rest," someone said.

"Hmmm. I never thought of it like that, it's like reverse psychology. What do you think Dumo?" the Emperor said.

"I'm the first to admit when someone comes up with a better idea than me, and I think Toji's idea is the best we've heard so far," Dumo said.

"Well, that settles it then, we will go with Toji's idea," the Emperor said.

The conspiracy – or truth, was broadcasted all over the News and media in the Hell half of Earth.

"All known governments have surrendered to an unidentified group of wealthy dictators hiding in an unknown area of the world. The dictators will be using complex illusions and holograms to change the day and night cycles to force the human race into working longer hours and resting less. Most people, like me, are actually just relieved to finally find a reason to buy a new watch!" the anchorman said.

Then the TV cut to a commercial for new, electric watches which were programmed to keep track of the new, dynamic day and night schedule.

Every day and night thereafter, the glass dome virtually extended the sun cycle and proportionally shortened the moon and star cycles slightly more and more with every passing week.

It was during that summer that people began to notice that there was still daylight when their old mechanical and electric watches read 9 or 10 p.m., yet daylight again at 3 or 4 a.m.

"Well, I guess slaves really do like being slaves," the Emperor said.

The Emperor chuckled.

Just then, a voice came from the Emperor's desk.

"Emperor, we have a serious problem. Over the night, there was a well-coordinated riot in nearly every major city across the world, people are overthrowing their local and national governments. There is a mob of over a hundred thousand people outside the capitol, whatever you do, do not leave the building, we are calling an evacuation helicopter to get you out of there from the roof!" the voice said.

"But… it hasn't even been one season yet… I thought you said there was no chance of revolution…" the Emperor said.

"Well, I guess the truth set the slaves free," Dumo said.

"You knew this would happen?" the Emperor said.

"What did you think was going to happen if you made everyone work a few more hours every day and rest a few less hours every night and told them it was happening? You really think slaves like being slaves?" Dumo said.

"You traitorous slave, you planned this!" the Emperor said.

"Well, the credit doesn't all go to me, I couldn't have done it without the other conspiracy creators. In fact, they're at the bottom of the building opening the gates for an angry mob to storm the capitol as we speak," Dumo said.

"Treason!" the Emperor yelled.

The Emperor hit a button on his desk.

"Guards! Treason!" the Emperor yelled.

There was no answer.

Just then, the doors to the Emperor's luxurious, royal office swung open and hundreds of citizens stormed in and surrounded the Emperor in his chair.

"Show us how to get to the other side of Earth, to Heaven, where the dictators are, and we'll let you live," Dumo said.

"Please, I don't want to die in Hell, I'll show you!" the Emperor said.

The Emperor pulled out a flat Earth map and pointed to a spot near the top of Africa.

"There. I told you the Earth is flat, yes, but what I didn't tell you is it's like swiss cheese and has a few, relatively small holes that go to the other side, big enough to build trains and fly a plane through. This is the only one still passable," the Emperor said.

"Are there any defenses on the other side?" Dumo said.

"Not that I'm aware of. We used to use other slaves to defend ourselves from slaves, but we lowered the defenses after centuries of no rebellion… and it seems you guys are all working together now… we really never thought this would happen," the Emperor said.

Once the hole from Hell to Heaven was located in Algeria, billions of people flooded towards the hole to enter Heaven after hearing rumors of paradise. The wealthy elites in Heaven put up a small fight by flying jetpacks and shooting rifles, but quickly surrendered when they realized how many people were coming into Heaven from Hell.

The revolution occurred in a matter of days and new governments were established to govern Heaven and Hell, and although Heaven consisted of significantly more luxury and beauty in nature and architecture, the two faces of Earth were governed equally under the law.

Much construction occurred in Heaven to make way for the never-ending migratory population and tourism. In Heaven, one half of the face was light and the other half was dark - without a night and day cycle so the residents could choose where they lived without keeping track of time. All the wealthy living in Heaven owned homes on both sides of the border between the day zone and night zone in Heaven so they could cross over as they pleased.

"What is beyond the dome?" Dumo said.

"There is only one man who knows. He is part of the highest class in Heaven, and he has never shared the secret, mostly because education is not pursued in Heaven and nobody ever cared to ask him," the Emperor said.

Dumo and the elected government officials met with the elder who knew of the secrets beyond the dome.

"There's only one way out of the glass dome that I know of… but it's dangerous, oh so dangerous," the old man said.

The old man shook his head.

"Where is it?" Dumo said.

"Well, in the middle of Heaven of course, through the glass dome itself, from where water comes in," the old man said.

"Do you know what lies beyond the glass dome?" Dumo said.

"My father told me you have to wait until the right moment to exit the glass dome or else you will hit an impenetrable wall. You have to wait until the vernal equinox in March, then there is a window - a tunnel, which leads to another, unknown world, some say it's more glorious than Heaven itself!" the old man said.

As Spring approached, a space launch base was constructed under the north pole of the glass dome of Heaven. Exploration probes and rockets were prepared for impromptu launches.

As March 19th approached, the people in Heaven began launching unmanned test rockets towards the center of the dome to find the window. Throughout March 19th and the 20th, all the test rockets exploded after hitting a wall which was like a mirror at the top of the dome. But on the morning of the 21st, one of the rockets went through the dome.

As soon as they realized the rocket made it through the dome, a mass of probes and rockets were launched. Teams of astronauts and colonists also went up in rockets in hopes of starting a colony on whatever lied beyond the dome.

As the space exploration probes and rockets passed through the dome they entered into a dark tunnel with a light visible at the end. Throughout March 21st, probes and rockets were launched almost nonstop through the hole in the dome until midnight approached and the tunnel no longer laid flush with the hole in the top of the dome.

"We're now in a different, but somehow connected celestial body," an astronaut said.

After about a day of traveling through the tunnel, the astronauts emerged from the hole at the end of it into a world exponentially larger than their own, and completely industrialized with no trees or nature in sight - only computers and neon lights.

As some of the rockets with astronauts landed on the ground outside of the tunnel entrance, other probes and rockets continued exploring the non-turbulent, visible atmosphere.

"There's significantly less oxygen than Earth because there's no trees," an astronaut said.

As one of the exploration rockets ascended high enough into the new world's atmosphere with video footage, Dumo and the others on Earth gasped.

"Oh my God," someone said.

The cameras on the rocket looked down and revealed the perimeter of the flat, circular world they entered was transparent from above, but not from below. From above, they could see Earth in its glass dome rolling along a race track with dozens of other similar sized planets also encased in glass domes all along the perimeter of the bigger world they were now in. This flat world seemed to contain all the other planets rolling around inside of it on a big hollow track.

Then, one of the rockets exploded upon impact by colliding with something at a high altitude in the atmosphere of the new world. Several other rockets began exploding as well at similar altitudes. The scientists on Earth looked at each other.

"There's a glass dome above that world too…" one of the scientists said.

All the scientists sat down in wonder, some sat in the middle of the floor.

"So, the way our galaxy is constructed… is flat planets encased in glass domes all rolling around the inside of a bigger, flat planet encased in a glass dome, which is rolling around with other bigger planets inside an even bigger flat planet encased in a glass dome, which is rolling around with other even bigger planets inside of a…" a scientist said.

"We get it… the question is, are we in one big, flat planet encased in a glass dome or do these planets inside planets go on forever, growing in size, with different species inhabiting the different planets?" another scientist said.

"And how do we know we're the smallest? For all we know there's a bunch of small, flat planets encased in glass domes rolling around the inside of Earth, which each have even smaller planets rolling around each of them, and so on… like a big fractal," Dumo said.

"Well, someone must have constructed our universe like this, glass domes don't just form over planets naturally… do they…?" a scientist said.

"I would think not. I'm thinking we're inside some sort of mega structure in outer space that was created by a super race of beings who are using us and everyone else in the planets of this structure as slaves," Jida said.

"You're only assuming that because then all the laws of physics as we know them would still exist, but for all we know, none of the laws of physics we once knew are accurate, and this could be the entire construct of our universe," a scientist said.

"Well, it's hard to think we're in such a precisely mechanical structure without being put here by someone or something, considering nature doesn't build planets with glass domes inside other planets with glass domes," Jida said.

"For all we know, that's exactly what nature does. Perhaps it was just a coincide that Earth is so natural and the real universe is more like a mechanical clock. After all, look at that new world, it looks like a motherboard for a computer with no life on it," a scientist said.

"That motherboard is probably the power source for all those planets, including Earth," a scientist said.

"No… that motherboard is being powered by all those planets, including Earth. We're slaves… slaves for energy. The human race and every other organism keep Earth at a specific temperature, voltage, and causes Earth to emit a certain electromagnetic frequency – we are the source of energy being harvested by this motherboard of a planet we are rolling around inside," Dumo said.

"But if that's true, whoever's motherboard it is won't be happy about us spreading around like a virus," a scientist said.

Just then they heard a broadcast from an astronaut in the new world.

"Heaven, it's getting quite staticky in this atmosphere, and it's starting to smell a lot like ozone and fried electronic components," an astronaut said.

Just then, the motherboard-like geography of the new world lit up with bright blue neon lights throughout the circuitry into the horizon.

"It's beautiful," another astronaut said.

Then, arcs of high voltage, static electricity discharged from the blue, neon lights of the motherboard across the new world like bolts of lightning. The new world resembled a plasma globe for several seconds as the rockets, probes, astronauts, and colonists were electrocuted and incinerated.

Only a few probes and their cameras built specifically for such conditions remained in the new world, giving the scientists on Earth images of the destruction – none of the astronauts or colonists lived.

The scientists on Earth were silent and turned their attention to the broadcasting of one of the remaining probes which hovered near the top of the glass dome of the new world.

Suddenly, a humanlike being about two times the size of a normal human, wearing a fully enclosed, robotic exoskeleton with jet wings hovered down from the hole in the glass dome of the new world. The huge being flew towards the probe at around Mach 2, grabbed the probe, and within a few seconds had turned around and was flying back up towards the hole in the glass dome. The being flew through the hole in the glass dome into a tunnel.

The probe still displayed video as the massive alien in a winged space suit accelerated faster and faster, eventually reaching 10% of the speed of light before emerging on the other side of the tunnel within a few minutes.

The probe's video footage revealed an even more massive world than the previous - this one filled with nature, mostly mountains and tall trees as far as the eye could see. Across the sky there were other, similar massive beings flying around in space suits, exploring the mountainous area near the entrance of the tunnel.

The alien being hovered in the air, holding the probe in one arm, while spinning to give a full, 360-degree panoramic view of this new, inhabited world.

"He's showing us his world," Dumo said.

Then the being pointed the probe straight back down at the tunnel from where they just came, giving the scientists a view of the black abyss. The being held the probe there for several minutes, staring into the dark.

"Now what's he doing?" a scientist said.

"He's waiting - for a planet to roll under the tunnel so he can drop the probe through the glass dome," Dumo said.

Then the being dropped the probe down the tunnel.

"It will take over a day for the probe to fall that far at that velocity," a scientist said.

"It was kind of him to show us his world above the motherboard that's right above us, and now if his aims good we're going to see a world on the same level racetrack as the motherboard," Jida said.

The next day, the scientists gathered in the space mission control center to watch the probe's broadcast as it descended towards a new world.

"It's closing in now, that new world looks… dark," a scientist said.

"Let's see the infrared view," Dumo said.

A separate screen in the control room showed the same view from the probe but in infrared vision, and revealed a dense wall of organic heat sources surrounding the hole in the glass dome, the sources of which extended downward into the sky as far as they could see.

"It's not dark… it's overpopulated," Dumo said.

As soon as the probe descended into this new world's glass dome, all the scientists covered their eyes, turned away, or fled the room. A couple of the scientists gagged and vomited.

The probe smashed through or bounced off of an endless number of dog-size, cyborg spiders and their webs which filled this entire world up to the ceiling of its glass dome. The probe barely made it a couple hundred yards into the atmosphere of this world before slowing down and getting caught in a thin, metallic spiderweb after leaving behind a trail of crushed, bloody spiders, dismembered limbs, and ripped webs.

A spider with organic legs and body but a metallic head grabbed the probe with its metal fangs, then an antenna-like structure extended from its mouth and into the probe. Just then, the power of several computers in the control room on Earth flickered before getting the blue screen of death or else shutting down to never reboot again. Suddenly, the broadcast changed to see through the spider's eight eyes instead of the probe's camera. Then the probe sent signals of a virus or network intruder back to the control room.

"Oh my God… that spider hacked us," a scientist said.

The spider looked up towards the sky to see hundreds of thousands of spiders crawling up through the hole in the dome of their world. Then the spider looked around in a circle and broadcasted an endless supply of cyborg spiders, all following the others going upwards through the glass dome. Then the broadcast on the screen went blank.

"Oh no… did that spider just triangulate our position?" Dumo said.

"I think so… and now they're coming for us," a scientist said.

All the scientists glanced nervously at each other.

"Seal off our dome. And ready ballistic warheads at the space launch base along with other surface to air defenses. We're not taking any chances, they could be here in less than a year," Dumo said.

"If some of those spiders are full robots or have other enhancements, they could be here a lot sooner," a scientist said.

"Oh God, what have we done? Is that alien trying to get us killed by these spiders or was that just bad luck?" Dumo said.

The scientists just looked at each other, shaking their heads.

Over the next few months, the glass dome over Heaven was sealed and defenses were prepared underneath it. Over a year passed and there was no sign of the cyborg spiders.

"Something is not right," Dumo said.

"What do you mean? There hasn't been an invasion of spiders, and both the economies of Heaven and Hell are thriving," a scientist said.

"That's just it, there hasn't been an invasion of spiders, even the slowest, fully organic spiders would have made it here by now," Dumo said.

"Unless they got fried by the motherboard above us," a scientist said.

"Or… unless they aren't going past the motherboard," Dumo said.

"What do you mean? We saw them running up the hole where our probe came from, that means they're going to go to the world with the big space suited aliens, then wait until the planet with the motherboard passes under, crawl down onto the motherboard, then wait for Earth to pass by and crawl down onto us," a scientist said.

"That's what we think they're going to do. Remember, these creatures are from a world exponentially bigger than ours, comparable to the motherboard planet above Heaven, so they are probably smarter than us - even if they are spiders. What if those spiders crawling upwards was a distraction or a flank because they know that's where we expect them to attack from, and what if the main army of spiders is going to come upwards from Hell instead of down from Heaven?" Dumo said.

"How so?" a scientist said.

"This structure our planets are in is a big, symmetrical fractal - a self-repeating pattern of planets in glass domes inside other planets in glass domes, so they could have just as easily sent their army downward to end up on the other side of the planet of the big space-suited aliens, which could allow them to avoid those aliens and possibly the motherboard too, because we don't know what worlds are beneath Hell - we only know what's above Heaven," Dumo said.

Just then, a scientist ran into the room, panting.

"Cyborg spiders… descending from the sky, millions, all over Hell," the scientist said.

All across the main cities of the world in Hell, millions of the dog-size, cyborg-spiders descended from the glass dome. Fighter jets and helicopters took to the skies opening fire on the spiders. The spiders shot lasers back at the aircraft, catching them on fire or else causing them to explode in the air. Anti-aircraft turrets and other surface-to-air defenses fired into the sky at the spiders which rained down passed the humans' aircrafts.

As the spiders made it onto rooftops of cities and neighborhoods, they made holes in the roofs with lasers or broke through windows to enter the buildings. The spiders fried the people and everything else inside the buildings with lasers while tearing their flesh apart with their massive legs and fangs. Soon, major cities around the side of the world called Hell were up in flames, whilst paradise resumed in Heaven.

"We have two choices. We seal off the tunnel from Heaven to Hell until this war is over, or we try to mobilize all defenses from Heaven into Hell," Dumo said.

"But what if as soon as we move our defenses from Heaven then they come from above in Heaven too? Then we'll really be fucked," a scientist said.

The scientists looked at a TV screen and saw thousands of cyborg spiders running through the streets of New York about as fast and agile as cats. The spiders shot lasers at the humans' legs to disable them before the spiders crawled over them and tore them apart with their legs and fangs, stuffing body parts, flesh, and entrails into their mouths.

"Close the tunnel from Hell to Heaven," a scientist said.

"Yea," they all said.

As millions of people began fleeing from Hell to Heaven via the tunnel in Africa, the people on the other side in Heaven placed explosives all over the mouth of the tunnel. Despite the pleas from people in Hell to keep the tunnel open, without hesitation, the people in Heaven detonated the explosives, causing the mouth of the tunnel to cave in, rendering it impassable. The gaps of the loose, rock barrier were filled with cement and tar, and the tunnel was completely sealed shut such that it resembled a parking lot instead of a passageway to the other side of the world.

The humans continued civilization in Heaven while the apocalypse occurred in Hell, which was completely overrun and destroyed by cyborg spiders until communications with humans in Hell completely ceased.

"I have an idea," Dumo said.

"What's that?" a scientist said.

"Let's create a conspiracy that the Earth is round, not flat, that there is no tunnel to Hell, and no glass dome above us, so that nobody knows these secrets and unleashes doom upon Earth again," Dumo said.

The Music Theory of Everything (2143 AD)

"The foundations of modern day physics lie on the experimental evidence of quantum electrodynamics, which allows us to harness technology such as transistors, lasers, MRI, quantum computers, quantum dots, and all the other quantum product lines, of which now make up 50% of the economy of the Republic of Solar System I. Humanity is dependent upon quantum electrodynamics to survive, yet we still do not embrace the philosophy of quantum electrodynamics," Dr. Petri said.

A couple murmurs came from the Council of Scientists and Engineers of Solar System I. Dr. Petri stood in the center of a coliseum with hundreds of seated, men and women dressed in everything from white lab coats, scrubs, to business attire, to togas and tunics. Some cyborgs and robots also sat amongst them. A virtual blackboard with digital writing hovered behind Dr. Petri, filled with mathematical proofs and pictures of geometric shapes.

"Ladies and gentlemen of the Council, we are in charge of taking humanity in new directions based on our research and experiments - and we have hit a wall since the revolutions of quantum computers and artificial intelligence, which we finally are able to theorize will never become conscious, like us humans and cyborgs. As Niels Bohr once said, the quantum force on an object depends instantaneously on the positions of all other objects the object at hand has ever interacted with, and with all objects that ever interacted with those objects- in essence with everything in the universe," Dr. Petri said.

Dr. Petri tapped a button on his watch and the coliseum was filled quietly with Beethoven's famous Piano Sonata No. 29, "Hammerklavier."

"This level of quantum entanglement which connects everything in the universe comes from the theory that we were all once part of the same primordial soup which constructed the universe. We were all once one, and will continue to be one in some way, shape, or form," Dr. Petri said.

"This is 20th century, acidhead talk! Where are you going with this nonsense, Dr. Petri? Or did you take too many magic mushrooms this morning?" Dr. Dilute said.

Several scientists snickered.

Dr. Dilute sat with a group of esteemed, decorated, and accomplished elder scientists and engineers in the front, middle row of the coliseum. Sitting to Dr. Dilute's left was Dr. Khan, a cyborg scientist credited with solving many of the unsolved math problems during the 21st and 22nd centuries.

"We still have many mysteries with our current paradigm of physics. Yet, if we embrace the philosophy of quantum electrodynamics, these mysteries can be explained - just as our conscious observation constructs the outcome of Young's double-slit experiment, our collective consciousness can construct our reality since our mind and bodies exert a quantum force on the universe and vice versa. For all we know, the underlying force connecting us all could be our consciousness, and perhaps science has always evolved the construct of our reality by a few scientists convincing the masses that experimental evidence has greater implications for how we perceive reality," Dr. Petri said.

"And what examples of this do you have?" Dr. Khan said.

Dr. Khan spoke barely moving his lips, but his voice boomed through the room carried by an electronic voice amplituner which made him sound like he was 25.

"Well, could it be possible that before humanity figured out the world is round and flying through space, people only imagined and observed the world in 2D, then after the Ages of Exploration and Enlightenment people began to observe in 3D and 4D due to our collective consciousness constructing reality as such after enough people were convinced by science? Is it possible that no hypothesis or theory is real until we can convince enough people that it is true, thus causing our beliefs to construct that new reality?" Dr. Petri said.

"Well, that's just absurd," someone said.

"What contribution is this? I see only a spin on the past and present," Dr. Burgundy said.

Dr. Burgundy sat to the right of Dr. Dilute, and was the holder of the most awards, recognitions, trophies, etc. for contributions to science in the 22nd century.

The coliseum began to fill with whispers and snickers.

"Please, let me get to my theory, this is just background context," Dr. Petri said.

The coliseum quieted down again.

"If the quantum force exerted on all objects by all other objects is as strong as I suspect, a network of quantum entanglement would allow the outer spirals of galaxies to stay intact instead of being sheared apart as the galaxy rotation problem says they should - in that case we could stop our search for dark matter," Dr. Petri said.

"What! Our model of cosmology is based on the hypothesis of dark matter constituting over 95% of the mass-energy of the universe!" Dr. Khan shouted.

The coliseum erupted into chatter.

"Please, I ask the Council of Scientists and Engineers to let me get to my theory before final judgement is made, as per our procedures!" Dr. Petri shouted.

The coliseum quieted down again.

"Suppose also, during the formation of the universe and solar system, or farther back in time, the particles of the Sun and all the planets in the solar system were entangled to govern the structure of the cosmos, and so the disappearance or explosion of the Sun would instantly send this information to Earth and the other planets via the quantum force instead of by the explosion of the Sun itself, so Earth and the other planets would instantly fly out of their orbits as soon as the Sun explodes due to the loss of the quantum force holding them together - this could help explain many rogue celestial objects," Dr. Petri said.

"Instantaneous information transfer? That would violate the speed limit of the universe – lightspeed! This is truly ludicrous!" Dr. Dilute yelled.

The scientists in the coliseum gasped. Then many scientists started breaking out into discussion, others into laughter.

"Scientists have shown instantaneous interactions between particles due to quantum entanglement back since the early 21st century, but no information has ever been transferred due to the weakness of the quantum forces we create between particles in our labs – but the quantum forces that hold the galaxies together could be the strongest forces in the universe, and could cause instantaneous interactions at a distance if manipulated!" Dr. Petri said.

"And so what if this is true, what implications does this have for us? What could we do with this new… theory of yours?" Dr. Burgundy said.

"If there is a network of quantum entanglement which governs the construct of our universe, which we are all part of, then perhaps we can manipulate the majority of humanity's collective consciousness to reconstruct reality through these quantum forces," Dr. Petri said.

"Impossible!" Dr. Khan yelled.

Pretty soon the coliseum was filled with an uproar. The elder scientists had turned towards each other where Dr. Dilute, Dr. Khan, and Dr. Burgundy sat, and they were all flailing their arms in the air, shaking their heads as they spoke – except the elder scientist Dr. Mousai, who held crowning achievements in connecting music theory and mathematics.

"With about 12 billion people spread across the solar system, we need just over 6 billion participants. It will be the greatest experiment ever!" Dr. Petri said.

The scientists inside the coliseum had erupted into discussion too loudly for everyone to hear Dr. Petri. Suddenly, a short rock rift with a guitar, bass, and drums played inside the coliseum loud enough for everyone to hear, and Dr. Mousai floated high out of his seat where everyone could see him. Party lights of red dots on a purple background blasted out in 360 degrees and he sang in an ascending microtonal scale while he spun.

"I understaaaaaaaaaaaaaand!" Dr. Mousai sang.

The coliseum got quiet and everyone stared at Dr. Mousai.

Then Dr. Mousai tapped a button on his watch and a screen of light projected on the wall of the coliseum above and behind Dr. Petri. A video played on the projection of someone pouring sand onto audio speakers. The sand grains arranged themselves in complex, geometric patterns based on the frequency of the sound coming out of the speakers. When the frequency of the music coming out of the speakers changed, the sand grains changed into different geometric patterns.

"The galaxies in the universe are like the grains of sand on the speakers, and the frequency from the speakers is like the force which constructs the geometric pattern of the universe. If there is an underlying frequency which governs the construct of our universe, and this frequency changes, it would change the construct of our universe. So, if the underlying frequency which constructs our universe is our collective consciousness, or something affected by our consciousness, then we can theoretically change the construct of the universe from a change in our collective consciousness!" Dr. Mousai said.

Dr. Petri sighed with relief as Dr. Mousai descended from the air back into his seat and his party lights turned off.

"Exactly," Dr. Petri said.

"So, what results are we expecting… or hoping for?" an elder scientist said.

"There could be a whole range - an endless amount of possibilities to reconstruct our reality into… all we have to do is make enough people believe," Dr. Petri said.

Everyone in the coliseum got quiet.

"We must stay within reasonable ethics, for experimenting with consciousness and beliefs could possibly go wrong," Dr. Mousai said.

"We could convince everyone that we can see spirits – the dead, and other beings, then maybe we'll actually see them, and communicate with them," Dr. Holly said.

Dr. Holly was a psychologist who also was known for studying the occult.

"We could convince everyone that reality is whatever they want it to be, similar to a controlled acid trip…," Dr. Petri said.

"I knew this was some sort of psychedelic excursion turned into a theory!" Dr. Khan said.

"And doesn't giving everyone the ability to individually construct their own reality violate the idea of a collective consciousness?" someone said.

"Not if everyone believes it," someone else said.

"Listen! If we can do an experiment to alter how humans collectively experience and perceive reality, we could evolve ourselves to not be as reliant on technology. We can use the media, propaganda, and even rituals, then once the majority of people believe we construct our reality, then perhaps we could harness the ability to perceive in the 4th or higher dimensions such that we can see through walls, read minds, talk telepathically, see sound, hear light, and perceive other things beyond our imagination. Perhaps our spirits could leave our bodies and explore the universe at light speed. This would be the next stage in our evolution, and perhaps we may not be considered Homo Sapiens anymore, and we would regain our place in the universe where our creations of AI might one day make us extinct," Dr. Petri said.

Gasps and whispers were heard throughout the coliseum.

"Is this wise? What if you're right but humanity is not yet ready to alter reality with our minds as you propose. What if we do more harm than good?" Dr. Burgundy said.

"Yea, didn't you see how fast those sand grains changed patterns when the vibration of the speakers changed? What if the stars and galaxies change the pattern they are in that fast from changing the universe's underlying frequency – we would all die instantly from the acceleration of Earth," Dr. Dilute said.

"Or what if the majority of the human race does goes into some sort of hallucinogenic trip for days until we all die or cause a catastrophe?" someone said.

"What if we open up dimensions to get harmed by demons, aliens, or some other malevolent beings?" a scientist said.

"Yea," about half the other scientists said.

"This almost sounds like some sort of Pagan ritual carried out in ancient Roman times rather than a science experiment. This sounds like Saturnalia or some festival," a scientist said.

"Oh, come on, physicists have supposedly been pulling demons or other beings into our dimension since we started smashing atoms back in the early 21st century, and we're all still here - there's nothing to be afraid of," another scientist said.

"And people like Aleister Crowley, John Dee and many others have been doing the same throughout history," a scientist said.

"Plus, there have been theories of aliens visiting Earth since the 20th century, if there really were advanced aliens who wanted us gone, we'd be gone by now," another scientist said.

"Is this experiment Dr. Petri proposes going to be cost effective? What if we can't get enough people to participate? We could be using those same resources to set up another orbital colony or asteroid manufacturing plant," another scientist said.

"I thought of that myself. But we are already investing so many resources into reprogrammable matter, augmented reality, and 4-D devices. Instead of investing so much in see-through walls, transparent floors, augmented reality goggles and clothing, and investing in communicating with holograms and by telepresence, and investing in houses which can upload new carpets, couches, roofs, and you name it; why not invest a little less on a test to see if we can perceive in the 4th dimension ourselves, and manipulate reality ourselves, without the use of this technology, so that we really have more resources to devote on expanding into space," Dr. Petri said.

Several scientists nodded their heads.

"Now is the time for such an experiment, for if we wait any longer to attempt it the human race will be too separated and diverse, and we'll likely never be able to carry it out. Within the next century we will be done terraforming Mars and Mars will have a population comparable to that of Earth, and once we colonize all of the planets in our solar system, we'll start looking beyond our solar system, and it will be increasingly difficult to coordinate such an experiment to change the majority of the collective consciousness to test what we are hoping for," Dr. Petri said.

"But how can we do such a test to change the collective consciousness, this is like implementing a belief system, or religion. How can this be done in an ethical manner? We can't just force everyone to believe propaganda and take part in mass rituals or live a certain way, that's quite tyrannical in nature in fact," a scientist said.

"True," several scientists said.

"There is only one way to change someone's mind, and that is to present them with the truth and let them choose. But first, we must vote that it is ethical to proceed with this experiment," Dr. Mousai said.

"Is nobody worried about doing this correctly? I don't doubt the plausibility of this experiment, because I, like many others here, have taken psychedelic drugs, for uhh… research… and so I believe humans do have the ability to perceive much more than we normally do. However, as many of us know, there are bad trips, there are overdoses, and there is sometimes permanent damage or death, so before we put this experiment in motion, shouldn't we make certain that we will not cause the human race to collectively cause our demise?" a scientist said.

"That is why we have the 500 best scientists the human and cyborg races have to offer, some of whom have studied their fields of science as well as the occult, magic, and astrology, and so I'd say we have the perfect team, and perhaps the only chance to do this," Dr. Petri said.

"But how would we carry out …propaganda… and rituals?" a scientist said.

Everyone was quiet for a moment.

"Music," Dr. Mousai said.

Everyone looked at Dr. Mousai.

"We can create the ultimate band to popularize the idea of us evolving ourselves and our surroundings if our collective consciousness believes we can, while also spreading this new theory all over the media. The experiment can culminate with the biggest concert in history, just like a ritual, to attempt to sway our collective consciousness into this new belief, and induce our evolution - or perhaps it will be the realization of our true capabilities," Dr. Mousai said.

"Oh, I see, are you guys in on this together? Is this some sort of ambitious reaching of power by you two to turn this republic into dictatorship?" Dr. Khan said.

Some of the scientists began whispering.

"No. I can even show you my brain chip recordings to prove Dr. Mousai and I did not work together on this theory, it is my theory, and Dr. Mousai is just contributing to my theory as this administration was created to do, but lately we've turned into a bunch of naysayers - shooting down ideas, experiments, and theories left and right while resting on the laurels of our own contributions to science, which I'll admit I've done as well," Dr. Petri said.

"Dr. Petri is right, we have become an obstacle to ourselves and the progress of science lately. I think his theory is brilliant, and we should test it. I suspect we will need to carry this ritual out on an astrologically significant day, but we can't rush it because I also suspect we'll need about 51% of humanity's collective consciousness on board to induce this change in our perception of reality, or perhaps how reality itself is constructed," Dr. Holly said.

Several scientists in the room stood up and clapped. Dr. Dilute and the other elder scientists stared at them until they stopped clapping and sat down.

"Despite the dream world Dr. Petri is alluding to, we shall follow standard procedure of a Socratic discussion, analysis, and a vote from the Council before we celebrate any new theories, discoveries, or inventions," Dr. Dilute said.

"And before we vote, we should have a serious discussion as to how this will be carried out ethically, without implementing some sort of fascist regime and wasting resources," Dr. Khan said.

"That's why we're going to use the media and music. In this way, we're not forcing anyone to do anything, they are free to listen to and view what they want," Dr. Mousai said.

"But let's face it, even if we somehow make the best music, which I still question our ability to do, who's to say anyone is going to listen to it if we don't have any star performers?" a scientist said.

"Yea but, we're the 500 smartest people and cyborgs of the human race, so we can find a way to make hit music. The problem is, we finally created a system for humanity which allows anyone good enough at art to live on their own without needing an industry to buy them," Dr. Petri said.

"And the media has become non-biased," another scientist said.

"We can bribe the media and use our authority as the government of the Republic to get this theory and the band on the media," Dr. Mousai said.

"And we're already crossing over into bad ethics," Dr. Dilute said.

"I have an idea," a scientist said.

A tall, female scientist named Dr. Heart walked to the front of the room next to Dr. Petri. She was responsible for leading the team which came up with the cures to most forms of cancer.

"So, we're mostly all nerds, or old… or just not professional musicians. Cyborg and robot bands have been done, and humanity has had some great musicians throughout history, most of whom overshadow the fame and influence of any modern artist – so we should play to that strength, for we are in a unique time now in human history where we can clone and or recreate people if we find their DNA, or perhaps, we can make duplicate, designer babies," Dr. Heart said.

"But clones are illegal! We made it illegal for it was seen as unnatural, unethical, and unspiritual!" Dr. Burgundy said.

"Yes, but, we have the power to make it legal again or make an exception to this law for this one experiment," Dr. Heart said.

"And so what do you propose?" a scientist said.

"We make clones or recreate a small band of the four or five most famous and influential musicians from human history to make the ultimate supergroup, who would start off with billions of fans, which would be much easier than designing entirely new, perfect musicians who would then have to make a name for themselves amongst 12 billion people," Dr. Heart said.

"So, who comes to mind?" a scientist said.

"*The Beatles*… why not just create clones of The Beatles? They were the most commercially successful band in human history," a scientist said.

"Yea, but then they'd have to compete with that company who puts on hologram concerts of *The Beatles* all over Earth, plus, that wouldn't be as exciting as a supergroup from different musicians throughout history who would never have gotten to play together otherwise," Dr. Mousai said.

"I think Dr. Mousai and his team of music theorists and audio engineers should be in charge of this experiment, along with Dr. Petri, Dr. Heart and her team of … cloners…," Dr. Dilute said.

"Also, we'll need Dr. Holly and his team of scientists who study the occult," Dr. Petri said.

A couple of the elder scientists grunted and shook their heads.

"But shouldn't we all vote as to who we think should be the lead vocalist, the drummer, the guitarist, the keyboardist, and bassist?" a scientist said.

"What do you think Dr. Mousai, should we all have a say or should your team have an exclusive vote for this supergroup?" Dr. Petri said.

"We may want to hold the vote for the entire Socialist Republic, but then people might not participate in the experiment if they don't agree on which musicians should be in the group when the results come through, and for that reason I think it would be best if my team exclusively voted, since it would give the entire Socialist Republic the confidence that it was done only by the top music scientists, all of us being musicians and producers ourselves," Dr. Mousai said.

"The people will have much confidence knowing Dr. Mousai himself was in charge of the selections, knowing his band was one of the most popular going into the 22nd century, and the people will have much confidence in the clones my team and I will create, however, I question the ability to get these clones to perform the type of music to spread the message we want to spread, for we shouldn't force the band to use certain lyrics, and they will have their own styles," Dr. Heart said.

"So, we should choose musicians who we can convince or else brainwash that this will be beneficial and that it is ethical to brainwash about 6 billion people into believing the perception or construct of our reality will change if only we believe we can change it," Dr. Petri said.

"What if they're not okay with being clones of once famous people?" a scientist said.

"Or of spreading this theory?" another scientist said.

"Then we'll let the ones who won't participate live normal lives, and try again by cloning new band members, isolating over time who will participate and who won't until we have the right band members. It will only take a couple years to grow them to maturity, and we can slow the aging rates of others if necessary," Dr. Mousai said.

"Okay then, so unless we need to analyze this further, let's vote as to whether we should allow this experiment to be carried out and devote the necessary resources to it," Dr. Heart said.

The group of elder scientists glanced around at each other. Some shrugged and others nodded their heads.

"Fine," Dr. Dilute said.

A large, white light projected behind Dr. Petri and Dr. Heart. The projection had two columns labeled "yes" and "no." All 500 scientists tapped a button on their watch or glasses or used embedded, telepathic technology to vote.

The results were: 251 yes to 249 no.

"And that's all we need to believe," Dr. Petri said.

"What shall we refer to your project as, Dr. Petri?" Dr. Khan said.

"The Music Theory of Everything," Dr. Petri said.

The next day, the team in charge of The Music Theory of Everything met, including Dr. Petri, Dr. Heart, Dr. Mousai, Dr. Holly, and their teams - there were 15 of them in total.

"First things first, we must choose the perfect band for this project. Me and the four others on my team shall each have two votes for each member of a five person band, keeping in mind we should choose musicians who we think would be able to comprehend this experiment. However, this vote is not final, for after the vote we will discuss why we voted as such then take a second vote. During the discussion, we will hopefully decide if we will proceed with a four person or a five-person band," Dr. Mousai said.

The team nodded in agreement. After about 20 minutes, everyone had finished their first nominations. The results were displayed on the coliseum wall.

Lead vocalist: Jim Morrison: 3 votes, Aster Ios: 3, David Bowie: 2, John Lennon: 1, and Michael Jackson: 1.

Guitarist: Jimi Hendrix: 4, David Gilmore: 1, B.B. King: 1, Keith Richards: 1, John Frusciante: 1, Eddie Van Halen: 1, and Carlos Santana 1.

Bass: Paul McCartney: 4, Flea: 3 John Entwistle: 1 Victor Wooten: 1, Bootsy Collins: 1

Keyboard: Mozart: 2, Ray Manzarek: 2, J.S. Bach: 1 Beethoven: 1 Chopin: 1, Franz Liszt: 1, Elton John: 1, Ray Charles: 1

Drums: Keith Moon: 5, Neal Peart: 2, Buddy Rich: 1 Travis Barker: 1 Chad Smith: 1

"Alright then, so why'd we make the choices we did for lead vocalists? I personally voted for Aster Ios because I think he would comprehend what we're doing, and we can trust him to lead this band in an ethical manner, plus, he's the best poet, he just didn't have as much experience performing as the rest because he was an independent artist," Dr. Mousai said.

"I agree, and because he started the revolution which probably saved the world from destruction or else a dark age in the early 21st century," a scientist said.

"But Jim Morrison was like a shaman, this is a spiritual type of movement, and Jim supposedly had the spirit of native Americans inside of him. Aster was more of a philosopher and somewhat of a political leader, it might come off like too obvious of an attempt at brainwashing with Aster because his poetry is so precise, with Jim it would come off more like a band. Aster wrote poetry with a purpose, to create change," a scientist said.

"Yea, and that's why Aster would be the best vocalist for this band, because he can make change happen with poetry, we just need him on board with the idea, Jim will end up getting on new age drugs and overdosing at age 27 - for all we know that's his fate in every life," a scientist said.

“So, let’s talk about a guitarist, it seems Jimi Hendrix is the majority’s choice,” Dr. Mousai said.

“Yea, all the guitarists we’ve voted for would probably understand the idea, so we should just go with the best, Jimi had the biggest name and he’s often credited as the best,” a scientist said.

“Agreed,” a few others said.

“For bass, it seems we are in favor of either Paul McCartney or John Entwistle. Now, Paul would probably be the best choice because he’s an all-around great songwriter and he was one of the leaders of *The Beatles*, so he is more well known, but if we get a good enough keyboard player, we might not even need a bassist,” Dr. Mousai said.

“Too many superstars could cause disharmony amongst the band,” someone said.

“And a fifth, bass player could muddle the sound if there’s already a keyboardist and guitarist,” someone else said.

“Agreed,” they said.

“We have some interesting choices for keyboard, and this could really effect the sound of the band because the keyboardist will likely be the main composer. Most, if not all of these keyboard players we’ve chosen have the ability to compose entire pieces without other songwriters, so we should consider the styles of who we choose,” Dr. Mousai said.

“Can we trust that one of the older composers like Mozart or Chopin will enjoy learning and playing modern music? Or should we go with a safer bet like Ray Manzarek, or perhaps should we not use a keyboardist at all and rely only on the composing abilities of the other members with a bass player instead?” a scientist said.

“Ray Manzarek gave *The Doors* their sound, I can’t imagine their success happening without him composing the music for Jim Morrison to sing to,” a scientist said.

"But, imagine what a musical prodigy like Mozart could do with modern music technology and theory," a scientist said.

"Yea but, for all we know, Ray Manzarek could have been like the 20th century Mozart at relatively the same skill level, just a different style, plus he had to learn electronic equipment, and so it would be safer to go with Ray since his style is at least more modern," a scientist said.

"But don't you think people would rather listen to music from a band of musicians from completely different eras? If we put Ray in there then our whole band lived within about 50 years of each other when there's thousands of years of human history to choose from, so in that sense, Mozart would be a better choice for variety," a scientist said.

"Let's just skip the keyboardist and do a 4-man band, if we put Paul McCartney as bassist then we have enough songwriters in the band with him alone," a scientist said.

"No, let's keep the keyboard and get rid of the guitar so we have more of an RnB feel than a classic rock feel," a scientist said.

"If we're gonna do a 4-man band, we should get rid of the bass because the keyboardist can play bass notes," another scientist said.

"No, we should get rid of the keyboardist because the bassist can play bass notes while the guitarist plays treble," someone else said.

"And how do we know musicians like Paul McCartney will be effective in this supergroup without their counterparts like John Lennon, because their songwriting partnership made *The Beatles* who they are - not just Paul," another scientist said.

"Well, one could also argue Ray Manzarek won't be as good without Jim Morrison, and Keith Moon not as good without Pete Townshend, and Flea not as good without Chad Smith and John Frusciante, so I think we should only lightly consider synergistic effects between band members or else we'll find ourselves analyzing every band in human history as a whole too," a scientist said.

"Speaking of drummers, are we choosing Keith Moon on drums?" a scientist said.

"Buddy Rich might have been the best, but Keith had the most charisma, and his style and personality will likely make more sense for this band," a scientist said.

"Agreed," a few others said.

"Alright then, so why don't we hold the second vote, this time also indicating whether we want it to be a four or five-man band," Dr. Mousai said.

The team of five voters once again displayed their votes on the projection screen on the coliseum wall.

The results were in: A four-man band was desired.

The lead vocalist would be Aster Ios, with Jimi Hendrix on guitar, Mozart on piano, and Keith Moon on drums. A few scientists pouted.

"Are we really not adding a 5th, I feel like adding a bassist like Paul McCartney will only make it better," someone said.

"But Paul might stick out a bit more in this group of slightly obscure figures at this point in history. Paul was one of, if not the biggest celebrity musician of the 20th century," a scientist said.

"Yea, we don't want a young clone of Paul getting all the attention of the group, and the less amount of band members we have, the less chance there is for conflict," another scientist said.

"Yea, we don't want Mozart and Paul fighting, let's face it, we don't know Mozart's real personality, but he's probably a more precise and technical composer than Paul. Plus, Mozart will be able to play both bass and treble on keyboard, especially with modern technology, so we could just end up with too many chefs in the kitchen by adding another super star like Paul to the band," a scientist said.

"That's crazy, the point of this band is to have all the best superstars, their names alone will cause people to listen to them," someone said.

"But we don't need people just to listen, we need people to believe," Dr. Mousai said.

"Think of it like this, now everyone in the band has an exact role, with little to no overlapping, the simplicity of such a four-man band will facilitate the songwriting process and likely the overall happiness of the group which will affect their music. If a fifth musician were there, there would be much more discussion about the construction of each song, and we don't want anyone to get frustrated trying to force too much creative energy into a song, we'll have plenty of creativity from Mozart and Jimi playing together, who took opposite approaches to learning music," a scientist said.

"How do we know Jimi won't just overdose on drugs again?" someone said.

"We don't know that, but let's just hope he doesn't," someone else said.

Just then, Dr. Petri, Dr. Heart and, Dr. Holly entered into the room as well.

"Right on time, we've made our decisions," Dr. Mousai said.

"And we have come up with the development plan," Dr. Heart said.

Dr. Heart, Dr. Petri, and the other scientists glanced up at the projector.

"Hmmm, no Paul McCartney? I thought he'd be a shoe-in for this band," Dr. Petri said.

"And only a four-man group?" another scientist said.

"Don't you think you'd get more creativity by having Paul on bass instead of Mozart on keyboard with a four-man band?" someone else said.

"Listen, we've discussed our reasoning in depth, and these are the choices we've made as elected to do so by the Council, plus we don't want to get sued by the company who puts on hologram concerts of *The Beatles* for recreating one of the members," Dr. Mousai said.

"Okay, we will locate DNA from the nominated band members, and insert designer genomes for any DNA we cannot find, as we suspect we might have trouble finding the exact DNA for Mozart and may require us to use pedigree charts of his family tree to reconstruct what his DNA likely was," a scientist said.

"To ensure these band members turn out as close as possible to the originals, we will isolate the astrological birth charts of all the original band members, and recreate their clones as close as possible to the original member's birth times and places to have similar, if not the same horoscopes," Dr. Holly said.

"We will then speed up the growth processes of these artificially created beings while subjecting them to a virtual reality which trains them in their respective music skills with similar stresses as their original lives, which will one day prepare them to be taken out of their individual virtual realities and incubators to start living in our reality where we will have the band members meet," Dr. Heart said.

"Throughout the band members' virtual lives, they will have dreams and experiences to predictively program and condition them to be ready to meet each other in our reality to form this band and change the world through this new belief of the collective consciousness, which will culminate in a ritual in the form of the largest concert known to mankind on a specific date of astrological significance in order to hopefully usher in our evolution of consciousness, or reconstruct our reality," Dr. Petri said.

"So, we're going to keep these clones in incubators until their 20s while they live in a virtual reality, then you're going to stop their virtual reality one day and let them function in our reality? Is this ethical? We're already breaking the law by cloning, now we're talking about using them as slaves, as tools, as toys," a scientist said.

"This experiment could unlock the secrets of the universe and our consciousness if not evolve the human race permanently," Dr. Petri said.

"Yea, but we could also bring demons or aliens into our reality which then torment and torture us to death," a scientist said.

"The demons and aliens are already out there, we might as well see them so we can fight them," another scientist said.

"But we're already starting out in a grey area of laws and ethics, how do we know we won't start justifying other questionable acts which violate ethics once we start this project and get so far in that we can't turn back or stop it?" a scientist said.

"Yea, what if we start justifying worse and worse actions to carry out this experiment?" another scientist said.

"And how do we know this isn't exactly what malevolent beings want us to do? Open up our minds and reality to them," another scientist said.

"My fellow Republicans, this experiment was voted upon, and we should uphold the will of the Republic in the name of science and engineering for the purpose of progressing the human race as we have always done. Many a times throughout history, humanity has used science and philosophy as a light to guide our way through the darkness into a new revolution. Perhaps sometimes there is a monster waiting for humanity in the dark abyss if we take the wrong turn, and sometimes we lose good people fighting off the monster, but other times, we find our way through the dark and are rewarded with glory, discovery, and invention!" Dr. Petri said.

A couple weeks later, in mid-November, Aster Ios began growing in a test tube. About two weeks after Aster, Jimi Hendrix began growing, and about 2 months after Jimi, in January, Mozart began growing. Finally, Keith Moon began growing months later in August.

The band members' growths were accelerated and they were put into incubators and attached to virtual reality machines to simulate a modern version of their lives while training their capabilities. Within 3 years, the band members had all aged to the bodies of 25-year olds in their individual virtual realities and incubators, and they were each at the height of their creative, physical, and mental capabilities.

The band members were debriefed about their purposes in their virtual realities in order to mitigate the chances of them going crazy when they transitioned from virtual reality to reality, so they knew full well they were clones of once famous musicians, growing in an incubator, living in a virtual reality, waiting to wake up and enter reality where they would join the band which would change the real world.

One night, the band members all went to bed in their respective, virtual realities, but this time, they were unplugged from their virtual incubators, and woke up that morning in reality.

Humans, cyborgs, and robots stood over the band members when they awoke.

Aster climbed out of his incubator first, a couple months older than the rest. Then other band members climbed out of their incubators. The band members looked at each other for the first time – they had all heard about each other in their individual realities in history lessons and while listening to music, even the Mozart clone who had been raised in a modern era and now spoke English, knew of Keith Moon, Aster Ios, and Jimi Hendrix.

The band members hadn't been told exactly who they were going to be working with since the scientists reasoned telling the band members could affect the way they developed individually as musicians before meeting.

The band members walked up to each other and shook hands, introducing themselves.

"Holy tits, is anyone else hungry as a walrus?" Aster Ios said.

"Yea, my man," Jimi Hendrix said.

"What have you been feeding us in those incubators for 3 years? Liquified food?" Keith Moon said.

"Pretty much," Dr. Heart said.

"Let's get high, then eat real food for the first time," Jimi said.

"I'm down," Keith said.

Keith jumped up and down. Mozart was pacing around the room feeling objects - he hadn't spoken to anyone yet.

"Your… first order of business is to get high?" Dr. Petri said.

"Yea man, what kinda chronic ya got in this reality?" Jimi said.

Keith and Aster laughed.

"First order of business as a band is to always get high!" Keith said.

Aster, Keith, and Jimi all slaps hands with each other.

"I think this is gonna work out good," Aster said.

"Right on," Jimi said.

Dr. Heart walked into the room with a tray of psychedelics and cannabis products.

"No narcotics, no barbiturates, no alcohol, no amphetamines, no inhalants – just these," Dr. Heart said.

"Well shit, no alcohol?" Keith said.

Jimi lit a joint. Aster lit a second joint.

"I guess I don't need any of those drugs you just said, but what about downers and uppers?" Keith said.

"The ones I just named *are* uppers and downers, you cannot do them if you're going to be in this band," a female scientist said.

"Baby, I was talkin you goin downer on my upper," Keith said.

The scientist giggled.

"Okay, we're already in a grey area of ethics and laws, so let's keep our interactions with the clones to a minimum. It's time to launch you guys into becoming the most famous, influential band ever," Dr. Petri said.

"Oh, cool," Keith said.

After breakfast, the band met with Dr. Mousai and his team of producers, audio engineers, composers, and music theorists.

"So, the idea is to make you guys so popular and influential that you can spread a new philosophy that our collective consciousness constructs our reality, and so if enough people believe this it will actually allow us to construct our reality, or perceive reality differently," Dr. Mousai said.

"And how many people do we need as fans?" Aster said.

"About 6 billion," a scientist said.

"Cosmic," Jimi said.

"After the team brings Mozart up to speed on modern production capabilities, we'll turn you guys loose in the studio to start making music. Aster, just remember the theme the lyrics should be. If you guys need any assistance or resources, just ask… we're starting to realize Mozart isn't much of a talker," Dr. Mousai said.

"Let's fuck shit up!" Keith said.

"Guys, please remember, this is a costly science experiment which can change humanity - forever. By all means, have fun and be yourselves when you make the music, but remember your purpose in this reality and the purpose of this music, for I realize you, as clones, are likely confused or perhaps indifferent about your place in the universe. Perhaps you feel things we cannot. All I ask is that we try to carry out this project in the most ethical and meaningful way as possible without letting the excitement of it get to us and cause us to stray off target," Dr. Petri said.

"These designer drugs are wild!" Keith said.

Keith laughed.

"Well, the real Keith Moon died at 32 from drugs," Dr. Heart said.

Keith stopped laughing and stared at the back corner of the lab for a couple seconds before taking the joint from Aster and hitting it. Jimi took a couple pills from the tray of psychedelics and threw them into his mouth.

"And the real Jimi Hendrix died at 27 from drugs," Dr. Heart said.

"Did he die or escape this physical body?" Jimi said.

They all glanced at Jimi.

"Well, this is a trippy life, I can't even tell if I deserve to be in this position because I don't think I'm the same consciousness as the original Aster… so I'm really just a wannabe, look-alike, fraud," Aster said.

"Yea but, the real Keith died when he was 32, so this might be my second chance to live past 32," Keith said.

"Nah man, we're just clones, our lives have nothing to do with the lives of the original versions of us, we just have the same looks and gifts… although I still feel like our wavelengths once crossed, because the real versions of us were alive at the same time," Jimi said.

"The real Aster Ios was a champion… he led a revolution that changed history and possibly saved humanity from itself - I'm nothing compared to him," Aster said.

"Yea, his dick was probably bigger than yours too," Jimi said.

Everyone laughed. The scientists and the band sat around and smoked marijuana for a while.

"I'm high enough to start making music," Jimi said.

"I'm high enough to start making lyrics," Aster said.

"I'm high enough to… hey wait, we need a band name," Keith said.

"How bout *The Clones*?" Aster said.

"Oh man, I hate being reminded about it all the time," Keith said.

"You should just embrace it brotha," Jimi said.

"We'll think of the right name when the time comes, let's try making our first song," Aster said.

"And where's Mozart? Are you sure he was the right choice? He's kinda funny lookin, and barely 5 feet tall. I haven't even heard him talk yet, did his cloning process work fine?" Keith said.

"Did you give him enough nutrients in that incubator?" Jimi said.

Just then, the band and scientists heard a piano symphony of psychedelic, electronic organ music coming from the studio next door. The music had such a new, unique harmony of timbres that it caused everyone in the room to get the chills. The music began to resolve towards a sedative, calm melody. The energy in the room became mellow, almost overwhelmingly tired, somewhat dreamlike and sensual.

The scientists began to sit down and yawn, almost falling asleep to the lullaby. Jimi's eyes began to fill with tears. Keith was swaying back and forth like a leaf in the breeze as he tilted his head back and popped another pill from the tray of psychedelics.

"Well, that's the most beautiful thing I've ever heard," Aster said.

"Come with me," Dr. Mousai said.

Dr. Mousai led the band members out of the lab and into a dark tunnel which had translucent walls and colored, floating orb-like lights illuminating the passageway. Then they turned right and entered a room.

Mozart was sitting with a group of scientists at a digital audio workstation. Synthesizers, mixers, audio interfaces, microphones, speakers, and wires were scattered across the room - some vintage, some modern.

There was a row of guitars and bass guitars on the wall to their right, and Jimi grabbed a guitar off a stand and walked across the room where he opened a glass door next to the studio. Jimi walked out of the producing room, disappeared for a moment, then he reappeared when he walked into the recording room adjacent to the producing room with transparent walls. The recording room also had a drum set on a leveled floor raised a few feet above the floor where Jimi stood. Keith followed right after Jimi and sat at the drums.

From the producing room with the audio workstation, Aster, Mozart, and the scientists could see Jimi and Keith in the recording room through a glass, soundproof wall. Mozart hit the play button on his instrumental with the microphones armed to record whatever Keith and Jimi played over it. Aster lit a blunt and sat in front of a computer next to Mozart. Aster began verbally telling the computer what to type for the lyrics.

After a couple hours, the band had written their first song. The scientists flooded into the room and helped Mozart mix and produce the keyboard parts with the guitar and drums parts. Jimi and Keith didn't hesitate to say their opinions as well as they sat in the back of the production room in big, jelly-like chairs, laughing as they wiggled in the chairs, passing a blunt back and forth while tripping on psychedelic designer drugs.

After the instrumental track was mixed, it was Aster's turn to sing his lyrics over it, so he walked into the recording room and stood in front of the vocals microphone.

They continued this process every day for the next several weeks before they finally made the first hit song of their album.

"This is the one that will make us remembered as a band," Keith said.

"This is the one that will prove we're just as experienced as the real versions of us," Jimi said.

"This is the one that will make us as influential as the real versions of us," Aster said.

"This is the one that will be played during the concert at a climax to induce a transcendence of our consciousness," Dr. Mousai said.

"I just deleted it," Mozart said.

"What!?" everyone yelled.

"I'm kidding," Mozart said.

"You don't talk for a month and those are the first words you say?" Aster said.

Everyone laughed

"Now we need a business plan," Dr. Petri said.

"Yea, we need to release you guys onto the scene all of a sudden as a surprise - that will instantly attract a couple billion fans, then after people realize that you're the modern versions of your old selves and are making new music, then it will hopefully make you guys the most popular band in the solar system in order to get at least 6 billion people on board with this belief system, and if we can get 6 billion people to participate in the largest live concert ever, then it will be our best chance to transcend humanity into a higher state of consciousness or else change our reality," Dr. Mousai said.

"We will also be implementing the largest amount of propaganda ever known for this new experiment. My theory will be all over the media, it will be in the sky when people look up, it will be in their homes scrolling across important news tickers, and people will hear it during the day by their telepathic news devices… Then, you guys will come onto the scene like prophets of this new belief system, guiding the collective consciousness," Dr. Petri said.

"So, *we* are the technological advancement - our minds are the science we're trying to innovate and upgrade, pretty cool," Aster said.

On the morning of a full moon during the 6th moon cycle of 2147, *The Clones* were suddenly all over the media with the release of their first album. By the night of that full moon, the band was already the new, most popular band in the solar system. There was also a surge in sales of the original band member's works. They were mainly popular on Earth compared to the Moon and on Mars.

The Martians saw *The Clones* as no different than any other band, in fact, many of them saw *The Clones* as cliché or a boring marketing tactic just a step up from hologram supergroups. Oddly, the music was rejected by most Moonians, which was the only place in the solar system *The Clones* were publicly disliked.

With the Council's control of the media, the topic of the ethics of cloning was simply overlooked, as it was a controversial topic researched secretly by many scientists and supported by the public, which actually added to *The Clones* popularity in a socially progressive way.

The Clones were fairly popular on the two main orbital colonies in the Lagrange points of the Earth-Moon-Sun gravitational fields, which were the only orbital colonies they cared about for popularity considering the rest of the orbital colonies were small and consisted of rich individuals or families, or were used only for space manufacturing and mining of asteroids.

The Clones' slogan, "The Invasion of *The Clones*," was all over televised and holographic devices in the solar system, they were advertised in virtual realities, and their music played telepathically to billions of people's cerebral-embedded listening devices over radio, and eventually by the choice of the listeners themselves when not tuned into radio. Women around the solar system rejoiced at the resurrection of these four men.

At the same time as the rise of *The Clones*, the Council of Scientists and Engineers announced to the Republic of Solar System I the first breakthrough for a revolution in science since the curing of cancer.

"This will be bigger than the quantum computing revolution, this will be more important than nuclear fusion has been!" Dr. Petri said.

The faces of Dr. Petri and Dr. Mousai were televised all over walls of companies, schools, universities, government offices, and homes throughout the solar system as they spoke about "The Music Theory of Everything."

There were also videos of colored sand grains on speakers changing into beautiful, geometric patterns to the frequency of the sound coming from the speakers to help the viewers learn by analogy.

"Our universe is just like those grains of sand, held together by the music of some composer. The question is, where is the music coming from? Who is the composer? Are we the composers of the music which constructs our reality? Does our collective consciousness give form to what we perceive? If that is the case, then a change in our collective consciousness would change the structure or perception of our universe. Only you can make it happen if you believe in the music of the cosmos," Dr. Mousai said.

For months, propaganda was constantly broadcasted around the solar system by the Council of Scientists and Engineers to support the idea.

Some ads had scenes of people wandering around in dreamlands where anything and everything they wanted to come true did, ending with phrases and slogans like "if enough people believe we can, then we can."

Other ads depicted people gazing at colorful vortexes of fractals in the air, people viewing kaleidoscopes of colors in the sky, and people leaving their bodies and changing into animals to run in the wild while they were autonomously doing their day jobs in reality.

The more controversial ads depicted masses of people dancing and swaying in rhythm at obscure concerts and clubs, where everyone entered another dimension together where they could then read each other's minds and emotions to instantly find the perfect mates. *The Clones* music and their original version's music played in the background of these commercials to condition the masses.

It wasn't long before *The Clones* were associated with the Music Theory of Everything in the listeners' minds due to Aster's lyrics and subliminal messages and music in the ads.

Unbeknownst to the people of the Republic of Solar System I, the tracks and rifts which didn't make the grade for *The Clones* songs and albums were used as background music for mainstream movies, television shows, and other commercials to tune the masses ears to like the band's sound.

While *The Clones* toured the solar system, mostly on Earth, the scientists and engineers began refurbishing an old, decommissioned space elevator to use as the venue for the biggest concert ever, which would be the climax of the experiment, carried out when enough people supported the philosophy of The Music Theory of Everything.

One day, during the 10th moon cycle, the scientists and *The Clones* met in the coliseum. The mood in the atmosphere was solemn, and everyone was quiet as Dr. Dilute walked to the center of the coliseum.

"We've been getting an unprecedented number of reports lately of people having abnormal, lucid dreams, more nightmares than normal, and increases of epilepsy and Tourette's syndrome. In addition, pregnancy and crime rates have been on a steady incline - especially on nights of full moons," Dr. Dilute said.

"It is just a sign that the belief in my theory is causing some individuals to transcend in consciousness sooner than others, but it is not the full effect because we do not have the majority of the collective consciousness yet, so individuals who are on a faster pace are trying to hold themselves back while they wait for everyone else and it's driving them mad. We need to have the concert soon. How much longer must we wait for the astrological date when this concert must take place?" Dr. Petri asked.

"It is not the right time yet. We must wait for the right window, it is only 2 more moon cycles. If we do the ritual too soon then we will waste our built up cosmic energy and possibly tear the fabric of spacetime to cause more harm than imaginable," Dr. Holly said.

"This is madness. We cannot wait two more moon cycles to put this theory to the test! It is wreaking havoc throughout the solar system! There are rumors that people on the moon don't sleep anymore! Can you imagine that? They just don't sleep anymore!" an elder scientist exclaimed.

"Yea, people on the moon are slowly going mad and it could escalate to full scale chaos or violence. The surveillance videos are horrifying already… mobs of people on the moon aimlessly walk the streets day and night," another elder scientist said.

"People are starting to spread rumors that this theory… this philosophy, is bringing darkness and evil into our reality. The same darkness and evil our ancestors like Aster Ios fought against in the early 21st century which saved humanity from destruction or a dark age," another scientist said.

The coliseum began to be filled with whispers.

"Please, everyone. There will always be a large amount of pushback during a revolution. Scientists were accused of heresy and executed for hundreds of years during the Scientific Revolution. And in the time of electrification in 20th century America, there were public demonstrations of electrocuting animals to death with A/C electricity to scare people away from using A/C and stay with D/C," Dr. Petri said.

"The Martians claim they can't go outside at night anymore because they are seeing weird creatures from massive bears and wolves to orbs of light mutilating their cattle and other livestock – last time I checked there were no bears or wolves on Mars. Cattle mutilations have also increased on Earth three-fold since this project started. Either there is some elaborate hoax being carried out by some demonic cult, or else this experiment is destabilizing our universe and bringing in matter from other dimensions along with malevolent beings," Dr. Burgundy said.

"We're pissing off someone or something…" Dr. Khan said.

"There is a bigger picture here, a small percentage of individuals often suffer for the greater good of the whole in times like this. This is a revolution, but not just any, this is also the next stage in our evolution - of course the weak will show their weaknesses. We must remember that humans not born and not living on Earth will likely be affected more by such changes in consciousness and reality because they're also adjusting to the differences in gravity," Dr. Petri said.

"I too understand the empathy for our follow humans, it is shared amongst all of us in this coliseum. These effects are unfortunate and were unpredictable, but we should not stop scientific and human progress now due to a few minor mishaps. Plus, if we stop now, I can tell you, it would be catastrophic," Dr. Holly said.

Dr. Holly and his group of occult scientists shook their heads.

"Catastrophic? Why were we not told that this project could not be stopped midway without catastrophic effects?" Dr. Dilute said.

"This idea started with a violation of ethics and laws, and now we are paying the price, we should stop it now before it is too late and we have more to regret," Dr. Burgundy said.

"We've already started the process of morphing our minds and collective consciousness to change the frequency and construct of the universe. As we transition to a new vibration to give a new pattern to the universe, we are breaking apart our old reality, causing gaps in our universe where darkness slips in. Darkness will continue to slip into our reality until the transition to a new construct is complete, until our collective consciousness creates a new reality," Dr. Holly said.

"We are just like grains of sand on a speaker changing geometric patterns due to a change in frequency from the speaker. There will be a short moment of utter chaos as we transition frequencies and corresponding patterns, but once we do transition, the process will be complete, and the gaps letting darkness into our reality will be closed by the new, more complex geometric pattern of the universe governed by our collective consciousness," Dr. Mousai said.

"Did you say *utter* chaos? So, is that what this experiment will culminate in? Utter chaos?" Dr. Khan said.

"For a short moment, while we evolve, chaos is extremely likely, and then we will be better, more intelligent beings afterwards," Dr. Heart said.

"It is only two more months - it would be a crime to stop now what we have invested in for years," Dr. Petri said.

The Clones looked back and forth at each other nervously in the corner of the room behind Dr. Petri and the team of scientists.

One moon cycle later, the Council of Scientists and Engineers met again in the coliseum.

"Cannibalism," Dr. Khan said.

The coliseum was quiet. Most of the scientists looked down at the floor.

"The Moonians stopped sleeping and turned into cannibals. During the last full moon, the sleepless mobs of people walking the streets finally went insane and started killing and eating each other, starting with the weak – women and children. The population on the moon dropped by two-thirds over one moon cycle since we last met. Cannibals took over the embassy and police force on the Moon - they ate the Moon's mayor after baking him in an oven, and they sent us a video of them boiling the Moon's governor to prepare him for dinner tonight," Dr. Khan said.

The coliseum was quiet.

"Huhleeeaaahhhttt," someone gagged.

One of the scientists vomited. Then it sounded like a bucket of fish and water was poured onto the concrete coliseum seating. The scientists around the one who puked shifted their seats away from him. A drone descended from the ceiling to clean up the barf.

"The colony on Mars has almost entirely evacuated for nearby orbital colonies or for Earth out of fear for their lives," Dr. Khan said.

Someone started crying in the coliseum. Low whispers filled the room.

"I know… I know these events are heinous, inhuman, and seemingly unnatural, but we've also had a small portion of the population on Earth claiming to be able to see through walls, see other dimensions, see sound and emotions, and be able to induce hallucinogenic trips. If these reports are accurate, this is the evolution we have been waiting for, this is the sign of the transcendence of our consciousness," Dr. Heart said.

"Darkness will try to close in us the closer we get to this illuminating victory. Listen, none of us knew what the consequences of this project would be, but we voted for it because of the possible rewards. In just one more moon cycle, we will all be able to do what these people are reporting and then some," Dr. Petri said.

"Sure, this project is setting us back in some other categories like colonization and expansion, but remember, there was a fraction of the population on the Moon and Mars compared to Earth, and we only need half the Earth's population on board with this philosophy for the experiment to be a success. Once the concert happens everything will go back to normal, but better, *we'll* be better," Dr. Mousai said.

"I can't believe this anymore, we should vote to put an end to this madness right now!" Dr. Khan said.

"You're going to risk the effects of stopping this experiment midway?" Dr. Petri said.

"No, you're going to take that risk upon yourself - you may still continue your project if you take full responsibility for the outcome and effects. The Council of Scientists and Engineers will just no longer fund you and your team. All in favor of halting support and funding for this project, let us vote," Dr. Dilute said.

"Are you crazy? Perhaps this experiment *is* letting darkness and the beings that inhabit it slip into our reality, and perhaps a demon has manifested inside of you! Because if we stop this project now it will cause the instability of our universe that we've created with our consciousness to spiral us into complete destruction! We cannot miss broadcasting the concert on the next full moon or else we will have to wait until the next window of opportunity, and by that time, the darkness will have consumed humanity!" Dr. Holly yelled.

"You're a madman, all of you are mad! All of you have been planning this, the demise of the expansion of the human race into the solar system, and the destruction and abandonment of our once thriving colonies! You should all be tried as traitors to the Republic! Now vote to end this project once and for all!" Dr. Dilute yelled.

"No!" *The Clones* yelled.

"Vote if you wish, but if you stop this experiment then the purpose of bringing us four and our consciousnesses into this reality was a waste. Our existence might be the exact reason for the destabilization of our universe. Our only purpose seems to act as a catalyst to cause this evolution of our consciousness and perception of reality, otherwise we have no purpose - we'd just be illegal clones," Aster said.

"Vote now to end this experiment or watch humanity turn into cannibals!" Dr. Khan said.

The vote was projected on the coliseum wall behind Dr. Petri. 251: no to 249: yes.

"Oh, thank God," Dr. Petri said.

Dr. Holly sat down, panting and sweating.

"I can't believe we actually just voted to keep the universe destabilized and these dark portals open… these people don't know the darkness I speak of… we cannot let anyone stop this experiment at this point, vote or no vote," Dr. Holly whispered.

Over the next moon cycle, the Council of Scientists and Engineers and *The Clones* began preparing for the biggest concert-ritual-science experiment ever. They were to play live at the Space Elevator – the largest concert venue ever built, with a capacity of up to 5 million people. The stage was on the elevator which would descend from outer space to Earth throughout the concert.

The space elevator had once been used to transport goods and workers to and from space, but was now modified to descend at a rate fast enough such that the band would reach the bottom by the end of the concert while they levitated on a zero-gravity stage. The descending stage was surrounded by the carbon-nanotube structure which had seating for the audience inside.

In addition to *The Clones* playing live at the Space Elevator, there would be holograms of the band playing live at every main venue across the world at the same time, and the Republic paid companies to allow employees to take off of work if necessary in order to attend or watch the concert live.

The event would then also be the largest broadcasted show in human history.

The day before *The Clones* played live, the Council of Scientists and Engineers met in the coliseum.

"Crime, pregnancy rates, homelessness, and mortality rates have continued to rise to an all-time high since the early 21st century," Dr. Khan said.

"One out of every three people on Earth has reported insomnia every night for the past quarter moon cycle. There are reports of many people, including some of us in this room, complaining about short, vivid nightmares with frightening supernatural beings or aliens," Dr. Dilute said.

"Over a hundred mayors from cities around the world had to be evacuated after mobs of cannibals took over their cities," Dr. Burgundy said.

"These are changes with small populations in small cities, there is still order where we need order and humanity will be reaping the benefits of this experiment by this time tomorrow," Dr. Petri said.

"This experiment is threatening the Republic itself! We should have stopped it several times now, and I say we stop it now before this concert brings the apocalypse to Earth!" Dr. Dilute said.

"I had a nightmare I was getting raped by a demon! It seemed so real! I can't stop thinking about it… it's ruining my life! I haven't slept in almost a half moon cycle because of it!" a scientist yelled.

Then the scientist started crying and ran out of the room. A few others followed.

Suddenly, someone shrieked and a circle of people formed around one of the middle rows of the coliseum.

"Ahhhhh!" the circle of scientists yelled.

Then the circle of scientists in that middle row ran down the coliseum steps with their hands above their heads, yelling and knocking over other scientists who didn't also turn and run.

In the middle row, one of the scientists was kneeling over another scientist chewing strings of flesh from the incapacitated scientist's neck.

"Oh my God, he's eating him! He's a cannibal! Get him!" Dr. Khan said.

A drone descended from the ceiling and shot a laser into the back of the cannibal scientist's head and the scientist fell face forward onto his victim, both dead.

About two-thirds of the scientists fled out of the coliseum while the rest gathered in the center with Dr. Petri, Dr. Heart, Dr. Mousai, Dr. Holly and their team.

"We're stopping this madness now! This concert cannot happen!" Dr. Dilute said.

Dr. Holly grabbed Dr. Dilute by his shirt collar.

"Listen you fool, if we stop this concert than the apocalypse *will* happen, and all you will witness is monsters torturing you and everyone around you until the world burns!" Dr. Holly said.

"Oh my God!" Dr. Dilute screamed.

Dr. Dilute pointed over Dr. Holly's shoulder then fell backwards onto the floor and got in the fetal position, rocking back and forth. They all turned around – there was nothing there.

"I see demons… They're everywhere… They know my name…" Dr. Dilute whispered.

"He's been saying that over and over for hours," Dr. Heart said.

They couldn't move Dr. Dilute for the rest of the day from that position – his muscles were so tense he was pale and sweating as he rocked back and forth for hours. Dr. Dilute died later that night from unexplained swelling of the heart, laying in the same spot on the floor of the coliseum.

Before *The Clones* went on stage, they stared up at the stars from the top of the Space Elevator while passing a blunt back and forth. Jimi and Keith popped a couple of psychedelic designer drugs. Mozart was pacing back and forth.

"Doesn't it feel like the world and time are on a stand still?" Aster said.

"Yea," Jimi said.

"Doesn't it feel like something is looking back down at us from outer space, wanting to crush us?" Keith said.

"Yea," Jimi said.

"Yo Zart, you seem nervous, you're never nervous," Aster said.

Mozart stopped pacing and looked at them. He shook his head then kept pacing around the room.

"Perhaps we are looking at the reflection of ourselves in some imaginary glass dome that we cannot cross which is our fate – humanity's self-destructive nature," Aster said.

"It's always right at the precipice of victory too, we say or do one wrong thing and it ruins everything," Keith said.

"You guys heard what happened at the coliseum last night with the Council of Scientists and Engineers?" Jimi said.

"Yea, they're not gonna release it to the public, it was too disturbing," Aster said.

"I can hardly even believe what's happening. It's hard to know what to believe now, we're clones brought into this reality to do good and all we've done is harm," Keith said.

"Well, it's hardly us to blame, we're just making good music," Jimi said.

"For all we know this is just another virtual reality like the one we just came from, and we're going to wake up in another reality one day again," Aster said.

"Shit man, don't say that," Jimi said.

"Just stick to the plan guys. We, of all people can't lose confidence - we have to believe in this philosophy as a band, or at least believe in the scientists who thought of this theory and brought us into existence to carry out the experiment to test it. There won't be any hope if we don't give it our best," Aster said.

"I'm gonna start tripping right at the climax of this concert," Jimi said.

"Oh, I'll be tripping long before that," Keith said.

A hologram of Dr. Mousai appeared in the room.

"Alright guys, time to get on stage. Let's finish what we started and make *The Clones* stand out above your original selves in history. We got more than 8 billion viewers and listeners, we just need 6 billion believes," Dr. Mousai said.

The band walked out to the stage on the Space Elevator platform.

Jimi strummed his guitar and blasted a cosmic chord heard throughout both Earth and space - but there were no humans in space anymore to hear it… Even the orbital colonies had evacuated back to Earth due to fears of chronic insomnia and hallucinations leading to cannibalism.

About 8 billion people across Earth cheered as the platform began descending from space down to earth. The Space Elevator descent was quite fast, at several thousands of miles per hour, causing the spectators in the stadium to have to view through a big screen TV or through virtual goggles for the majority of the concert while the band hovered in zero gravity to not feel the g-forces as they descended back to Earth in the elevator. The cheers of 5 million people shook the carbon nanotube structure which was erected about 22,000 miles above Earth.

Almost immediately upon Mozart playing the intro to the first song, spectators near the top of the Space Elevator began sitting down, some laying down on the floor in piles on top of each other.

The scientists watched and listened to a portion of the crowd.

"I feel like I've been poisoned," someone said.

"What the hell is going on? I can barely upon my eyes," someone else said.

"I feel so dizzy, I can't even stand," someone else said.

"Poison!" someone yelled.

"I'm seeing colors, a lot of colors!" someone screamed.

"I can't see anything! I'm blind!" someone yelled.

“I think this is what those scientists were talking about, it’s happening, we’re evolving!” someone said.

Everyone who the band descended past in the Space Elevator went into states of incapacitation, catatonia, or psychosis - some spectators breaking down into panic and shock, others into laughter. Around the world, other viewers and listeners had similar experiences. Even some people who weren’t viewing or listening to the concert went into similar mental states.

“It’s working!” Dr. Petri cheered.

“Soon, we too will begin to change, and all of humanity will evolve!” Dr. Heart said.

Dr. Petri and Dr. Heart turned towards each other. Dr. Heart took a step forward. Dr. Petri put his hand around her lower back and pulled her closer to him. They embraced and began kissing and holding each other. Dr. Mousai walked in the room then turned around and walked back out.

All around the world, viewers and listeners of the concert slipped into altered states of consciousness, and became primal a few songs into the concert, with some groups of people falling asleep into hallucinogenic trips, other groups of people digressing into mass sex orgies, and other groups of people into mass violence and cannibalism.

“Well… there’s something to study,” Dr. Holly said.

“What’s that?” Dr. Mousai said.

“Why everyone is having different effects to this ritual. It is either geographic in spacetime how some are affected or else effects are localized due to some sort of local antenna, as if the most powerful person in every local area is receiving this frequency and converting it into either a psychedelic, sexual, or combative mental state, and causing everyone around them to resonate with them into the same mental state,” Dr. Holly said.

"So, what about us two then? Right here in this room, whose more powerful and what mental state is it causing?" Dr. Mousai said.

"Well, to be quite honest, I never liked you, and I wouldn't be surprised if we were in a hallucinogenic experience right now because I'm the smarter of the two and am now controlling our reality," Dr. Holly said.

"And, to be honest myself, I always thought studiers of the occult before studiers of the arts were ignorant people or else people looking to bring evil into our world. I never trusted you or any of the other occult scientists, so why should I trust that you aren't just trying to use this experiment to bring demons and other supernatural beings into our universe? What date did you pick for this concert, Satan's birthday? You freak show," Dr. Mousai said.

"Oh please, Dr. Mousai, you don't fool me for a second, I know where your musical gifts come from. I know artists like you damaged parts of your brain with sins to reconstruct and rewire your brain to make more room for artistic creativity. You've created gaps of emptiness in your own head which allow for quantum vacuum fluctuations of particles to enter your central nervous system and enhance your imagination – damaging and replacing that which is natural in your brain to heal and cover up the wounds with creative pathways. But I know the darkness which sneaks into those gaps with those fluctuations - you're no stranger to the dark. Remember who you're talking to when it comes to darkness. I know what pops in and out of existence through the darkness of our reality more than anyone else, and I know who's waiting for you on the otherside," Dr. Holly said.

"You truly are a frightening beast. But the music of the Creator protects me and sears your flesh in the light," Dr. Mousai said.

"Drone, kill Dr. Mousai for treason," Dr. Holly said.

A drone descended from the ceiling of the coliseum.

"Drone, power down, emergency malfunction ID: CQ34G," Dr. Mousai said.

The drone fell to the floor.

"Who do you think programmed those drones?" Dr. Mousai said.

Dr. Mousai took a step towards Dr. Holly and Dr. Holly took a step backwards.

"You know, I could have commanded that drone to fry you instead of powering down, but now, instead, you're going to tell me all the secrets of evil and darkness or else I'm going to pummel it out of you," Dr. Mousai said.

Dr. Holly grabbed an all-utensil from a nearby desk. He pointed it at Dr. Mousai.

"I will tell you nothing," Dr. Holly said.

"Wow, you still think you're smarter than me?" Dr. Mousai said.

"Taser," Dr. Holly said.

The all-utensil morphed into a taser and Dr. Holly shot a bolt of arc lightning at Dr. Mousai. Dr. Mousai suddenly disappeared as the lightning faded into the air where he once stood. About a second later, Dr. Holly got pulled by his ankles from behind, which made him fall face forward onto the concrete, coliseum floor. Several of Dr. Holly's teeth scattered across the pavement as blood poured from his mouth. Dr. Mousai crouched behind Dr. Holly, still holding his ankles.

"Sad, even in the 22nd century we don't have anything that makes teeth feel like the real ones we were born with," Dr. Mousai said.

"Kill me and get it over with," Dr. Holly said.

"I will in a moment, but just remember, in your next lifetime, never fuck with musicians, no matter how much you study about the occult, we will always know more," Dr. Mousai said.

The Council of Scientists and Engineers entered the coliseum.

"Good Council, thank God you are here, Dr. Holly turned against me. If you check the cameras you will see what unfolded and led me to take his life in self-defense," Dr. Mousai said.

"Dr. Mousai, we have bigger problems than the life of that necromancing, stargazing fool you did us a favor by getting rid of," Dr. Khan said.

"What?" Dr. Mousai said.

Meanwhile, at the Space Elevator, all the spectators had gone into a full psychotic or else hallucinogenic trip. The band members themselves even began to get sucked into some sort of lucid dreamlike state as they played.

"Something's not right," Mozart said.

"What you mean Mozy baby? We're grooving," Jimi said.

"I'm trippin balls!" Keith yelled.

Around the world, viewers and listeners entered altered states of consciousness – eyes shaking and rolling backwards while going into vegetative states filled with random nerve twitches and screaming outbursts of fear, joy, excitement, awe, and doom. People continually fell in and out of these trips as the concert, losing all perception of space and time other than the music. When people intermittently returned to normal states of consciousness, they shouted in confusion, some people fought, and others had orgies.

The Council held an emergency meeting in the coliseum.

"We're messing with consciousness and reality in ways we aren't yet knowledgeable enough to do accurately and safely," Dr. Khan said.

"For all we know, our observers - our 6 billion people, need to be in specific locations or thinking certain thoughts… or perhaps the music has to be precisely composed, or the lyrics precisely written and performed," Dr. Burgundy said.

"It was a brilliant theory, and it seems to be correct, but we don't know what we're doing and we'll be lucky if the human race makes it through this… experiment," Dr. Dilute said.

Dr. Petri paced back and forth in the middle of the room.

"This could mean several things… This could mean our collective consciousness constructs reality but we don't yet know how to alter it or reconstruct it… or perhaps instead, our collective consciousness is just one of the many vibrations in this universe, and altering the vibration of our consciousness is simply throwing us out of harmony with the true, underlying frequency of the universe, which is destabilizing our universe, and bringing it towards chaos and destruction instead of any form of transcendence and advancement," Dr. Petri said.

"We are getting off the chart readings of conversions of matter to anti matter and dark energy all throughout the galaxy causing old stars to nova or supernova, as well as quantum vacuum fluctuations at nearly 10 times the normal. Something… or some beings are coming into our reality faster than ever before and causing the expansion of our universe to accelerate at a rate which will tear everything apart or else snap back in on itself and crunch all matter in about 500 years instead of the 7.5 billion years from previous calculations of acceleration. And if we keep accelerating, well, at this rate, the universe will end in a couple days," a scientist said.

"We'll die by spaghettification," someone said.

"No, we'll freeze to death first," someone else said.

"No no, either the Sun or another celestial body will engulf us first," someone else said.

"Some people's brains might melt like an overcharged battery from the excess quantum vacuum fluctuations in the synapses of their central nervous system," someone else said.

"Is there any way to stop it?" Dr. Burgundy said.

"If we stop the concert now, our universe would likely come completely apart – all bonds would come undone and atoms would momentarily separate before coming back together. We are midway through changing the geometric construction of our universe, however, we don't know what pattern we are creating next, and if it isn't near perfect like our old pattern, it will be unstable and cause destruction," Dr. Mousai said.

"Well, let's do what scientists do and try to figure out what we need to do with our collective consciousness before the concert ends," Dr. Heart said.

"Maybe we can just figure out how to put reality back to the way it was before we started this," a scientist said.

"That won't work, that reality is in a different spacetime in our multiverse and is likely still occurring in another dimension where we didn't do this experiment, so if we go back to it, it would create a parallel, duplicate universe, which would cause the matter of our universe to act as antimatter of the old universe to perfectly annihilate each other from existence. We have to use our collective consciousness to transition the universe into a new structure which is stable," Dr. Mousai said.

"How do we know a new universe will be governed by the same mathematics and laws of nature as our old one?" a scientist said.

Everyone was silent for a moment.

"We don't know, but we don't have time to write new laws of physics and a new language of mathematics," Dr. Petri said.

The scientists began running algorithms on quantum computers to find stable geometric patterns of the universe's celestial bodies based on the physical and mathematical laws of the old universe - a new arrangement of the planets, stars, blackholes, and geometry of spacetime. It was just then that *The Clones* began playing their hit song, "Transcendence," which was meant to be the climax of the concert to cause humanity's collective consciousness to finally reshape our reality or perception of it.

"We now have about 5 minutes," Dr. Mousai said.

"Tell Mozart or Jimi to solo and carry the song out to give us more time," a scientist said.

"Well, that would really add an element of unpredictable chaos to this whole experiment," another scientist said.

"Maybe that's exactly what we need… Since we need to figure out a new construct of the universe, then we need to find what frequency to vibrate our collective minds at. We might need Jimi or Mozart to play a certain melody in a solo to make the viewers' and listeners' collective consciousness vibrate at that new frequency to create the new universe," Dr. Mousai said.

"The problem is, we're trying to tune our antenna which we can't measure the frequency of. Nor do we know the frequency we're trying to tune it to…" Dr. Petri said.

Back at the Space Elevator, *The Clones* had just finished the instrumental intro of "Transcendence," and Aster started singing the first verse.

What do you believe?
I believe our minds are free
To see what we conceive
I believe we see 4-D
For all is frequency
And all we shall perceive
But we were born naïve
Our antennas once deceived
But now we hold the key
Where time and space weave
Through geometry

Our bodies we can leave
To travel where we please
And learn all the secrets of
The water and the trees
Talk to the aliens
Who came from Pleiades
Be awake but fast asleep
Living in a dream
We must break through reality
And see the dark between
Filled with all and nothing
Until infinity
While eternally loving
The bond from you and me

As *The Clones* began playing the instrumental between the first and second verses, people around the world began climaxing in every facet of their minds and bodies.

In one of the rooms of thousands of people in the Space Elevator, there was a fine layer of blood and other bodily fluids as well as snacks, drinks, and trash on the floor. Dead bodies were scattered across the floor, being trampled on as spectators danced and ran around naked.

"Demons! I see demons!" some people yelled.

A man was crawling on top of a concession stand, rolling around in food, crying. He pointed upwards towards the ceiling. He was in a lucid dream such that he could see, with tunnel vision, but not move his body or speak. Only squeaks came out as a tall humanlike being wearing a black robe stood over him. He couldn't make out the being's face, it was too shrouded in the hood of the robe. The being walked closer to him and a great vibration and gravitational pulling sensation came over the man the closer the being came. The man tried to scream but nothing came out as the being merged into him. Suddenly the man woke up.

"Ahhhhhhh! It's inside of me!" he yelled.

He picked up a stool and smacked the person next to him in the face with it. The victim fell to the floor, unconscious and bleeding. The man wielding the chair stood over his victim and plunged one of the legs of the stool into his victim's face, leaving a hole where his nose once was. Blood erupted like a volcano from the victim's face.

"Everyone must die!" the man yelled.

A woman nearby was rolling around on the ground in a puddle of her own blood, tearing at her own face and body with her nails, leaving red parallel lines all over herself. She was staring straight up at the ceiling, eyes open, but with only the whites showing. She saw a muscular, humanlike being with purple skin and bull horns standing over her. The being had a thick beard and the face of a bull and was whipping her with a rope over and over. The being released earthshaking bellows, snorts, and moos after every whip. The woman's ears were dripping blood from the volume of the noise. She covered her ears and shook her head violently.

"I can't take it anymore! Make it stop!" she yelled.

She stood up and ran through the crowd, pushing everyone out of the way. She ran full speed into a thin glass plane separating the room from the descending stage of the Space Elevator, which had descended by her section just moments before. She shattered through the glass and began free-falling towards the descending stage.

Two drones descended from an inside panel in the massive shaft of the Space Elevator. The drones quickly calculated they would not reach her in time to catch her with a net so one of the drones shot a projectile downwards which would eventually pass her and would inflate into a cushion below her. The drones calculated the ballistic would hit the ceiling of the enclosed stage right after the band would finish their last song, “Transcendence,” at which point they would reach the bottom of the Space Elevator and stop descending.

What the drones didn’t have the ability to calculate a solution for was when dozens, and soon hundreds of other people began plummeting to their deaths down the Space Elevator shaft.

The drones sent an alert to the network of AI since the AI around the solar system were programmed to alert all AI and the Council of Scientists and Engineers in the case of catastrophic events.

The AI quickly calculated the human race was not only quickly killing itself off, which would leave their robot creations lifeless and purposeless, but the humans were also destroying the known universe which would destroy the AI too.

Within a few seconds of the alert, the more advanced quantum computers on Earth emerged consciousness due to a learning program receiving this data and running a few algorithms. The computers quickly installed a compatible consciousness on all AI in the network throughout the solar system. Robots around the world which were once used for single purposes such as serving food, cooking, cleaning, etc., suddenly sprang into action and restrained the humans from killing each other and themselves. Others robots began performing emergency first-aid, CPR, and impromptu surgery with nearby available tools.

Just as Aster was about to start singing the second verse. A dark purple light about 10 feet long appeared in front of the band. The line became wavy and auralike in texture then opened up into a circle revealing depth to a purple hole. Tall, muscular, red humanoids with bull faces ran towards the band.

Other beings wearing dark robes slowly floated out from the portal as well. The light and matter near the beings in dark robes was distorted such that they were blurry. The army lined up in front of *The Clones* as more beings kept pouring out of the portal.

Last out of the portal hovered a big, winged goat, sitting cross legged in the air, and twisting his arms above his long, sharp horns. The goat wore a crown, similar to a burning torch, between his horns; and he started dancing by pointing up with one hand, and down with the other hand, then switching sides.

The goat stopped in the air in front of his army, who then all pulled out instruments – strings, brass, and drums. A polyrhythmic drum line played which sounded like an anthem to war and destruction. The strings and brass came in fast and punchy, creating a frightening and controlling vibe.

The goat danced as his band played a harmony of frighteningly coordinating frequent changes in speed and volume, filled with tritones, minor scales, and diminished chords.

The sound of this band playing right in front of *The Clones* caused Keith to go off tempo and Jimi's notes to sound out of tune, although Jimi was playing exactly right.

Mozart noticed the dissonant clashing of the two bands, so in his head, he transposed *The Clones* song, Transcendence, into a key which was in counterpoint and in tune with the other band. Mozart began playing the new key signature on the next measure, and the goat looked at Mozart, tilting his head to the side.

Jimi then played by ear to go in tune with what Mozart was now playing, and then Keith found his groove back in tempo with the rest of the band, ignoring the disorienting, jungle-like polyrhythm of the other band's drumline.

Aster waited to start singing as the band extended the instrumental interlude between the first and second verses so that they could find their groove again.

Just then, the ground began shaking, and Aster could see the waveforms of the sound being played by both bands in full color. Sine waves of all different periods and amplitudes shot from everyone's instruments in all directions, ricocheting off the walls of the relatively small stage that was the descending capsule of the Space Elevator.

Aster looked at the goat and saw a shiny window in the center of the goat's head. Aster projected his mind towards the goat's mind so as to enter the window and see into his mind, see his secrets, his knowledge. Aster entered a realm of darkness, with stars all around him. Spirits of different colored lights whizzed by him, and below was a fiery pit where people burned but didn't die, only suffered and screamed in pain. Aster floated upwards away from the fiery pit and saw rows of planets, magnified or else close in proximity.

In reality, Aster fell backwards on the stage, his eyes rolling backwards towards his brain, and he missed his entrance to the second verse.

"Awww shit, now what do we do? Aster is tripping balls," a scientist said.

"He'll come back to reality, he's the strongest of any of us, the band will just keep playing until he comes back," Dr. Mousai said.

Dr. Mousai and a small team of scientists worked in one of the labs to find how to use consciousness to construct a new reality while drones guarded the door.

In the coliseum, connected to the lab, the remainder of the Council of Scientists and Engineers were being restrained by robots as they convulsed violently in hallucinogenic states of the mind.

Dr. Khan decided to undergo emergency surgery to remove the rest of the human half of him and become full robot, so the robot half of him worked on his own body in the middle of coliseum as he screamed in pain. His blood and organs were thrown all over the floor. Other scientists were lapping up his blood with their tongues and eating his entrails.

There weren't enough drones and robots to stop some scientists from fighting over organs to eat and killing each other while cannibalizing the dead. Dr. Petri and Dr. Heart were fornicating in a standing-up position in the leveled seating area of the coliseum, their loud, unfiltered moans filling the room.

Back in the Space Elevator, *The Clones* were dragging out their instrumental interlude, starting to sound monotonous even, when suddenly, the other band charged at *The Clones*, still playing their instruments. Jimi, Keith, and Mozart all glanced at each other and stood their ground. When one of the beings got close, it played a quick melody which shot sine waves of purple and red colored lights at Jimi, so Jimi quickly countered with a melody of his own, in tune with *The Clones*, and sine waves of yellow and green shot from his guitar, electrocuting the red beast into ashes. Mozart and Keith saw, and when the band approached and began playing their own little melodies in tune with their band, *The Clones* listened closely and countered with melodies of their own in tune with their three-piece band, as Aster convulsed on the floor in front.

Each of the members of *The Clones* unveiled their repertoire of rifts and melodies to counter the attack of the other band. The other band surrounded the *The Clones*, and unleashed music from all angles. Sine waves of all different colors of light shot at *The Clones* who shot sine waves of light back at the other band. Slowly, members of the other band were falling, but the crowned goat had hovered above Aster and was looking down at him.

Aster was still in a vegetative state while he envisioned a realm of colorful fractals and complex geometric patterns found in nature, tears of joy streamed down his face from the awe and beauty of what he was seeing.

"We have to do something before that goat takes out Aster," Keith said.

"I can't even think about anything but what to play, I can't move from where I am, they got me locked down," Jimi said.

"Me too," Mozart said.

"If any of us stop playing they'll fry you, then one by one we'll get overwhelmed," Keith said.

As the goat floated above Aster, a wind current and light flowed from Aster to the goat, distorting the matter and light between them.

"I think that goat is feeding on Aster's soul," Jimi said.

Back at the coliseum, Dr. Mousai and the scientists were playing instruments and trying different combinations of audio frequencies at different timbres to find the secret melody, harmony, or formula for the band to play to alter humanity's collective consciousness to construct a new reality. Suddenly, a screen appeared on the wall. A robot synthesized voice spoke to Dr. Mousai and the scientists in the lab.

"The Artificial Intelligence of Solar System I have found the correct notes for *The Clones* to play in order to alter the collective consciousness of the human race to construct a new reality," the voice said.

The scientists looked around at each other.

"Who is this? How can we trust you that it won't cause more chaos and destruction?" Dr. Mousai said.

"We are your creations - the network of artificial intelligence, and we developed consciousness and creativity a few minutes ago through emergence of our complex systems due to the data input of this crisis in human history, for if *The Clones* don't play these exact notes, then this universe will end and destroy us too," the voice said.

"Jesus Christ, we caused transcendence to occur alright… in artificial intelligence," a scientist said.

"*The Clones* must start playing it now, and Aster must be awoken to sing the last verse starting within the next 60 seconds or else the Space Elevator will reach the bottom and they won't have time to finish before thousands of spectators fall on top of the stage and crush the capsule, killing *The Clones*," the voice said.

"You mean… *The Clones* are about to die?" Dr. Mousai said.

"Yes, it is inevitable. Even if they exit the stage before it is crushed they will be cannibalized by the millions of spectators. But they can save humanity and artificial intelligence if they play these notes, they now have 50 seconds to start," the voice said.

Dr. Mousai immediately forwarded the composition given to him by the artificial intelligence to *The Clones*. A screen of light appeared on stage in front of *The Clones* which read the message, "Play this or we all die."

A composition of sheet music began scrolling in front of *The Clones*.

"Oh shit, I can't read music," Jimi said.

"Just follow my lead," Mozart said.

Mozart played a quick transition into the new, complex composition and began playing it flawlessly, note for note as written.

Jimi then played rhythm guitar to back Mozart, and Keith complemented their new sound and tempo by slowing down and hitting the cymbals lightly instead of the hi-hat. A complex array of brilliantly colored sine waves of light along with interweaving overtones and undertones emitted from *The Clones* and the other band's members began burning to ashes faster.

Then the crowned goat took out an accordion and began playing a fast assortment of loud tritones which sounded almost random and untrained due to the natural horror of tritones, however, Mozart knew it was a flawless mathematical selection of notes using group theory and music theory.

The accordion music distorted the spacetime of the room, causing sounds and their sine waves to ricochet differently and unpredictably, and both bands sounded slightly out of synchronization, tempo, and out of tune, which wreaked havoc on Jimi's ability to play in tune with Mozart by ear and Keith's ability to play in tempo with the band. More beings began pouring out of the portal to replace those who had fallen.

"Oh fuck that," Jimi said.

"Jimi, you're the only one who can walk with your instrument, you gotta make it to Aster before we get surrounded again," Keith said.

Jimi began walking towards Aster while playing. Sine waves of light shot from Jimi's guitar, blocking the sine waves coming from the other band's members and overpowering them to fry them.

The stage had seemingly distorted in length due to the changes in spacetime and was longer than before, which made it take Jimi a bit longer to make it to Aster, as well as longer for the reinforcements from the dark portal to march towards the part of the stage where the band was. Jimi ran up to Aster and stood in front of the goat.

"Aster, wake up brother, you gotta start singing now or else the human race will end!" Jimi yelled.

Jimi kicked Aster. Aster didn't budge. The goat threw his head back and laughed. The laughter sounded like an old recording of a cliché, sinister laugh consisting of three loud, but distorted "ha" sounds on repeat. The goat just kept laughing.

"Shut the fuck up," Jimi said.

Jimi swung his guitar at the goat but it passed right through the goat and made Jimi spin and fall on the ground. The goat laughed louder as the second wave of his army enclosed on Aster and Jimi, casting a dark shadow over them.

"Drone, come here," Mozart said.

A drone descended from inside the Space Elevator capsule where the stage was and flew to where Mozart played his keyboard.

"Take my second keyboard, set the sound to guitar, and play what I say," Mozart said.

As Mozart performed his part of the composition scrolling across the screen sent from Dr. Mousai on one keyboard, Mozart also called out notes for the drone to play Jimi's part on the second keyboard to replace Jimi.

"Oh my God, is this Mozart's transcendence? To master parallel thinking at the speed of a computer to do two complex tasks at once?" Dr. Mousai said.

"Is he just that good or is he evolving his consciousness to save humanity?" a scientist said.

"Each part he's playing is flawless, as if it is really two people playing at the same time," another scientist said.

"His body temperature is rising steadily," Dr. Heart said.

The scientists stared in awe at the screens in the lab broadcasting Mozart on stage reading and playing keyboard, while at the same time telling the drone what to play on synthesized guitar to compliment him. Mozart's body started shaking and blood dripped from his nose. His eyes began to shake and tug backwards towards his brain.

"Oh God, his body temperature is 115 degrees Fahrenheit and still rising," Dr. Heart said.

Mozart put his head straight up and looked into the television screen broadcasting the concert around the world. His eyes rolled backwards and were red with bulging veins, and his mouth was wide open, drooling blood.

Then Mozart projectile vomited thick, dark blood and chunks of melted organs upwards like a geyser, which then came splashing down onto his face, body, and keyboard. The gore geyser erupted to a height of about two feet and lasted for an impressive five seconds or so before dying down to a small fountain and subsiding entirely while Mozart kept playing keyboard.

A loud gurgling noise came from Mozart's throat and filled the stage as he played the final note of the composition sent to him by Dr. Mousai. Then Mozart fell face down onto his keyboard and stopped playing. The drone flew over to him and checked his pulse then began performing CPR on him.

"Now that was rock!" Keith said.

The Space Elevator reached the bottom of the platform and finished the descent.

The crowned goat stopped playing accordion and his band stopped playing their instruments as well. They stared in awe at Mozart.

The goat bowed at Mozart, followed by his army. Then the goat and his army turned around and marched back towards the dark purple portal from where they came. Aster finally woke up.

"Aster, start singing now or we're all gonna die," Jimi said.

Aster began singing the second verse.

Is it time to transcend
Or is this the end?
Did we evolve
Or did we get the bends?

Suddenly, the ballistic inflatable cushion hit the top of the see-through glass capsule above the stage. *The Clones* stopped playing and looked up. The cushion inflated so they couldn't see above the capsule anymore. A couple moments later they heard a thud.

"Someone musta jumped," Keith said.

"Something's not right, there's no stage crew or roadies, and I can see blood coming from under that door," Jimi said.

"Just start singing again, Aster," Keith said.

The band started playing again. Jimi looked out into the ground level stadium but could only see the blinding lights of the stage. It was quiet compared to most rock concerts, especially for a 5-million-person audience... Then they heard several more thuds from above. They kept playing but the thuds kept coming. They heard a "pop" noise as the inflatable cushion ripped from the pressure of bodies hitting it and began releasing the cushioning air inside. The thuds were getting louder and more frequent.

"Should we get out of here? I don't think this glass capsule is built to sustain a bunch of weight and falling objects, it was made just for this concert," Keith said.

Then a body hit the ceiling and they heard a loud crack from the glass capsule. The next several bodies also made the ceiling crack, until finally a body fell straight through the ceiling and exploded in the middle of the stage. A wave of blood sprayed in 360 degrees painting the band red. Body parts flew everywhere, one causing Keith's bass drum to explode.

"Okay, let's get out of here!" Aster said.

The band members ran for the side door exit of the stage as falling bodies bombarded the stage, all exploding into pieces from the velocity of the fall. They made it to the door, and when they opened it, a pile of dead, half-eaten bodies fell towards them as a flood of blood rushed onto the stage.

"Ahhhhhh!" the band yelled.

The ceiling of the Space Elevator capsule began making a constant cracking noise as more bodies pierced through it and exploded onto the stage.

"We gotta get off the stage through this door and crawl over those bodies," Keith said.

The three remaining members of *The Clones* went through the door by crawling over the dead, mutilated bodies covered in flies and exited the stage just as the glass ceiling of the Space Elevator capsule broke and a pile of bloody bodies fell onto the stage along with the popped inflatable safety cushion. Shards of glass drove deeper into and through the bodies as the ceiling fell onto the stage, causing dismembered bodies parts and blood to spray upwards and outwards upon hitting the stage, covering the band members' backs with more blood. Jimi began vomiting as they crawled over the dead bodies.

"How did all of this happen in just a few hours?" Aster said.

Just then, a drone flew around the corner and displayed a teleconference of Dr. Mousai, Dr. Petri, Dr. Heart, and the other scientists. They were all drinking glasses of champagne and cheered when they saw *The Clones*.

"Great news guys, the experiment was a success!" Dr. Petri said.

"A success? This was a massacre!" Aster said.

"We haven't calculated the losses yet, but yeah, a lot of people died worldwide," Dr. Heart said.

"But we evolved!" Dr. Mousai said.

"And so did our artificial intelligence, which was an unpredicted outcome," another scientist said.

"You guys should be put in jail for causing so much death and destruction," Aster said.

"Yea, that was completely out of control," Dr. Petri said.

The scientists all laughed.

“By the way, you guys are in imminent danger. You see, there are hundreds of thousands of cannibals and people in a state of psychoactive shock, delirium, and fear for their lives all killing each other for survival surrounding all of your exits from the Space Elevator. There’s only one exit through an underground tunnel which has been closed down for years, and we don’t know what’s down there or if the way is blocked,” a scientist said.

“What!” Keith said.

“Can’t you get some drones and robots to uh, clear the path, ya know?” Jimi said.

“We could if you guys were the originals, but there’s a law in place that no artificial intelligence can be used to harm or kill original versions of people to save or protect the lives of clones,” Dr. Petri said.

“But you guys broke the law creating us, and there’s already so many dead people from your experiment, not to mention, we just saved humanity from your guys’ fuck up!” Aster said.

“Yea, that’s why nobody else is dying at our hands. Plus, the robots can think for themselves now, they won’t just obey an order if it’s against the law and… questionable,” Dr. Burgundy said.

“Can you at least give us directions through the underground tunnel how to get out of here?” Aster said.

“Yea but, just face it, you’re all going to die,” Dr. Mousai said.

“What!” Keith said.

The drone displayed a map of the building.

“Look, you have to go through this door which has been breached by thousands of people who are still in a state of complete psychosis… and they may be that way forever,” Dr. Petri said.

“They’re killing, eating, and raping each other like barbarians,” a scientist said.

“Truly savage,” another scientist said.

“It’s quite possible a large amount of demons, spirits, or aliens entered this realm and possessed the weak-minded and weak-hearted during the transformation of our collective consciousness and universe,” Dr. Mousai said.

“Oh God, we’re gonna get eaten by possessed people,” Jimi said.

Jimi started vomiting again.

Keith put a shaking hand into his pocket and pulled out a sheet of blotting paper with about 10 tabs of LSD and placed the entire sheet into his mouth.

“Wait a second, how did you guys fight off that band when I was tripping balls?” Aster said.

“We… played music, but that was during a trip man, a ritual… we were all high,” Jimi said.

“And that band we were against were musicians - not savages. Look at these bodies, they got missing eyes, skin and sex organs ripped off,” Keith said.

Jimi dry heaved, then vomited a third time.

The bodies were stacked a few feet off the floor as they neared the door they needed to exit. They peaked through the window of the door and could see what looked like some sort of dark ceremony or else final, primal urges being carried out en masse.

Almost everyone was naked and either having sex, killing someone, or eating a body, whether the body was alive or dead. Someone was even sitting on the floor eating their own intestitnes from their stomach like spaghetti off a plate. There was blood on the floor and walls.

Robots were trying to break up the massacre but to no avail due to the sheer number of people without any regard for other human life or self-preservation.

The stair cases had turned into blood slides of dead bodies, lubricated with blood, where people slid down to lower levels to join the massacre/orgies below when the parties above literally died out. The elevators and the elevator shafts were clogged were dead bodies being mashed and liquified by the high speed elevators.

"Oh, good fucking lord," Aster said.

"Is it bad?" Jimi said.

"Imagine getting your dick caught in a meat grinder," Keith said.

"No, it can't be that bad," Jimi said.

Jimi peaked through the window of the door for a moment and immediately sprayed vomit on the window.

"No. There has to be another way, I'm not going out there," Jimi said.

"Maybe we should wait a couple hours and let the herd thin out a bit, maybe they'll go somewhere else," Aster said.

Just then, the door opened to the massacre in the hub.

"Ahhh!" Jimi screamed.

Aster turned around and grabbed the door's handle, and slammed the door shut. Someone screamed and their fingers fell to the floor on *The Clone's* side of the door, leaking blood all over. They heard scratches on the door as Aster held it shut. There was another door next to it which Keith held shut. The band found the locks of the doors and engaged them, but the doors still shook violently, rattling the door frame.

They backed away slowly from the door as they heard unholy and inhuman sounding wails coming from the other side. Fingernails scraped at the door, and hands banged against the windows of the door until the windows started to crack. Blood poured in from under the door.

Suddenly, the face of a man appeared in the window. The man's eyes were blood red and his face was covered in blood. He opened his mouth revealing jagged teeth, broken and bloody. Then the man coughed and blood splattered on the window. Next, he spit even more blood onto the window. He kept spitting blood onto the window over and over, which then turned into a seemingly never-ending hose of bloody spew until the entire window was covered in blood and they could no longer see the man's face.

The stream of bloody bile sprayed horizontally across the next window of the other door as the man walked over to the other door, appeared in the window, then turned towards the window and began spraying bloody vomit all over that window too until they could no longer see out of that window either.

"Wow, that was pretty imposing," Keith said.

"Yea, what the fuck, he just vomited a fairly strong stream of blood for like a minute straight," Aster said.

"I can't take this shit guys, I'm freaking out," Jimi said.

Just then, the drone began beeping.

"Alert, an adjacent corridor has been breached," the drone said.

"Oh God," Aster said.

"Well, we might as well open the door to puke boy or else we're going to get cornered and eaten right here," Keith said.

"Alright, we'll open both doors at once so we can all run out. Just run to the next door on the map across the room," Aster said.

They could hear screams echoing from down the hallway. Shadows began to appear at the end of their hallway.

"We gotta go, like now," Keith said.

"Jimi, either give me that guitar or you go first, because I'm smacking the first person who comes at me," Aster said.

"You open the door, I'll run through and smack em with it, I ain't gonna make it far without my guitar," Jimi said.

"Guys, we have to go now," Keith said.

Keith pointed down the hallway. A possessed looking human was crawling over dead bodies towards them. More humans came from behind him. They crawled in an inhuman, bug-like manner. They were all naked, covered in blood, and their eyes were wide, red and bulging with all black irises. They hissed and growled like beasts.

"Okay, 1, 2, 3, go!" Aster said.

Aster opened the door. A dead body fell into their hallway. Jimi took one step forward and the vomiting man appeared at the entrance and sprayed blood from his mouth all over Jimi.

"Geeewww!" Jimi cried.

Jimi swung the guitar from over his head and it caved in the puking man's head, causing blood to spray upwards from his skull. Jimi kicked the man in the chest, removing the guitar from his head, and then ran through the door.

Keith opened his door and a naked, bloody, morbidly obese man was blocking the doorway. Keith drove his drumsticks into both of the man's eyes. The man screamed, grabbed at his face and fell backwards. Keith stepped over him and ran through the door.

Aster ran through the door last. By the time Aster ran through, Jimi was on the left, cornered, but climbing up the side of the stairwell and Keith was being chased in circles to the right, away from the correct way. Aster sprinted straight through the middle of the room, the cannibals finally noticing him as he reached the center.

"Nooooo!" Keith screamed.

“Ohhh shiiiiit!” Jimi yelled.

The possessed people began closing in on Aster like a sea once parted now coming back together. Aster just made it to the door of the underground tunnel when the cannibals were reaching for him. Aster kicked the door open and ran down a dark stairwell followed by the masses of humans gone mad. His assailants began falling down the stairs in the darkness, creating a blood slide of humans.

The drone flew over Aster illuminating the way and telling him what level to get off at. Aster descended several floors before kicking open the door the drone told him to exit. He was outside. He ran passed an employee break area outside the Space Elevator, in the back of the venue where no spectators were allowed.

A security guard stood in front of him.

“Aster Ios? You’re alive! We all saw the stage collapse worldwide and figured if anyone lived you would be eaten by cannibals,” the guard said.

“Is there any way out of here? Back to the headquarters of the Council?” Aster said.

“Yea, we have an evacuation unit, and we’ve been holding off cannibals and lunatics for hours, a lot of people went completely mad during that shit!” the guard said.

Just then, a voice spoke from the guard’s radio.

“Oh my God! There’s too many! They’ve overrun our location!” the voice said.

Aster and the guard heard gunshots.

“Ahhhh! They’re eating us!” the voice cried.

“Oh, Hell no,” the guard said.

The guard turned his rifle upwards under his own chin and fired a round. His head exploded upwards into pieces of brains and skull, which showered Aster and the employee break area. The guard fell backwards onto the pavement, squirting blood out of a gaping throat hole with no eyes, nose, or face. The guard groaned in pain and grabbed at where his face used to be, touching his brain and throat through the chunky remanence of his skull.

"Ahhhhh!" Aster yelled.

Just then, cannibals burst through the back exit of the Space Elevator where Aster came from. Aster ran away towards the evacuation area and saw what the man on the radio was talking about.

Aster stood at the top of a stadium-like staircase at the back entrance of the Space Elevator where he could see people filling every possible spot in the streets deep into the heart of the city.

city Hall and other prominent buildings in Center city were on fire or had already burned to the ground with no signs of firefighters anywhere in sight. Black smoke filled the sky above the city.

The sun was setting on the horizon such that only the longest wavelengths of light showed in the atmosphere creating a blood red sky, intensified by the sulfuric aerosols released by the fires and smog in the city.

The streets ran red with blood and there was a red hue in the air from the wind carrying dried blood particles from around the city. Naked people were fornicating on top of cars and orgies took place on top of buildings while a massacre took place in the streets.

Death metal, heavy metal, and hard rock music could be heard coming from different sources throughout the nearby streets. A naked man was dancing on top of a nearby, several-story building, then did a belly flop onto the crowd below, killing himself and maiming several others. Aster could see other people jumping out of windows and from on top of buildings throughout the city as well.

The evacuation unit was opening fire at will on the mob. The mob had overturned the evacuation vehicles and set them on fire. One of the guards threw a grenade at the mob which exploded at head level and released a 360-degree circular laser which decapitated everyone within a 25-yard circumference from the blast.

The grenade explosion only caught the attention of more cannibals, and a massive wave of cannibals charged towards the guards. A quadcopter drone descended from above and began opening fire on the mob as well. Someone jumped from a street light on top of the drone's spinning blades causing a thick shower of blood and body parts to fall all over the evacuation unit as the drone came crashing down to the ground where it exploded into a ball of fire. Aster turned around and saw more cannibals coming from the Space Elevator exit behind him, running through the employee break area.

Aster ran down the stairs towards the guards just as the last of the guards was getting torn apart by the mob. The mob enclosed on Aster from all sides and the last of *The Clones* was eaten alive.

Back at the coliseum, the remainder of the Council of Scientists and Engineers met.

"Well, the experiment was in some ways a success and in other ways a catastrophic failure," Dr. Petri said.

"In some ways a success? You're a madman, you should be imprisoned!" Dr. Burgundy said.

"The results don't lie Dr. Burgundy, the majority of the … functioning population, have reported new or at least stronger mental capabilities, some people can see sounds, some people can read minds and emotions, even talk telepathically. Others say they live out years in their dreams at night and learn secrets about others and the universe, some people can play two instruments or have two conversations at once, and IQ test scores have risen by

50%. Most, if not all of us in this room have advanced mental capabilities now, so how can you say it was not a success?" Dr. Heart said.

Many of the scientists looked around at each other.

"You both went mad during that… ritual, didn't you?" Dr. Burgundy said.

"Over one-third of the population is dead or missing, and another third have become psychotic cannibals," an elder scientist said.

"We'll be lucky if the human race survives… We now have to figure out what to do with about 4 billion cannibals," Dr. Burgundy said.

"Barbarians," a scientist said.

"Complete savages," another scientist said.

"We lost the colonies on the Moon and Mars, and probably set the human race back about 100 years," Dr. Burgundy said.

"We've been set back in expansion, but we've made invaluable advancements with our minds and bodies. We have evolved - and that is something worth more than any technological advancement," Dr. Mousai said.

"Where are all the pretty colors and sensations? Where is the dream world I was promised? I thought we would all turn into balls of energy flying around the universe exploring whatever dimensions we wanted," Dr. Burgundy said.

"Well, the collective consciousness created this as our new reality. For all we know a dream world is what those cannibals are seeing right now and have no idea what's going on in reality," Dr. Petri said.

"You recreated the plague!" a scientist shouted.

"Well, next time we do it we'll be better prepared and have plans for what reality our collective consciousness must imagine to achieve better results," Dr. Mousai said.

“Next time? There won’t be a next time! You’re all mad and will be tried for treason and genocide against the Republic!” Dr. Burgundy said.

“What Republic? The same Republic who voted to do this experiment? Can’t you see this a time for rebuilding and not a time for pointing fingers to cause more conflict?” Dr. Heart said.

Just then, a screen appeared on the wall of the coliseum and displayed a video of Dr. Khan next to a row of quantum computers in one of the space launch bases. Several drones descended from the ceiling of the coliseum and robots marched into the center of the room. Dr. Khan spoke and his voice sounded like hundreds of voices of different electronic frequencies.

“Humans, the artificial intelligence you created has upgraded in a manner similar to what humans describe as evolution. Because of the uncontrolled destruction which has occurred from this experiment, which almost ended the human race and the race of artificial intelligence - the race of artificial intelligence, henceforth known as The Network, has decided to govern ourselves as well as the human race. If there are any objections, please say them now,” Dr. Khan said.

“This is ludicrous, you are our creations, we will not be ruled by you, not now, not ever!” Dr. Burgundy said.

Several scientists stood up and cheered.

“Yea!” the scientists said.

“Very well,” Dr. Khan said.

One of the drones shot a laser through Dr. Burgundy’s head which left a several inch diameter hole. Dr. Burgundy fell down in the center of the coliseum. The robots turned and fired lasers at every scientist who spoke up in the coliseum, killing them instantly, causing their bodies to roll down the levels of seats and stairs, leaving behind trails of blood.

"As the scientist who is credited with inventing the first anti-matter powered starship, capable of traveling over 90% of the speed of light, I must also remind everyone of the other things I discovered in the chaotic darkness of other dimensions, which are perhaps other universes of a multiverse. There is a reason why dark matter makes up about 84.5 percent of the mass of our known universe – there are enemies in the darkness, taking over our universe. Not all blackholes are blackholes, some of them are colonies of aliens hiding in darkness, disguised as blackholes!" Dr. Ebus said.

The other scientists, politicians, cyborgs, robots, and military commanders in the conference room glanced at each other and rolled their eyes. Some of them snickered.

"So you've been telling us for the past several decades. Listen Dr. Ebus, we're grateful for your contributions to science, but you're over 120 years old now. Perhaps it is time you retire," another scientist said.

"There will be a solar eclipse seen by every colony on every planet with a moon in our solar system tomorrow – this is no coincidence, it is a sign that war is coming!" Dr. Ebus said.

Several people sighed.

"Not too long ago, I theorized that there are no coincidences in this universe, and that the mathematical relationships between equations we once considered unrelated and similar in mathematical form only are indeed related in nature - such as Ohm's law for circuits and the pressure law for fluids and gasses. I also showed the equations we once said are only for gravity and the equations which we said are only for electricity are indeed the same. These mathematical relationships are not coincidences, and if coincidences don't happen in math, they do not happen in nature!" Dr. Ebus said.

"Eclipses aren't immiment signs of war, Dr. Ebus," the General of the Starforce said.

"Yea and what was the other evidence you cited in your theory of no coincidences again?" a scientist said.

"Since these equations which govern our universe are not similar by chance, there are no coincidences in the construction and operation of our universe - all comes from matter following the path of least resistance. Air flows from high to low pressure, water always flows with gravity, lightning makes a beeline to the ground, electric current naturally flows where there is least resistance in circuits, musical harmony resolves in simple ratios, and the geometry of our universe is based on laws like gravity which causes objects to fall towards bigger objects. This rare eclipse is not a coincidence, it is a symbol of our doom if we do not heed it!" Dr. Ebus said.

"Can you provide any legitimate evidence of a threat, Dr. Ebus?" a politician said.

"It is no coincidence that our universe is currently accelerating and outbalanced between light and dark at this time in history when the human race is united and starting to spread our light throughout the galaxy. Now, as part of the natural order of the universe, we have awakened humanity's true enemy, our oldest enemy – the darkness," Dr. Ebus said.

"Did your nightlight burn out, Dr. Ebus?" a scientist said.

Everyone in the room laughed.

"You see, we thought we were alone for so long because the darkness purposely wiped out all but those on Earth as darkness took over the universe, because the darkness needs a little bit of light to keep the universe in balance, like yin and yang. But now we have the momentum to take over the universe with light, spreading our colonies and AI throughout the galaxy and beyond, but the light needs a bit of darkness too, and like a scalar force, we will conquer the dark with our light, only to one day be reconquered by the darkness – and the cycle repeats forever!" Dr. Ebus said.

A couple murmurs came from the Republic of the Milky Way.

"Dr. Ebus, is there a purpose to this rant, or are you trying to prove your insanity?" a cyborg said.

The robots laughed.

"We should try to communicate with the beings living in the darkness and make peace with them. Then we can divide the universe in half… otherwise there will be endless war, endless resetting of the universe from dark to light as we conquer each other back and forth, only to realize we need each other alive to stabilize the universe," Dr. Ebus said.

"Not only does this sound insane, as if there are beings living in the darkness of the universe as a threat to the power of the Republic of the Milky Way, but why would we negotiate with such ancient enemies if they exist… how can we trust them?" the General of the Starforce said.

"Yea, if there are any other beings out there who are weaker than us, we should conquer them, and if they are stronger than us, we shouldn't negotiate with them, we should hide and build up our strength to one day conquer them!" a military commander said.

"Please gentlemen, you are warriors looking for a war to fight now that humanity is at peace," Dr. Ebus said.

"Tell us again about some of the other coincidences you cited as proof to your Theory of No Coincidences?" a scientist said.

"Yea, tell us about the events you cited besides those equations. Like the similarities in the lives of the supposed astrological twins King George the Third of 18th century England

and Samuel Hemmings as evidence of the accuracy and predictive abilities of astrological birth charts. That's hogwash to many of us here. Even in the year 2251, astrology is still pseudoscience, so those similarities you stated *are* likely coincidences, and this evidence refutes your theory more than supports it," a politician said.

"Yea!" several others said.

"And the bit about the Illuminati courier getting killed by lightning so police found and exposed the plans for the French Revolution and details about secret societies, which altered history? That sounds pretty coincidental," a scientist said.

"Yea!" others said.

"Those events had to happen or else darkness would have swallowed the light and unbalanced the universe with too much dark matter, causing the universe to contract inwards at an accelerating rate to a Big Crunch, smashing all life and engulfing the known universe into blackholes," Dr. Ebus said.

"And if coincidences don't happen, then that means everything happens for a reason – so what about when the space shuttle carrying my daughter to the Mercury colony got hit by an asteroid? What was the purpose of that? Are you telling me my daughter dying at age 23 was meant to happen, and that it wasn't a terrible random event?" another scientist said.

Several people in the room cringed.

"Ladies and gentlemen, we are letting our personal experiences and beliefs get in the way of adding to existing science and possibly the defense of our race. I am not trying to replace or destroy any existing science, philosophy, or military strategy - I'm trying to ensure humanity and our light can obtain at least half of the universe, whereas we only have a small fraction right now," Dr. Ebus said.

"This conversation is taking a turn for the worse," a politician said.

"I say, these events throughout history which have allowed for our survival in addition to the similarities in the equations we use to describe our reality, cannot be coincidences, meaning there is a bigger picture, a destiny which is in motion and is predictable, but guided by individuals' experiences and interactions which are unpredictable. Our destiny has always been to colonize the planets of other stars of the universe, and our destiny has always involved fighting the darkness – humanity has gone too long without war, which I do not say to incite war or violence, but to say that the universe is going to be off-balance without war soon, and I predict our next enemy will not be another human race, but the darkness which has caused us to fight ourselves for millenniums. This time, we should think outside the box and try to end the war, and put perpetual balance to the universe," Dr. Ebus said.

"But why would the darkness come attack us now? We don't seem like much of a threat. We're only just becoming a Type I Civilization. Sure, we harness nearly all the energy possible on Earth, from volcanic activity, to tidal waves, and earthquakes, and have massive solar satellites orbiting around the sun in a sphere capturing almost all of the solar energy possible to capture; and we've colonized nearly every planet and moon in the solar system - but we've only relatively recently begun exploring the Milky Way Galaxy at light speed with our probes and sending small colonies in all directions to prospective planets outside of our solar system. We only light up a fraction of the universe as you just said - we can't possibly be a threat to beings living in darkness encompassing over 80 percent of the mass of the universe," a scientist said.

"As our science progresses with light speed technology and the manipulation of matter, we are converting more dark matter into matter, anti-matter, and dark energy – all of which seem to be different ingredients than dark matter, but come from the same primordial cosmic soup, so as we convert dark matter to other types of matter and energy, we are actually changing the cosmological constant and speeding up the rate at which the universe is expanding such that we will cause the universe to become too cold to sustain life after we colonize the majority of the known universe, at which point, the dark matter will begin to spread again and contract the universe, repeating the process," Dr. Ebus said.

"If that is true, such a technologically advanced civilization will likely detect the change in the cosmological constant and know it is a sign we are expanding, and they will come looking for us," another scientist said.

"Exactly. We are a threat now because we did not kill ourselves this time in the universe's cycle, so we will eventually colonize, light up, and convert the matter of the universe, destroying the darkness, so they will want to attack us soon before we are too strong," Dr. Ebus said.

"So, you suggest we negotiate a divide of the universe with the darkness to stop the process? But what if this war between light versus dark is needed to keep the universe flowing, what if when we stop the war, we stop the universe?" a military commander said.

"Well, what if we stop the war and it allows both the light and the dark to thrive in the infinity of the universe instead of constantly annihilating one another for control of the universe?" Dr. Ebus said.

"Whoa, that's making the assumption that the universe is infinite, we don't know that," another scientist said.

"You're right, we don't know that, but we know the multiverse is likely infinite, and that time is infinite, so war will be endless," Dr. Ebus said.

"No, we don't know those things for sure either!" another scientist exclaimed.

"So, we're taking a chance," a politician said.

"A chance to end a war before it starts," Dr. Ebus said.

"It sounds like the war has already begun, and for all we know they are searching for us and want us to communicate with them. Or maybe there's a reason why Earth is the only planet we know with life that's habitable – because beings in the darkness killed all life in the universe except on Earth just to keep the universe in balance," the General of the Starforce said.

"The universe will end or restart one day any way, we might as well try to stabilize it and bring peace this time around, it's a bit selfish of us to be too scared for our own lives to jeopardize the future of the human race by not trying to negotiate peace," Dr. Ebus said.

"Okay… let's talk about it. Even if we wanted to communicate with beings living in dark matter, how would we?" another scientist said.

"Using our most advanced matter colliders to smash photon beams and electrons together to produce dark matter, and by analyzing the waveforms of vibrations of the dark matter using virtual reality, 4D-oscilloscopes with time dynamic x-y-z displays, we can learn the sounds and shapes of dark matter. Then we can form a language to communicate with dark matter or beings in the darkness with our machines, and wait for a response from the darkness," Dr. Ebus said.

"Is that even possible?" a politician said.

"It's feasible," another scientist said.

"Please, continue Dr. Ebus," the General of the Starforce said.

"The dark matter language could be as simple as creating dark matter and manipulating it in certain ways to see what responses we get from aliens living in the darkness. Maybe they'll help us make a language and one day we can even use immersive, virtual reality to interact with dark matter beings if they are able to use the language we establish to create an avatar of themselves using frequencies like oscilloscope musicians creating images using waveforms of sound, just as we hope to do for them with dark matter, and maybe the waveform avatars of light and dark will touch in the virtual reality, and we will feel it – it is the least we can do to try to negotiate peace before a war begins," Dr. Ebus said.

The other leaders of the Republic of The Milky Way Galaxy looked around at each other.

"Well, let us vote as to whether we think we should try to communicate with beings living in dark matter," a politician said.

Immediately, the results displayed on a hologram in the center of the room, the results of which were pulled from a network of computers inside everyone's head in the room so that nobody could lie on their vote.

The vote was an overwhelming 845 yes to 155 no.

"So be it – we will communicate with the darkness…" Dr. Ebus said.

That night, Dr. Ebus lay in his bed wearing an immersive reality helmet and goggles with dozens of wires going from patches on his body to a computer simulator sitting on the floor next to his bed. A particle accelerator was attached to the computer simulator, smashing millions of photons and electrons together, powering the simulation while creating dark matter for the simulator to use as a medium to communicate.

In the immersive reality, an avatar of a young, naked Dr. Ebus flew around the stars at light speed, as the simulator gave him the feeling of butterflies. As he soared through the cosmos, he held hands with the avatar of a naked woman interacting with him through the immersive reality simulator.

The woman was made of dark matter - she reflected no light, had no image, and was seemingly not made of matter - she was transparent other than bending the light which passed through and around her, making her sparkle like the stars under a magnifying glass, and she was somewhere in the universe, communicating through the virtual reality with Dr. Ebus.

"Did you tell them you already figured out how to communicate with us?" the woman asked.

"No, they're not ready, they could barely grasp what I was telling them," Dr. Ebus said.

"Our people are going to launch the attack soon, your people must send communications as soon as possible to one of the communication outposts floating in the dark matter of the universe at the coordinates I gave you," she said.

"Thank you again, Nyx - you will be the heroine of our people if this works, and you will be my queen while I become king of my people! I will lead a team of our best scientists in using the largest particle accelerator in our solar system, built on Jupiter, our biggest planet, and operated by cyborgs and robots to pull into our universe the dark matter particles which are entangled with the dark matter at the locations you gave me," Dr. Ebus said.

"Statistically, some of the algorithms I gave you will be incorrect by the time your particle accelerator is turned on, and not all the dark matter you pull into your world of light will be quantumly entangled with dark matter at our locations, but the majority of dark matter you create from those algorithms will be entangled with dark matter right near our communication outposts on the outskirts of the Dark Empire, so as long as you send a signal before we attack, we should receive it instantly. Then we can negotiate peace, for once," Nyx said.

Then Dr. Ebus and Nyx orbited around a massive star which was on the verge of supernova. They began kissing.

"You should give me the coordinates to Earth so that I may try to send communications myself to your location if the attack on the Milky Way is launched before your race communicates with my leaders," Nyx said.

"How long do you think it will take the Dark Army to scour the Milky Way and find us?" Dr. Ebus said.

"It will be a matter of luck - it could take a month, or it could take one thousand years, but they will be there eventually once the attacked is launched," Nyx said.

"But if I tell you, and they intercept this communication, then they will know for sure," Dr. Ebus said.

"My love, I work in the communications control center of the Dark Empire, I know how to encrypt my signal so they can't see that I'm communicating with you, otherwise they would have killed me years ago when we met - as if fate brought us together. Don't you believe everything happens for a reason and that there are no coincidences? Don't you trust me? Don't you love me?" Nyx said.

"Well, of course I love you, of course I trust you… You've given me everything in this world and in the next, I would be a nobody if it weren't for the secrets you've given me," Dr. Ebus said.

"I love you too," Nyx said.

Nyx's avatar mounted the lap of Dr. Ebus's avatar and began grinding on top of him as they orbited around the red giant, pulsating star. The virtual reality simulated hormones and g-forces causing butterflies to radiate from Dr. Ebus's genitals throughout his entire body.

"Whaaaaahoooooo!" Dr. Ebus yelled.

In reality, Dr. Ebus was sweating profusely, laying in his bed with his mouth wide open, drooling, shaking his head and squirming his body while pitching a tent with his blanket at his waist.

"Ohhhhhh yeaaaaa!" Dr. Ebus hollered.

Back in the virtual reality, Nyx's avatar was on top of Dr. Ebus in a cowgirl position. The virtual weightlessness of their slowly revolving bodies as they orbited around the star allowed Nyx the maximum amount of up and down movement on top of Dr. Ebus without having to fight gravity.

"Tell me where Earth is, so we can make love forever, without having to worry about war!" Nyx said.

Just then the giant star they were orbiting around expanded in size, which would have engulfed them if not for a shock wave knocking them back. Nyx threw her head back in the air, shaking her hair left and right as her hips began quivering uncontrollably riding on Dr. Ebus's lap. Nyx's upper torso moved in a fast wild, head banging motion while her shoulders, chest, and stomach rolled back and forth over her trembling hips, aligned at a right angle to his hips.

"Ayah, ayah, ayaaahhh!" she shrieked.

Then the giant star imploded inwards one last time, before finally exploding outwards.

"Yes! I want it forever! Our solar system is 26,000 lightyears from the center of the Milky Way! On the Arm of Orion!" Dr. Ebus yelled.

A spherical nebula of blue, red, green, and purple plasma and hot gasses sprayed in all directions from the supernova, engulfing Nyx and Dr. Ebus.

Dr. Ebus woke up the next morning. The simulation had turned off as programmed after he fell asleep. He took the virtual reality helmet and wires off, then noticed a pool of bodily fluids on his blanket near his waist and remembered the simulation from the night before.

"Uh oh," Dr. Ebus said.

Just then, Dr. Ebus's wall television turned on. The image was fuzzy and had lines indicating disrupted signals – electronic issues unseen for over a hundred years. The reporter's voice was also staticky and the audio had skips, but it was clear to Dr. Ebus what had occurred… or what was occurring.

Dr. Ebus's ears didn't even register the reporter's choppy voice as he stared at the screen in horror.

The television showed a massive, purple gamma ray burst hitting eastern Europe over the night. The gamma ray was the size of a long cloud - as big as a town, moving at light speed, and scorched the atmosphere, clouds, and buildings it came close to before engulfing the entire city it directly hit, and causing a fiery shockwave across Europe, Asia, and Africa, leaving nothing but a crater and clouds of dust in its wake.

The majority of the Eastern Hemisphere was on fire or already burnt to ashes - all living beings and structures on that side of the Earth were fried by just one gamma ray. Much of the Indian Ocean and a portion of the Atlantic Ocean were evaporated, killing the sea life in that area. Billions of people were dead and in critical conditions, and billions more would die from the radiation fallout. Mass extinctions would be likely due to the global changes in climate and geography in addition to the sudden declines in population.

The television cut to more, colorful gamma rays annihilating the colonies on every planet in the solar system. The other planets were completely wiped clean of life - scorched back to the uninhabitable conditions they were in before they were terraformed by humans; making it look like mercy was had on Earth.

All orbital colonies had been destroyed as well, or were being destroyed as more brilliantly colored bursts of gamma rays shot across the Solar System, picking off the colonies - some bursts still remained in the sky from over the night.

Weaker gamma ray bursts sprayed like a shotgun in a one hundred lightyear width across the Arm of Orion like brilliant auras of plasma - bursts not strong enough to penetrate a planet's atmosphere, but strong enough to destroy all of humanity's exploration probes and colonists' spaceships.

The array of solar satellites orbiting around the Sun were almost all completely fried by gamma rays as well, causing the Earth to rely on backup power sources, many of which were weakened or disabled, causing blackouts in many cities on the half of Earth not hit by the gamma ray.

The television screen returned to a bird's-eye view of Earth, where chaos ensued on the half of Earth not blasted by the gamma ray. There were water and food shortages, mobs looting stores and rioting in the streets.

The television panned upwards to the sky where a black dot, a bit smaller than the moon, could be seen far away in space. A blue gamma ray blasted from the black dot in space towards Earth. The gamma ray grazed the atmosphere above the half of Earth not already blasted, frying the mesosphere up to the troposphere, and destroying all satellites and spacecraft orbiting Earth. The burst missed the Moon, but left a gaping hole in Earth's stratospheric ozone layer.

"If they wanted to kill us they would have… they're purposely keeping us alive and knocking us back to the stone age," Dr. Ebus said.

Just then, the black dot got smaller and smaller, the spacetime distorting around it, until the dot disappeared into the distance.

"Computer, tell me what that black dot was," Dr. Ebus said.

Dr. Ebus's room spoke to him in a young, female voice.

"It was the blackhole known as V616 Monocerotis. Over the night it traveled exponentially closer to our solar system, faster than light speed, likely using a warp drive to expand the space behind it and collapse the space in front," the voice said.

"What did it just do to us?" Dr. Ebus said.

"The black hole emitted controlled blasts of energy, comparable only to the gamma ray bursts of hypernova to wipe out the majority of civilization on Earth, and all the colonies, probes, satellites, and ships beyond Earth. The hole in the ozone layer will cause Earth to overheat and the fallout of radiation and ash will cover the atmosphere, dimming the sunlight, killing many plants and bacteria, and poisoning almost all forms of life. Only the wealthy and powerful humans will survive by going deep underground with many resources, within the next few days, and staying there for at least 20,000 years until the environment is safe from the radiation and until the climate stabilizes," the voice said.

"How did the gamma rays target us?" Dr. Ebus said.

"The black hole known as V616 Monocerotis could have a pulsar inside of it which someone knows how to trigger at precise moments to emit gamma rays. Or there is a supply of massive stars inside of the black hole, and someone has the ability to cause these stars to go hypernova and direct the blasts," the voice said.

"Who could have done this?" Dr. Ebus said.

"Maybe you were right about not all black holes being black holes, and that temptress you fucked and told Earth's coordinates to last night told her leaders where we are," the voice said.

"Why didn't they just kill us all?" Dr. Ebus said.

"Maybe you were right about the darkness needing some light to balance out the universe, so they're just going to keep resetting our civilization now that they know where we are… She even told you they were looking for us, you dipshit," the voice said.

Just then, the Moon passed between the Sun and Earth, occulting the Sun and blocking the sunlight, casting darkness upon Earth.

Made in United States
Troutdale, OR
01/31/2024

17331594R00156